MW01487154

Weevil Spirits

Freaky Florida Investigations, Volume 5

Margaret Lashley

Published by Zazzy Ideas, Inc., 2020.

Copyright

What Readers are Saying about Freaky Florida Investigations...

"The story lines are crazy, and all you want is more!"
"Hilarious, weird and entertaining."
"The X-Files has found its funny bone!"
"I read a lot, and Kindle suggested your book. This book is laugh out loud funny. Is everyone in Florida crazy?"
"I have read Tim Dorsey, Carl Hiaasen, and Randy Wayne White. Those writers are funny but they need to watch out for you."
"A funny cozy, science fiction, thriller, mystery all rolled into one great story!"
"I read the whole book in two days, something I've never done before! I just couldn't wait to find out what was going to happen next!"

"What's bugging the inhabitants of Liberty County? Bobbie and Grayson's trip to see an entomological wonder turns out to be causing folks to lose their heads. Literally! Rednecks abound and Cousin Earl fits right in. What is it about the area that is resulting in extinction, sinkholes and bug barbeques? You may laugh yourself into an insect frenzy! Her best so far!"

Prologue

Hi, I'm Bobbie Drex. After having an up-close and personal experience with a ricocheted bullet, I ditched my mall-cop gig to become a private eye. My mentor, Nick Grayson, is as sketchy as he is handsome. A bona-fide conspiracy-theory nut, he's teaching me how to spot the difference between an authentic, otherworldly being and your average, down-to-earth lunatic.

I guess I'll have earned my license when I figure out which one *he* is.

For the record, tracking down cryptids sucks. In fact, if you ask me, the job really puts the "rear" in career.

It's not like you can stake out Bigfoot's workplace. Or corner Mothman in his favorite bar. Aliens rarely leave credit-card trails. And ungodly Parasitic Organisms don't phone family and friends asking for money.

Well, not the *non-human* kind, anyway.

I signed up for a two-year stint as Grayson's P.I. intern. Since then, I've spent my days beside him, roaming the dirty backroads of Florida in a rundown Winnebago, interviewing people with missing teeth, marbles, and/or the occasional vital chromosome.

Pretty glamorous, eh?

Well, don't turn green with envy. At least, not in front of Grayson, anyway.

If you do, you might end up hog-tied and thrown into the monster trap in the back of his RV.

Chapter One

The cabinet door squeaked like a horror-movie staircase as Grayson unhooked the padlock, tugged on the handle, and allowed me a tentative peek inside.

Until today, the secret potions that my sort-of mad-scientist partner concocted and stored behind lock and key had been deemed strictly off limits to me. In fact, whenever I'd asked Grayson about them, he'd simply said, "That's on a need-to-know basis, Drex."

Why I needed to know *now*, I, ironically, didn't know.

But I wasn't about to blow my chance to see inside his secret stash by opening my mouth and asking dumb questions. Instead, I craned my neck to see over his shoulder in the tight hallway of his cramped motorhome.

In the jaundiced light cast by the yellowing ceiling fixture, I caught a glimpse of his private stash.

My gut dropped with disappointment.

Inside was a hodgepodge of bottles and jars that looked like something you'd find crammed under the sink of a kleptomaniacal cleaning lady's house.

I frowned. Then I noticed the ordinary household containers had all been repurposed. Their original labels had been pasted over with what appeared to be ID stickers stolen from a convention registration table.

Knowing Grayson, it was probably MUFON.

My eyes landed on the label stuck to a Windex spray bottle.

It read:

I REACHED FOR IT.

"No touching!" Grayson said, slapping my hand away.

"Then why show me?" I grumbled, rubbing my stinging hand.

"Because as my intern, it's time you learned the basics of chemical warfare. It's a subject not to be taken lightly."

No kidding. After four months of being cooped up in a twenty-four-foot Winnebago with a rogue, monster-chasing physicist, I didn't need any more ammunition to go ballistic.

"Chemical warfare?" I asked.

Grayson tipped the brim of his fedora up to get a better look at me ... or perhaps at his precious potions.

"Yes. Chemistry is destiny," he said, studying me with his all-seeing green eyes.

"I thought that *biology* was destiny," I countered.

Grayson's cheek dimpled. I'd amused him. The deep divot was the only hint that a smile was lurking underneath that ridiculous bushy moustache of his.

"Nice try," he said. "But Freud's belief that women's behaviors and personalities are compelled by their anatomy have been proven time and again to be merely observational stereotypes, not evidentiary proof."

"Right."

Tell that to my thighs.

"But your comment brings up an important point," Grayson continued. "When it comes to animal behavior, chemistry can trump biology, but biology can't supersede chemistry."

I pursed my lips in frustration. Grayson was right about that, too.

An electric buzz ran up my spine and settled behind my ears. Despite all the weird things about him that should've made me toss Grayson out the window as a potential romantic interest, the chemistry between us was undeniable. My whole body tingled every time we accidently touched. Sometimes even when I stood too near him, like I was now.

The RV's cramped living quarters didn't help on that score. Neither did the fact that, as of late, we'd had way too much time on our hands.

We hadn't worked a case in nearly three months.

After concluding our Skunk Ape investigation in the tropical, bug-infested swamps of Ochopee, Florida, news of the weird had grown scarce in the Sunshine State. Even Grayson's ham radio and its network of conspiracy-theory loons had gone eerily silent.

With no cryptid-related crises to guide us, we'd spent the last couple of months rambling the rural backroads, exploring some of the Sunshine State's lesser-known natural wonders.

Some of them weren't even taco stands.

Grayson used his spare time to brush up on his entomology interests. He spent hours in the woods collecting bugs in jars, then skewering them to pieces of Styrofoam with hatpins. What he did with them afterward, well, I didn't ask. Some things a girl's just better off not knowing.

As for me, I used *my* free time to hone my target-shooting skills. Not that I needed to. I still had the deadly aim I'd developed as a backwoods tomboy, shooting out baby-doll eyes with my trusty Daisy BB gun.

Of the two of us, I was definitely the sharp-shooter. But I had to admit, it was Grayson who had the sharper mind—when it came to book-learning, anyway. The random facts and otherworldly musings that tumbled casually from his lips both shocked and amazed me. And, Lord help me, some of them I was actually beginning to *believe*.

When Grayson wasn't bug hunting or scouring the internet for weird phenomena, he was fiddling with his pimped-out EEG brain-wave machine. As his intern—aka captive guinea pig—that meant I spent way too many evenings with electrodes pasted to my head, staring at computer-generated images of things I could never un-see.

According to Grayson, it was all in the name of science. He was desensitizing my fight-or-flight reactions to encounters with the bizarre and unexplained. Unfortunately, his program failed to desensitize me to my encounters with *him*.

Something had to give. And soon. Or I was going to have to either kiss the guy or kill him.

"What do you mean, chemistry can trump biology, but biology can't trump chemistry?" I asked, repeating Grayson's words like a model pupil.

He shrugged. "Just that, Drex. Examples exist—"

An electronic buzz crackled from the front cab of the RV. It echoed into the main cabin where we stood, causing Grayson to pause mid-sentence.

Someone was calling in on his ham radio.

"Better hurry and get that," I said, trying to hide my elation at escaping another of his mind-blowing info dumps.

Grayson's eyes darted in the direction of the radio, then back to me. "Right." He closed the cabinet door, set the padlock, and sprinted toward the driver's cab.

Rats.

I'd hoped Grayson would leave the door open and let me browse his collection of crazy concoctions.

No dice.

"Gray here. Come in," I heard him say into the crackling microphone.

I flopped onto the couch and closed my eyes. Then I crossed my fingers and said a little prayer.

Please, Universe. Let it be something normal *this time.*

A sharp, staccato noise sounded from somewhere outside the RV.

I opened my eyes.

Either I'd just heard the call of a pileated woodpecker, or the Universe was laughing at me.

Again.

Chapter Two

I was tucked into the booth of the banquette reading *Aliens & Ammo* on my laptop when Grayson emerged from the front cab of the RV. He'd just concluded a lengthy discussion with one of his conspiracy nutter friends on the ham radio. One glance and his animated fidgeting told me Grayson was anxious to share the news.

I kept my eyes on my screen and pretended not to notice.

In actuality, I was dying to know what hair-brained scheme he was cooking up now—and whether it seemed survivable. But I didn't give him the satisfaction. Why? Because I was miffed he hadn't involved me in the discussion.

So I'd decided to teach him a lesson of my own.

Chemistry can be a *bitch*, too.

Grayson scooted into the booth across from me and opened his laptop. I could feel the tingle of his energy as he studied me with that mad scientist look of his. I didn't look up. Instead, I clicked something on my laptop screen, then casually raised a hand and tucked my hair behind my ear.

It had been four months since my stint in the hospital that had left me with a shaved head. Since then, my auburn hair had grown out almost two inches—just long enough to be totally annoying. It was the choppy, shapeless cut of an escaped convict. But on the bright side, at least I was no longer at the mercy of cheap Walmart wigs.

Grayson cleared his throat to get my attention.

Totally not happening.

"Good news, Drex," he announced.

"What?" I said, keeping my eyes on my laptop. I held my breath, hoping he wasn't going to report another alien invasion in progress—or mention that "killer tomato" crapola in Ruskin again.

"Since we've got time on our hands, I thought we'd go witness firsthand one of the most remarkable events in nature. A spectacle that only happens once or twice a century."

I smirked and glanced up. "You've got a *date?*"

"What?" Grayson's face went slack. "No. I'm talking about one of nature's *true phenomena.*"

I raised an eyebrow. "And *that* doesn't qualify?"

Grayson blew a breath out his nose. "I'm *serious*, Drex. We have the opportunity to witness a gathering that could arguably rival the migratory activities of the monarch butterfly."

"Look," I said, "If this has anything to do with attending this year's Entomology Society of America convention—"

Grayson's brow furrowed. "Wrong again. Take a look at this video."

I grimaced. "Aw, crap! Not another one of your monster creep shows!"

"No. This intel came directly from Operative Garth."

My upper lip hooked skyward. That wasn't necessarily good news. Operative Garth was an even bigger conspiracy theorist than Grayson. From inside his prepper compound, the *Wayne's World* wannabe had helped instigate more than one of our past wild ghoul chases.

I shot a suspicious, sideways glance at Grayson's computer. "What is it?"

"See for yourself."

Grayson flipped his laptop around so I could see the screen. He tapped a key with a long, spidery index finger. A video began to play.

I glared at it through narrowed eyes. To my surprise, not a single rotten-faced zombie lurched out at me.

"What kind of birds are those?" I asked, watching the synchronous movement of the choreographed swarm as it danced against a pink, dusky sky. "Are they starlings?"

"Even better," Grayson said. "*Cicadas!*"

My nose crinkled. "Bugs?"

Grayson's shoulders straightened. "I prefer the term arthropods. But, technically, yes. Keep watching. It gets even more interesting."

My face puckered. "How could that *possibly* be?"

I stared at the video. It appeared to have been made with someone's cellphone as they rode along a highway.

Suddenly, the camera's viewfinder panned abruptly away from the cicadas swarming in the sky. It refocused on a jackknifed tanker truck. It was lying on its side, half in the road, half in the grassy median.

I looked up at Grayson. "What the?"

He nodded at the laptop. "Keep watching."

A moniker on the tanker's side revealed it belonged to Bong Chemical Company. In a matter of moments, the truck was overrun by hordes of greenish-brown cicadas the size of my thumb.

Like locusts in a Kansas wheat field, the flying insects swooped down from the sky and landed in undulating waves in the amber liquid pooling on the asphalt around the fractured tanker.

Seconds later, the insects began to buzz around erratically, then fall to the ground like dirty hail. In under a minute, the surrounding grass and roadway were covered in an ankle-deep layer of dead and dying bugs.

Gross.

"Uh ... I don't get it," I said. "Remind me again. What's the appeal here?"

Grayson's left eyebrow arched upward like Spock's. "Don't you see, Drex? This is a *mega year!*"

"Huh?"

"A year when the life cycles of the three-year, five-year, seven-year, and periodical thirteen- and seventeen-year cicadas all emerge at once!"

My stomach went slack. "Oh. Goody."

"Exciting, right?" Grayson's green eyes glowed with a nearly deranged scientific fervor. "And, as a bonus aside, I'll get to practice my new hobby. *Entomophagy.*"

I cringed. "Eating bugs? Geez, Grayson. Is that what you've been do—"

"Exactly," he said, cutting me off. "I read that cicada exoskeletons crunch like popcorn. Think of it, Drex. This is the chance of a lifetime!"

"*Your* lifetime, maybe."

Grayson rubbed his hands together. "Then it's settled. We leave at dawn."

I sat back and groaned.

Great. Just what I need.

Another compelling reason to die young.

Chapter Three

Heading westbound on I-10, I caught a glimpse of the sunrise in the rearview mirror. As Grayson drove on, I shifted in my seat and drank my first cup of coffee in blissful silence.

I didn't have many rules, but no talking before my cup was empty was one of them. Grayson had learned it was worthwhile to follow it.

As we approached Tallahassee, to my surprise Florida's monotonous, flat landscape began to make allowances for slight inclines and slopes, then for actual hills. The dull-olive forests of slash pines and scrub oaks became more and more peppered with vibrant green splotches of newly leafed-out chestnuts and maples.

The changes stirred a vague recollection lying dormant in my sleepy brain.

Oh, yeah. Up in the Florida Panhandle, they actually had seasons.

I sat up in my seat and smiled at the splashes of white and pink dancing in the shadows of the forest understory. On either side of the highway, the dogwoods and azaleas were in bloom. It was late March. Spring was in the air.

I rolled down the window. The air outside was fresh and cool.

"Are we still in Florida?" I joked.

"Yes," Grayson said, my sarcasm failing to register. "Did you know that these hills are the end of the Appalachian mountain chain?"

My left eyebrow dented downward. "Please. No quizzes. Not without a second cup of coffee."

"Think of it," Grayson said, ignoring my plea. "This terrain was formed by glaciers at the end of the last ice age. You're a native, Drex. I'm surprised you didn't know that already."

I blew out a sigh. "Gimme a break, Grayson. I saw you reading a copy of *Florida Roadside Geology* last night. You didn't know it yourself until a few hours ago. Am I right?"

Grayson shrugged. "There's no time limit on knowledge."

Rolling my eyes required too much effort so I sighed instead. "How much further?"

He glanced at the odometer. "After we get through Tallahassee, we've got about an hour, give or take a taco break."

I shot my partner an incredulous look. "Geez. It's barely seven-thirty in the morning. Would you settle for a churro and a cup of coffee?"

"Perhaps. Either way, we need to tank up before we get to Bristol. There may not be a gas station nearby."

I cringed. "How big *is* the place?"

"The last census taken of Bristol recorded 993 people living there."

"Right. If you call *that* living."

"GEEZ. AND I THOUGHT Point Paradise was bad," I said as we passed the homemade road sign welcoming us to Bristol, Florida. "At least *we* had the Stop & Shoppe drive-thru."

"What are you complaining about?" Grayson asked. His voice was way too cheery for the circumstances. "Didn't you see the sign back there?"

I pulled the chocolate Tootsie Pop from my mouth. "You mean the one that read, '*Welcome to Bristol, the* only *incorporated city in* all of *Liberty County*'?"

Grayson turned his head and stared at me blankly. "No. The one that said it was Taco Tuesday at Appaloosa Diner."

My gut went slack. "Well, we certainly wouldn't want to miss *that*. I mean, we haven't had tacos since ... let's see ... *eight o'clock*."

Grayson shifted the RV into a lower gear. "Fish tacos don't count."

My face puckered. "In what universe? Where is it, anyway?"

Grayson pushed the brim of his fedora up with an index finger. "Where's what? The restaurant or Bristol?"

I glanced out the windshield at a whole lot of nothing that wasn't even *trying* to be something. "At this point, I'd settle for either one."

"Well, then, the odds are in your favor. Both should be just up the road ahead."

"Awesome."

As we traversed the pothole-pocked, two-lane road to nowhere, I leaned down and grabbed my laptop from the floorboard. I powered it up and google-searched Bristol.

The first image to come up was a mangled port-a-potty lying beside a hiking trail. A caption under it read: *"World's worst case of explosive diarrhea."*

You've got to be shitting *me....*

I caught my unintended pun and chuckled under my breath. As I clicked through a few more images, I realized it could well be the last laugh I'd have for a while.

Besides a mysterious-looking white mansion, a gopher hole, and a picture of an impressive Chicken-of-the-Woods fungus, Bristol appeared to be losing its bid as the cultural epicenter of northern Florida.

I sighed, snapped my laptop closed, and groused at Grayson. "Why is it that everything you find interesting has to be in the middle of freaking nowhere?"

"Just lucky, I guess," he said. "Relax. Think of this as a vacation."

"From what? Civilization?"

Grayson's cheek dimpled. Then he had the audacity to start *humming a tune* as he maneuvered the ramshackle RV down State Road 20 straight into the heart of Bristol. If it were the Heart of Dixie, it would've needed life support.

"Looks like we've arrived," he said.

I stared sourly at the mismatched buildings masquerading as a county seat. "How can you tell?"

To our right stood a pair of sagging, paint-worn wooden shacks that could've come straight from a black-and-white picture book of a pre-electricity pioneer shantytown. Just past those two time-forgotten hovels, an anachronistic traffic light blinked tiredly at a run-down gas station.

"Geez," I muttered.

I glanced across the street, where an old-time clapboard storefront proclaimed to be a family-owned hardware store and florist shop combo. "Aww. Look. Just what everybody needs. One-stop shopping for daisies and drill bits."

Ignoring me, Grayson drove through the only intersection in town. A few feet past it stood the wooden façade of an old-timey barber shop and a small, boxy post office.

Across the street, completing our grand, two-block city tour, sat an anomaly—a brand-spanking-new building constructed of precise, beige brick. Its tidy, pristine exterior was in such contrast to the rest of faded, worn-out Bristol that I figured it must've fallen out of the sky like Dorothy did in *The Wizard of Oz*.

"Well, what have we here?" Grayson said, nodding toward the newly constructed town hall/fire station.

The sun glaring off its shiny metal roof made me wince. "How in the world can a town like Bristol afford such a fancy new building?"

Grayson shrugged. "My money's on governmental snafu."

I sighed. "Makes as much sense as my theory."

"Which is?"

I grimaced. "Never mind."

A quick glance over at the road signs marking the intersection re-vealed they all pointed the way back to the interstate. Given what I'd seen of Bristol so far, I could hardly blame them.

"Uh, Grayson, maybe we should—"

"There she is," Grayson said, nodding at the windshield.

I turned and stared. "Who?"

"Not who. *What.*"

Grayson punched the gas, plastering me to the back of my seat. Straight ahead, the rectangular hulk of a single-story, red-and-green building caught my eye.

As we grew closer, I realized the red of the bottom half of the structure was a cladding of fake brick. The dark green top half was actually an oversized metal awning. Just like the new town hall, the oddly disproportionate overhang appeared to have been originally intended for a much grander locale.

"What *is* that place?" I asked.

Grayson scrunched his eyebrows at me as if I should've already known. "Appaloosa Diner, of course. Our tacos await."

I burped back acid from the mystery-fish gas-station taco I'd scarfed for breakfast. "Good grief, Grayson. It's not even nine o'clock. It's too early to eat another taco."

Grayson shrugged and pulled into the parking lot. "No harm in checking out the place, is there? Besides, I could use another cup of coffee. Maybe some flapjacks. How about you?"

I squelched another burp and stared at the Taco Tuesday sign. "Uh ... sure, I guess."

Too bad it isn't Mylanta Monday.

Chapter Four

Grayson and I ducked under the massive awning clinging to Appaloosa Diner's façade like a swollen green caterpillar. Through the glass front door, I caught a glimpse inside.

The interior of the place appeared to be in line with most eateries of its ilk. The walls sported 1970s-era wood paneling. Standard-issue laminate-topped tables were heaped in the center with an assortment of sticky-looking condiments. A stack of well-worn highchairs stood to the left of the door, waiting for the next round of Jell-O-slinging toddlers to fill them.

But as we stepped inside, the red-and-beige checkerboard floor caught me off guard. So did the fancy red-vinyl chairs on rollers. The once-chic office chairs now sagged under the weight of their current predicament, as if doing penance for squandering their youth as impudent fashion divas gracing some elite advertising firm's luxury digs.

But what amazed me the most about the diner was that—on a random Tuesday morning in the middle of nowhere—it was chock-a-block with customers.

The fact that most of the clientele were bearded guys in hunting camo was a tad less surprising...

"Howdy, folks!" a Southern tenor rang out over the clatter of silverware and country conversation.

As Grayson closed the front door behind us, I glanced in the direction of the voice. It had emanated from a scrawny, fifty-something guy sporting a camo ball cap. A scraggly grey beard cascaded from under the guy's red nose to midway down his flannel-clad chest like a hank of soggy Spanish moss.

I elbowed Grayson. "You didn't tell me this is where they filmed *Duck Dynasty*."

"Y'all here for breakfast with eh stee-ranger?" the man asked in a cornpone accent as thick as cheese grits.

"Breakfast with a stranger?" I said, then smiled and cocked my head toward Grayson. "No need. I brought my own weirdo."

Confusion dented one of the old guy's bushy, half-grey eyebrows. "I meant *him*," he said, and turned in the direction of a man sitting at the end of a large table cobbled together from two smaller ones.

Unlike our hillbilly host, the man at the head of the table was clean cut. He had dark, thick hair, and a button nose that made him look boyish. Instead of flannel or camo, he wore a beige, crisply ironed shirt with a collar and brass-buttoned pockets on each side. I couldn't help but think he looked like an overgrown Boy Scout.

The bearded guy turned back to us and grinned. "That there's eh stee-ranger right over there, in the flesh."

As opposed to what? In the skeleton?

I took another gander at the troop leader. He smiled, got up, and ambled over to us.

"Nice to see some fresh faces in the crowd," he said, flashing a winning smile. He extended a hand to shake. "I'm the park ranger around these parts." He grinned at me. "Given my name, some people say I didn't have much choice in the matter."

I glanced at the shiny brass nameplate above his left shirt pocket. It read, *S.T. Ranger*.

Breakfast with "eh-stee-ranger."

"Oh," I blurted, unable to decide whether to laugh or groan.

Either S.T. Ranger was one of those rare souls who arrived on Earth with his destiny pre-known, or he shot out of his mother's womb equipped with absolutely no freaking imagination whatsoever.

I guess I was about to find out.

"I WAS HOOKED BY SMOKEY the Bear," S.T. Ranger said after waving Grayson and me toward the empty red office chairs loitering around his table.

"On what? Crack?" I quipped.

It was a lame attempt at humor. But all of a sudden, I felt kind of giddy. The smell of frying bacon and buttermilk biscuits could do that to a Southern gal.

So could the attention of a good-looking stranger.

S.T. Ranger stared at me blankly for a moment, then broke into a grin when my pathetic joke finally registered.

"Oh! Not crack," he said. "I caught the *forest bug* from Old Smokey. I've wanted to be a park ranger since I was a kid in knee pants. And now, ta-da! I am."

"Don't let him fool ya," *Duck Dynasty* dude said, plopping down in the seat beside me, enveloping me in his redneck bubble of chewing-tobacco stink. He nodded toward S.T. Ranger. "You're talkin' to the unofficial king of Liberty County."

"Thanks, Lamar," S.T. Ranger said, then glanced at me and shrugged. "But Liberty County's a mighty small kingdom. I'm not just the park ranger. I'm also a fill-in deputy and the county's only trained naturalist."

"Naturalist? How fortuitous," Grayson said from across the mountain of condiments on the table.

Lamar's beady eyes narrowed. "What you mean by that, mister?"

Grayson studied Lamar slowly and patiently, as if he'd just skewered him to Styrofoam with a hatpin. "I meant that it's fortunate we ran into you. We've come to Bristol expressly to experience the cicada swarm firsthand."

Lamar's eyes widened. "Are y'all cicada maniacs?"

My eyebrows shot up. "I beg your pardon?"

The wiry old buzzard grinned at me. "You know, members of *Cicada Mania*."

My jaw lost its tension and fell open a crack. "Is that a real thing?"

"Absolutely," S.T. Ranger said. "Check it out online. We're both members. Everybody in the LBH is."

"LBH?" Grayson asked.

"Liberty Bug Hunters," the good-looking ranger said proudly.

I forced a smile.

Just my luck. The only handsome guy in the room turns out to be the leader of Bugsy and the Bug-Nuts.

"Cicada mania, you say," Grayson said. "I wasn't aware there was a website dedicated solely to cicada aficionados. Sounds like my kind of organization."

"Honestly, I don't get what all the 'buzz' is about," I quipped.

The three men stared back at me blankly. I watched as my joke wobbled lamely over their heads and splatted against the wood paneling like a one-winged cockroach.

I grimaced out an apologetic smile, then posed a question I hoped would redeem me. "Why cicadas, gentlemen?"

"Because," S.T. Ranger said, shooting me a GQ-worthy smile. "Like the Cicada Mania website says, 'Cicadas are the most amazing insects in the world.'"

I nearly let out a whimper for all of womankind.

"In fact, that's the topic of this morning's LBH meeting," the ranger continued. "The mega event happening right here, right now, in little-old Bristol itself!"

"Outstanding!" Grayson beamed. "Like I said, that's *exactly* why we've come to town. By the way, I'm Nick Grayson. This is my partner, Bobbie Drex."

"Steve," S.T. Ranger said. "But most folks around here call me Ranger. Nice to meet you both. And I guess you've already figured out the name of this guy," he said, nodding at *Duck Dynasty* dude. "That's Lamar Cinders."

"Yes," I said, blocking Lamar's hug attempt. "Thanks. But let's keep this professional, shall we?"

Ranger glanced in the direction of the front door and bolted to his feet. "It's about time you two got here!" he hollered at two men approaching the table. Both were dressed for either a long hike in the woods or an afternoon of serial killing.

"Sorry we're late," one said. "We were—"

"No worries," Ranger said. "We were just doing introductions. I want y'all to welcome ... uh ..."

"Nick Grayson," Grayson said, standing up and extending a hand to shake. "And this is my partner, Bobbie Drex."

"Russel Stokes. Rusty for short," said a slim guy in his late thirties. He reached out a slender, ruddy hand covered with more freckles than the legal limit should allow.

"Everybody 'round here knows me as Whitey," grunted the second man, removing his camo cap. The leathery-skinned old man sported an impressive paunch and a headful of shockingly white hair that, despite his advanced age, was still as thick as an animal pelt.

"Okay," Ranger said. "Everybody sit. Let's call this meeting of the Liberty Bug Hunters to order." He clomped on the table with a coffee spoon. "Fellow entomologists and ento-wannabes, any *biz*-ness before we get down to *bugs*-ness?"

I stifled a groan. I should've seen that one coming.

"Yeah," Lamar said. "Where's Darryl and Dale? It ain't like them to miss a meetin' of the LBH."

I glanced around at the other men. Rusty, Ranger and Whitey shook their heads and shrugged.

"Well, their loss is your gain," Ranger said, beaming his perfect smile at me and Grayson. "You're filling their seats right now. It'll be interesting to see if you can fill their shoes, too. Now, let's order up some breakfast and get down to some serious cicada chat. We need to set the date for this year's festivities."

"Uh, you have cicada *festivities?*" I asked.

"Of course," Ranger said. "Every year. The highlight's the annual bug barbeque."

My gut flopped. I glanced over at Grayson. He was grinning like a nerd with a new chemistry set.

"I hope we're invited," Grayson said.

"Of course," Ranger said. "The more the merrier!"

Lamar elbowed me. "Play your cards right and you could be this year's Cicada Queen."

Then my life on Earth would be complete.

I held my breath against Lamar's body odor and felt my own body go limp in my chair. The men's chatter slowly faded away, along with my will to live.

I was about to succumb to death by gutted hopes when a miracle happened. A waitress came over, leaned against my shoulder, and poured me a heavenly smelling cup of coffee.

She winked at me and said, "Ladies first," in a sweet Southern drawl.

I smiled, grateful not only for the coffee, but for the proof the server delivered along with it; I no longer needed a wig for strangers to recognize that I was female.

As the waitress made the rounds with the coffee pot, I took a sip and felt my feelings of hopelessness fall away, kicked to the curb by potent caffeine. I smirked.

More proof that Grayson's right. Chemicals really do *beat out biology.*

"I see someone appreciates my coffee," the waitress said, pouring Lamar a cup.

I looked down and realized I'd drained mine dry. I held it out for her to refill it.

"Best I've had in quite a while," I said. "Honestly. In fact, it may've just saved my life."

She laughed and handed me a menu. "Wouldn't be the first time, sweetie."

I grinned and decided to nip my bad mood in the bud and count my blessings instead.

One, I had an endless supply of great coffee at my fingertips. *Two*, Grayson didn't have electrodes pasted to my head. And *three*, nowhere on the menu was the slightest mention of cicada exoskeletons.

Maybe it wasn't going to be such a bad day after all.

Chapter Five

"**A**nd now a few facts for you new-*bees*," Ranger said, addressing me with a wink.

He handed the waitress his menu, then continued officiating the Liberty Bug Hunters meeting.

"I thought it would be interesting for you to know there are over three thousand known species of cicada," he said from his chairman's position at the head of the table. "Florida is lucky enough to host nineteen of them."

I smiled and nodded. That really *was* pretty lucky, considering there could've been 2,981 more varieties of the creepy pests crawling all over the place.

I enviously eyed someone's breakfast as it passed by—sausages and biscuits heaped high in one of those sectioned plastic plates used by prisons and school cafeterias.

"Uh ... how long will this cicada event last?" I asked, partly to win favor with the cute ranger, partly to know how many days I had left before this crap would finally be over.

Ranger nodded appreciatively at me. "Good question, Miss Drex. It's a known fact that periodic cicadas typically continue to emerge in waves until late June. They are, of course, different from *seasonal* cicadas. They're emerging now, all at once."

"But it's still March," I said.

Ranger grinned. "Yes. We got lucky. They're all emerging early this year, thanks to the warm winter we had."

Yeah. That's pretty lucky all right.

"How can you tell the nineteen species apart?" I asked, batting my eyelashes at Ranger.

Ranger's smile skipped a beat. "Uh ... by their appearance, mainly."

Grayson cleared his throat. "Cicadas vary widely in size and shape, Drex. Therefore, the best species determinants are eye color and wing size."

After having listened to Grayson drone on for months about his bug collection, I was ready for a second opinion. I shot my partner some cicada-inspired side-eye, then turned my attention back to Ranger. "Can cicadas be distinguished by the sounds they make?"

Ranger's brow furrowed while he contemplated my question. "Well, the males of both periodic and seasonal cicadas are infamous for their shrill calls, that's for sure. They can get quite loud when they're gathered in large numbers."

"What drives them to call?" I blurted before Grayson could stick his nose in again. I already knew the answer. The males called out in the hopes of getting laid. Why else did any guy do anything?

"To attract a mate," Lamar said, confirming my theory. The old man stared at me with his beady eyes, then scratched something either on or living inside his ragged beard.

I grimaced and reached for the red plastic drinking glass. As I took a sip of water, Lamar's hand shot toward my head.

"What lady could resist this?" he asked.

Suddenly, a sound akin to a buzz saw on helium reverberated beside my ear canal.

"Argh!" I yelled, spewing my mouthful of water. "What the hell was that?"

Lamar grinned and opened his palm, revealing a black object the size and shape of a key fob. I flinched at first, thinking it was a palmetto bug, Florida's native, mutant-sized cockroach.

It wasn't.

"This here's my handy-dandy cicada recorder," Lamar said. "And what you just heard was the distress call of *Diceroprocta olympusa*, also known as the Olympic Scrub Cicada."

I shot him a look that, in my mind's eye, set his mangy beard ablaze. "Stick that thing near my ear again and you're gonna be letting out your *own* distress call."

Lamar shrank back in his seat, taking his stupid micro recorder with him.

"I thought the Olympic Scrub Cicada didn't emerge until June," Grayson said.

Lamar studied me with a wary eye, then turned to Grayson. "That's right. I recorded that one last year."

"But with this year's early emergence, you might get lucky and hear one in the wild today," Ranger said. Then, to my surprise, he winked at me again.

One of my eyebrows rose an inch.

Either he's flirting with me, or the guy's got an inbred facial tick. Given the state of my love life, I guess I could live with that...

"That must explain the giant swarm we saw on the video," Grayson said.

Ranger's gaze jerked from me to Grayson. "Video?"

Grayson nodded. "Yes. The one involving the overturned tanker truck."

"You *saw* that?" Rusty asked, choking on a slurp of coffee.

"Well, second-hand," Grayson said. "An operative ... I mean *associate*. He sent me the YouTube video. I was hoping someone here could take us to the exact location."

"Why?" Whitey and I asked simultaneously.

"To take documentary photos," Grayson said. "After all, this is a swarm for the history books, correct?"

"Oh. Sure," Lamar blurted, his eyes darting to Ranger. "I thought it might be on account of the legend—"

"Legendary it *is*," Ranger said loudly. He grabbed his coffee cup and raised it to the center of the table. "I say let's toast to being here to witness this historic event!"

"Here, here!" the other men cheered, grabbing up their mugs.

I raised my coffee cup too, and clinked it against the others' half-heartedly. But as I turned to touch mugs with Lamar, he was staring into his cup, gnawing his lip.

"What's wrong?" I asked over the din of the other men talking.

"You going with them? Out there in the woods?" he asked.

"Uh ... yeah. Why?"

"Nothing."

I shrugged and started to glance back over at the other men. Lamar grabbed my arm.

"You got a gun?" he asked.

"Yeah."

He nodded. "Good. I hope you know how to use it."

"Why?"

"There's some spooky shit going on around here."

I suddenly realized my ears were ringing.

Was Lamar's cicada recording still buzzing in my eardrum, or was it a warning bell?

Chapter Six

The hair on my neck pricked up. Lamar's words of warning echoed in my head.

"You got a gun?"

I felt for my Glock.

What the hell are we doing out here?

Stupidly, Grayson and I had just followed four strange men down a narrow dirt road into a thicket of unfamiliar forest.

As I stood there fingering the trigger in my right pants-pocket, I couldn't decide which was spooking me more—Lamar's warning or the fact that the men had just led us to the site of a huge, unmarked grave.

"Right here's where we buried 'em," Whitey said, adjusting his camo pants around his ample middle. He pointed a rifle butt at a rectangular mound of raw, red clay the size of an Olympic swimming pool.

"You *buried* the dead cicadas?" Grayson asked, taking the words right out of my mouth. "Why?"

"Because of the legend—" Lamar said, shooting me a knowing glance.

"*Legend*ary numbers," Ranger said, cutting his fellow bug-hunter off.

"But Ranger, don't you think—" Lamar protested.

Ranger's eyes narrowed, silencing Lamar. Then they locked on me and Grayson. "You saw the video. Those cicadas died in heaps. We had to get them off the roadway A-S-A-P. The gawkers were causing traffic jams. Besides, Rusty here was itching to try out his new backhoe, weren't you?"

The freckled redneck chuckled as he pulled off his camo ball cap, revealing a pate of thinning, red hair. At the speed his hairline was receding, I figured it'd be two years tops before Rusty's new nickname was "Bozo."

"Well, yeah," Rusty said. "And the fifty bucks you paid me for the job didn't hurt none, neither, Ranger."

Lamar pulled his cap off his mangy head and held it to his heart. "And seeing's how we consider the critters our brethren, well, it seemed plum wrong to just dump 'em out on the ground like garbage."

My nose crinkled. "Brethren?"

"All God's creatures deserve respect," Lamar said, wagging his eyebrows at me. "Even skinny old rascals with shaggy beards."

Disgust ran a cold, randy finger down my spine.

"Well, it's still a shame they had to die," Grayson said. "But at least they had a semi-full life."

"Semi-full?" I asked.

"They survived all five of their life stages," Grayson said. "Ovum, larval, subterranean grub, nymph, and winged adult." He sighed. "Granted, they didn't last long after they emerged and shed their exoskeletons, but they did get a brief chance to fly free."

"Maybe even to mate," Lamar added, winking at me. "That's purty much all they do once they git their wings."

"Oh." I stared at the cicadas' mass grave, feeling both repulsed and oddly jealous.

Grayson put his hands on his hips and inhaled deeply. "It's a shame their short lives were cut even shorter. But at least they went to their rest amidst the smell of fresh forest pines."

"That ain't pines you're smellin'," Rusty said. "That'd be the detergent."

Grayson's eyebrow crooked upward. "Detergent?"

"Yeah," Rusty said. "That tanker was in-between runs when it jackknifed. It was hauling a load of detergent-water to clean out the tank."

"I don't get the connection," I said.

Lamar grinned lewdly at me. "Bet you didn't know this, Missy, but Bong Chemical's the maker of world-famous Pine-Solve-It."

"He's right," Ranger said. "That strong pine smell is from the wash-water. The cicadas were covered in it."

"From what I saw on the video, it's also what killed them," Grayson said. "Is this Pine-Solve-It stuff toxic?"

"No," Ranger said. "Not to humans, at least."

"What caused the tanker to jackknife?" Grayson asked.

Ranger shrugged. "Don't know."

"What does the driver say?" I asked.

"Virgil Stubbs? Nothing, yet. We haven't been able to interview him."

"Why not?" Grayson asked.

Ranger glanced away for a second. "We can't find him." He looked down and toed a pinecone. "He's been declared missing."

"Missing?" Grayson said. "Did he flee the scene of the accident?"

"I can't comment on an ongoing investigation."

"I understand," Grayson said. "But let me know if I can help." He whipped out his wallet and flashed his P.I. badge. "I'm a private investigator."

Ranger's eyebrows shot up, then he nodded toward me. "What about her?"

Grayson smirked. "She's working on it. If you need any help, let us know."

"I appreciate that," Ranger said. "But I think we'd better leave this to the Sheriff's Department."

"When did the accident happen?" Grayson asked.

"Three days ago. The woman who reported it said it must've happened just about dawn on the seventeenth."

Grayson's eyebrow shot up. "How would she know that?"

Ranger chewed his lip for a moment. "She said when she passed by the tanker, the front wheel was still spinning."

"Hmm," Grayson said. "Anything else?"

"No."

"Yeah there was," Rusty said. "She said she saw someone with long, red hair run into the woods."

"Hacksaw Hattie!" Lamar gasped.

"There's no such thing!" Ranger hissed at Lamar, then shot Rusty a dirty look.

"Humor me," Grayson said. "Who's Hacksaw Hattie?"

"Just some local superstition," Ranger said as if the words tasted bad in his mouth.

"It is *not*, Ranger, and you know it!" scraggly bearded Lamar protested. "It really happened!"

"What happened?" I asked.

Ranger blew out a breath. "Nothing. It's an old wives' tale. This woman named Hattie supposedly cut off her husband's head with a hacksaw when he came home drunk on St. Patrick's Day."

I grimaced, recalling the green tacos and beer I'd been forced to eat three days ago. "Wait. That was the same day as the tanker accident."

"Just a coincidence," Ranger said.

"Is not!" Lamar said.

"Look," Ranger barked. "Hacksaw Hattie is nothing but a silly ghost story. She's been dead and buried for God knows how long."

"Exactly a hundred years," Lamar said, "and three days."

"Intriguing," Grayson said. "So there's a ghost legend involved here."

"Not *legend*," Lamar said. "*True history*. A hundred years ago, Hattie was hanged for killin' her husband. Says so right on her tombstone. With her final breath, she vowed she'd come back and get her revenge one day."

Ranger scowled. "Don't listen to that nonsense."

"Nonsense?" Lamar hissed. "If it's all nonsense, why don't you go ahead and tell them her real name?"

"Oh, geez," Ranger said, exasperated.

Lamar locked eyes with Grayson. "It was *Stubbs,* mister. Hattie *Stubbs*. And her husband's name? It was Virgil."

My eyebrows met. "The same as the truck driver?"

"Identical," Lamar said.

Ranger threw his hands in the air. "It's all just a stupid coincidence."

"I would tend to agree," Grayson said. "That is, I would if I believed in coincidences."

Chapter Seven

I couldn't shake the eerie vibe of the place.

Next to me, beady-eyed, lecherous Lamar was going on and on about a killer ghost. A few yards away, Grayson was poking around, taking photos of a mass grave. Untold hundreds of thousands of cicadas had died during their fifteen minutes of fame, their tragic end commemorated on YouTube for our entertainment pleasure.

Sometimes the world was just too strange to fathom.

I turned away from Lamar and his kooky rantings, and tried to change the subject.

"So what do you think happened to Virgil Stubbs?" I asked Ranger, waving a gnat away from my face.

One of his dark eyebrows rose. "Hattie's husband? Like everyone says, she sawed his head off while he was passed out drunk, I suppose. I do wonder, though. If she really did, why would her kin still see fit to bury her in the cemetery right beside him?"

Lamar snorted. "His *body* might be buried beside her. But from what I hear, they never did find his head."

I grimaced. "Uh ... thanks. But I meant Virgil Stubbs *the truck driver*."

"Oh." Lamar shrugged. "If you ask me, I think—"

I glanced over at Ranger. His face was the color of a ripe pomegranate. I couldn't tell if he was angry, embarrassed, or about to have a stroke. I decided to pose my question anyway.

"Could Virgil have been the red-haired person that was reportedly seen running into the woods after the accident?"

Ranger shook his head. "Not possible. Virgil's bald."

"Not completely," Whitey said. "He's got a ponytail."

"Fine," Ranger said. "But his hair's not red. It's dirty blond."

"With an emphasis on *dirty*," Rusty said, his freckled nose crinkling like he smelled a skunk. "Virgil never was partial to regular bathing."

"So what do you think happened to Virgil after he wrecked?" I asked.

"Hacksaw Hattie got him!" Lamar said.

Ranger blew out a breath. "The most likely scenario is he suffered a concussion during the accident. Virgil hit his head on the windshield, got disoriented, and wandered off. Or he was unconscious and some Good Samaritan picked him up and is taking care of him as we speak. He'll turn up directly."

"The Sheriff's Department's been searching for *two days* already," Lamar said. "From what I heard, they ain't found a single sign of him."

Grayson studied Ranger. "Is that true?"

The Boy Scout's button nose bristled. "As far as I know. Look, they don't always tell me everything. I'm just a part-time, fill-in deputy, remember."

Grayson nodded amiably. "I understand. But you were *there*, right? You saw the actual accident scene."

"Yes. But I'm not at liberty to discuss it."

"Right," Grayson said. "Were you able to conclude what caused the truck to jackknife?"

"There was a rubber skid-mark trail big as King Kong's under britches," Lamar said. "Seen it myself."

The tendons in Ranger's neck made an appearance. "There was a *sizeable* trail of burnt rubber on the asphalt," he said, giving Lamar the stank eye. "Apparently, Virgil hit the brakes hard for something. But whatever it was didn't leave a trace, as far as I've been told."

"That's because ghosts don't leave traces," Lamar said.

Ranger's eyes narrowed. "Enough with this Hacksaw Hattie nonsense!"

"From the video I saw, it looked to me as if the tanker's windshield was completely gone," Grayson said.

Ranger sighed. "It was. The safety glass shattered and fell out in one big sheet. Virgil must've crawled through it."

Grayson's eyebrow flat-lined. "Why do you say that?"

"Because it would've been easier than going out the door, seeing as how the truck was on its side. Also, the tanker's doors were still locked. Like I said, Virgil must've bumped his head and wandered off. Now please, can we give this whole thing a rest and let the Sheriff's Department do their job?"

"Fine by me," Whitey said.

Rusty nodded and tugged at the cap on his half-bald pate. "I wonder if Bong's lookin' to hire a replacement driver."

Lamar sneered. "Who'd want the job?"

Whitey grinned. "Why? You afraid Hattie will come get the next one, too?"

"No, you ignoramus," Lamar hissed. "Bong don't pay enough to keep a church mouse in cheese. You know that."

"You worked there?" I asked.

Lamar nodded. "We've all took us a turn workin' at the plant at one time or another, ain't we, boys?"

To my surprise, all four men nodded, including Ranger.

"In a town this small, there aren't a lot of options," Ranger said almost apologetically.

I nodded in empathy. Growing up in dead-end Point Paradise, I totally understood just how non-bright a future could be.

"Speaking of cheese," Grayson said. "Anybody else hungry?" He reached into his jacket and pulled out a shaker of popcorn seasoning.

"I was hoping to taste-test some cicada exoskeletons. Know where we can find some?"

My jaw went slack.

"Seriously?" Ranger said, echoing my thoughts. His lip twisted slightly in disgust, earning him another gold star in my little black book.

"Absolutely," Grayson said. "Where could we find enough to share?"

"Uh ...," Ranger fumbled. "You've probably got plenty around your place, don't you think, Rusty?"

"Prolly," he replied, scratching a freckled ear. "By the sound of the matin' calls coming out of the woods around my house, I figure the ground's gotta be plum loaded with 'em."

"So where *is* your place, Rusty?" Grayson asked.

Rusty hooked a thumb over his shoulder. "Just down the road a piece." He turned to Ranger. "What say you, chief?"

Ranger gave Rusty a quick nod. "Think Bonnie will mind?"

Rusty shook his head. "Naw. Just so long as nobody drags mud in the house, she'll be all right."

"Okay, then. Everybody, load up," Ranger announced. "Looks like the LBH crew is heading to Rusty's."

"Excellent!" Grayson turned to me, a gleam in his green eyes. He rubbed his hands together. "I for one can't *wait* to savor the Olympic Scrub Cicada in its natural habitat."

I swallowed the bile rising up my throat. I for one certainly *could*.

"YOU'RE NOT THINKING about getting involved in this Hacksaw Hattie crap, are you?" I asked Grayson as we walked to the RV.

He shrugged. "You have to admit the story's got legs."

"But no head," I quipped. "And I don't feel like being the next to lose mine."

"Come on, Drex. How dangerous can a hundred-year-old ghost be?"

"She killed her husband, Grayson."

"Sure, but how long can a woman stay mad?"

Oh, you have no idea.

Chapter Eight

On the way to Rusty's hometown exoskeleton buffet, I'd hoped to catch a moment alone with Grayson.

To my annoyance, my head was still vaguely buzzing. Was it just a headache, or had Lamar's cicada call disturbed the mass a recent MRI had uncovered inside my brain? Was my vestigial tumor-twin trying to warn me of something, or was it merely laughing at the absurdity of my life and rattling my Pineal gland like a maraca?

Whatever the reason, my enquiring mind would have to wait. Without consulting me, Grayson had invited Ranger to join us in the RV for the trip to Rusty's. Given how soundly Ranger had put the kibosh on Lamar's mention of Hacksaw Hattie, I figured I'd best keep my mouth shut about my own vanishing twin.

"How far to Rusty's place?" I asked, looking up at Ranger from the floorboard.

Rather than sit on the couch in the back of the RV, I'd chosen to kneel on the floorboard in the space between the two swiveling chairs in the driver's cab. I hadn't wanted to miss a word of the guys' riveting conversation. But so far, their discussion had been duller than a dusty flip-flop. I swore if I heard either one of them utter another word in Latin, I was going to slap them upside the head with a flyswatter.

"And that's how I discovered the residual effects of long-term iridium exposure," Grayson said, snapping me out of my boredom stupor.

WTH?

"Almost there," Ranger said. "Just follow the road and take a right past the giant sinkhole."

I choked on my own air supply. "Sinkhole?"

"Yes."

Ranger turned and looked down at me. "It's a natural phenomenon caused when rainwater erodes the rocks and minerals forming the underground structure of a piece of land until it collapses under its own weight. Given that Florida's substrate is comprised mainly of soft limestone, sinkholes are practically a forgone conclusion."

"I *know* what a stupid sinkhole is," I said sourly.

Ranger's brow crinkled. "Then why did you ask?"

"I didn't—"

"Is the sinkhole natural or manmade?" Grayson asked, cutting me off.

Ranger turned his attention back to Grayson. "A bit of both, I suppose. Man started the hole, then nature came along and gave it a helping hand."

"What do you mean?" I asked.

Ranger sighed like a man who'd told the story more times than he cared to remember. "It all began a couple of years ago, right before Michael came to town. You know, a lot of us think Bristol would've finally topped a thousand residents if it wasn't for that blasted Michael."

My nose crinkled inquisitively. "Who's Michael?"

"Oh." Ranger sat up straight in his chair. "Sorry. I figured you knew. I guess I should've said *Hurricane* Michael. He blew through here back in October of 2018. Lots of folks around here blamed the sinkhole on that storm. But the truth is, a small hole had already opened up a few days before, due to an underground pipe leak. Then Michael came by and dumped so much rain on top of us that it caused the hole to collapse in on itself until it was the size of a football field."

"Intriguing," Grayson said.

Ranger nodded at the windshield. "See? There it is, straight ahead."

I got up off my knees, crouched over, and peered out the windshield. Off to the right, surrounded by barricades and blockade fencing, stood the remains of a crumbling building. Eating away at its foundation was a crater in the orange-clay earth as big as a Walmart parking lot.

"Holy smokes!" I gasped.

"Amazing, isn't it?" Ranger said. "When it collapsed, it took out a couple of duplexes and half the old cemetery."

"Why don't they fill it in?" I asked.

"Can't. When a hole like that gets started, it can keep going for years. There's no telling when the edges will cave in again. With sinkholes, all you can do is evacuate the area and hope for the best."

"Geez." I craned my neck for a better view as we drove closer to the massive hole in the ground.

"You have to admit it's impressive, huh?" Ranger said. "Every time it rains, the sides give way a little more. If it ever stabilizes, well, then we can think about filling it in. But honestly, what for? Who in their right mind would ever trust that patch of land again? Besides, it's not like we've got the budget for such a major project."

"What will happen to this place, then?" I asked as we drove past the humongous, gaping abyss. Teetering on its ragged edge, a couple of old limestone headstones stood at weird angles, on the verge of toppling in.

Ranger shrugged and smiled wistfully. "With any luck, in a decade or two, the good folks of Bristol will have themselves a new fishing spot." He turned to face the windshield and said, "Turn right just ahead."

"Roger that." Grayson maneuvered the RV onto a narrow, unpaved road made of the same red clay as the sinkhole we'd just passed.

Dread cascaded over me as I imagined the earth beneath us collapsing and swallowing us whole.

"Uh ... is this entire area prone to sinkholes?" I asked, holding onto the back of the passenger seat for dear life.

"Not particularly," Ranger said. "Actually, this was the first one we've had in decades. Why?"

"Well, we're going to need a place to park the RV," I said. "I'd rather not end up getting buried alive in it overnight."

Ranger chuckled. "I don't think you have to worry about that."

"I saw there are a number if state parks around here," Grayson said. "Any you'd recommend? I was thinking about Torreya. It sounded interesting."

"And a whole lot nicer sounding than Tate's Hell," I said. "Is that place for real?"

Ranger laughed. "Yes. And I have to say, they both have their own unique draws. But since you're asking I prefer the first one. And, for the record, it's pronounced TORE-*ee-ya*. It rhymes with Gloria."

Right. Just like Bristol rhymes with piss-hole.

"TORE-ee-ya," Grayson said, trying on the word. He hit the brakes and nodded at the windshield. "What now?"

A line of battered pickups were parked bumper-to-bumper along the shoulder of the narrow dirt road, making it too tight for the RV to pass. I recognized them as belonging to the rest of the bug-hunter bunch.

"Looks like this is as close as we can get," Ranger said. "Park anywhere you can find a spot and we'll walk from here."

"Will do," Grayson said, then maneuvered us onto the soft shoulder and turned off the ignition.

Ranger cracked open the passenger door, then hesitated. "Hope y'all brought some serious bug repellent with you."

My brow creased. "Wait. I thought you L-B-H-ers *revered* insects."

Ranger grinned. "We do. But when it comes down to it, if somebody's gonna get chomped on, I'm with Grayson."

"What do you mean?" I asked.

Ranger winked a devilish blue eye at me. "I'd rather be the eat*er* than the eat*ee*."

I only had a second to ponder the innuendo potential of his remark before I felt a sharp sting. A mosquito had stuck its nasty little proboscis into my neck.

Not sexy. Not sexy at all.

Chapter Nine

I spritzed on what Ranger promised was "industrial-strength bug repellent" as we walked in tandem down the clay-dirt road leading to Rusty's place. After squirting it on my arms, I rubbed a bit on my face and neck and handed the bottle back to the overgrown Boy Scout.

Ranger tucked the repellent into his shirt pocket and said, "That ought to do it."

At least, I *think* that's what he said. I could barely hear him over the relentless chorus of cicadas. It sounded like millions of them were letting out their shrill calls from the forest surrounding us.

"Thanks," I yelled, then noticed that Ranger had stopped in his tracks and was staring straight ahead.

I turned and followed his gaze. We'd come to an illegal dumpsite by the side of the road. A well-used one, at that. I expected Ranger to get angry and start writing a citation or something.

"We're here," Ranger said.

"What?" I asked.

Ranger took another step toward the garbage-strewn ground. As he did, a monstrous buzz rang out above the others. It came from somewhere within the heaps of dead appliances and abandoned auto parts nearby.

I flinched. "What the hell was that?"

Suddenly, something emerged from behind the rusted-out chassis of an old Volkswagen beetle.

I opened my mouth to scream, then closed it again.

"Lug nut come loose," Rusty said, standing to his full height.

He grinned and pulled the trigger on the oversized gun in his hand. It whirred and let out another resounding buzz. "Love me some pneumatic drill in the mornin'!" he called out, and waved us over.

Please. Someone tell me I've been slipped some LSD.

I suddenly felt dizzy. And a bit nauseated.

This shit was *real*.

"What're you working on now?" Ranger asked Rusty, as if living in a garbage heap was completely ordinary.

"Bonnie's tire's gone hinky again," the freckled freak replied. "What do you think, Miss?" he asked, then waved his free hand in Vanna-White fashion across the sea of vehicular debris.

I think you should spin the wheel again. You obviously landed on Bankrupt.

I gawked, trying to take it all in. Next to the faded-tan rust-bucket beetle Rusty was working on stood a junky white Jetta missing its front bumper and hood. Beside the Jetta was a dark-brown, 1980s-era Westfalia camper van. Half disassembled, the van's parts were scattered like shrapnel all over the clearing in the forest that Rusty called home.

A well-worn footpath through the junk-strewn patch of land wound its way to a clearing at the top of a small hill. There, a conga line of old VW camper-vans stood, welded together end-to-end, like a giant junk centipede. Attached to the middle of the thing was an old pontoon boat. Steps leading up its side bore witness to the sad fact that the old party barge was now serving time as a makeshift front porch.

"Uh ... I've never seen anything like it," I said.

Rusty beamed. "Thanks!" He leaned over, switched off the compressor powering his pneumatic drill, then stood arrow straight with redneck pride.

"Welcome to my little slice of heaven," he announced, then grinned wide enough to reveal a missing molar.

I forced a smile and hoped like hell that if I ever made it to heaven, Rusty wouldn't be my next-door neighbor. Given my family upbringing, I'd already suffered enough junk-hoarding rednecks and broken-down vehicles to last me *ten* lifetimes.

"Earl would love this place," I said absently, thinking of my cousin back in Point Paradise.

"Nice Westfalia," Grayson said, coming up behind us and slapping a palm on the front side-panel of the gutted camper van.

"Thanks," Rusty said. "When I'm done with it, that's gonna be my man cave."

Of course. Just what every modern Neanderthal needs.

"What do you do with all the spare parts?" Grayson asked.

"Sell 'em on eBay or Craig's list, mostly," Rusty said. "Why? You need something? I got a real beaut of an engine block I can let go pretty cheap."

Grayson rubbed his chin. "Tempting, but—"

"So, where can we find these delicious cicada exoskeletons?" I asked Rusty, knowing that the sooner Grayson got his hands on some, the sooner we could get the hell out of there.

"Right yonder, I 'spect." Rusty nodded toward a patch of woods behind us.

I turned to see Lamar and Whitey tromping out of the underbrush in our direction. Whitey's leathery right hand held a rusty Maxwell House coffee can.

"Here you go," Whitey said as he walked up to us. He handed the can to me. "Got you up a good batch."

I peered into the old tin can. It was a quarter full of what appeared to be the outer husks of dried dates—if dried dates had bulging eyes and creepy, crab-like legs.

Yuck!

"Some of 'em looks pretty fresh, too," Lamar said proudly.

"Uh ... how can you tell?" I asked, plucking one from the bucket. I held it up to the light and examined the rigid, opaque-amber shell.

Gross. If Quasimodo ever came back reincarnated as a bug, he'd surely be one of these ugly-ass things.

"Well, the fresh ones is the ones ain't got much dirt on 'em, right?" Lamar said, then laughed.

Grayson snatched the coffee can from my hand and began fishing around inside it—for the cleanest exoskeleton, I presumed.

"I ain't never heard of no one eatin' no exoskeletons," Rusty said, shaking his freckled head. "No sir. The best eating cicada's the ones what just crawled outta their shells. Right, Whitey?"

"Yep."

I tried to hitch the corners of my mouth into a smile, but my lips weren't having it. "So you've all uh ... *tried* them?"

The men chuckled.

"Sure have," Whitey said, nodding at the exoskeleton in my hand. "When they first crack out of those nymph husks is when they're at their softest and juiciest. Goes without saying, that's when they make the best eating, too."

And yet you said it anyway.

Grayson popped a cicada hull into his mouth and crunched down on it.

My gut recoiled. "What do they taste like?"

Grayson grimaced and spat out a mouthful of brown shards. "Definitely not popcorn."

I smirked. "I was talking to *Whitey*."

"Oh," the old man grunted. He ran a hand through his shock of white hair. "When they're fresh, I'd say corn, mostly."

"With or without the cob?" Grayson said sourly, then raked his tongue with his teeth and spat again.

Whitey laughed. "I told you it's the *fresh ones* you want. And not those blasted hulls. Fresh-hatched cicada *bugs*. They make a tasty meal—especially served alongside the larvae of the sago palm weevil. Those critters taste like bacon, don't they, Ranger?"

"Somewhat," Ranger agreed. "But in my opinion, the best eating bug is the tarantula. It has a delicate flavor. Something between crab and shrimp. Too bad we don't have any tarantula species indigenous to Florida."

"Yeah," I said, shaking my head. "Too bad."

"Which method do you prefer when preparing cicadas for consumption?" Grayson asked.

"You mean how do we cook 'em?" Whitey asked. He chuckled. "Any old way you can. Steam 'em, sauté 'em. Boil 'em. Grill 'em on the barbeque. Whichever way you like."

Lamar's beady brown eyes darted around at the treetops. "If you think about it. This here mega-event is like a free restaurant."

"Yeah," I quipped. "A regular In-and-Out Bug-er."

Ranger laughed. "If you don't like catching your own, you could always try some prepared ones. I think they still sell canned cicadas online at Cicada Mania dot com."

My stomach flopped. "You're kidding."

Ranger glanced at the disgust etching my face and smirked. "Hey, don't knock it till you've tried it. Right, Whitey?" He nodded at his cotton-headed friend. "In case you haven't already figured it out, Whitey here is our club's entomophagy expert. That means—"

"We know what it means," I said, turning to Whitey. "You know which bugs are edible."

"That's right, missy." Whitey grinned proudly and tugged at the lapel of his faded blue corduroy jacket. Pinned to the breast pocket was a tin badge bearing the image of a grasshopper poised to jump from a frying pan into a blazing campfire.

I could totally relate to the poor bug's unenviable options.

"I earned this entomophagy badge with my recipe for cricket cacciatore," Whitey said, sticking a wrinkly thumb at his coronary-sized chest. He straightened his shoulders and eyed us with a hint of hillbilly smugness. "Did you know—and this is *official* from the UN Food and Agriculture Association—that around the world, on any given day, over *two billion* folks eat insects?"

I sneered. "Voluntarily?"

Ranger laughed. Whitey's grin faded a notch.

"I'll have you know insects are high in protein, vitamins and minerals, Miss," Whitey said defensively. "And they reproduce quick-er than rabbits. If more folks ate insects, we'd have an ecological, nev-er-ending supply of ready protein."

I grimaced. "Right. I can see the celebrity endorsements on TV now."

"You make fun, missy, but they'd probably come in hot and heavy," Whitey said. "I read where Angelina Jolie told *E! News* that when she was doing a photoshoot in Cambodia, her children scarfed down crickets like they were Doritos."

Yum. New Cool-Roach flavor.

I shook my head. "Sorry, but it's still revolting."

Lamar glared at me. "No it ain't. Right there in the Old Testa-ment it talks about eatin' crickets and grasshoppers. If they was good enough for Jesus, they's good enough for me."

I bit my upper lip. "Um...I'm no Bible expert, but wasn't Jesus born *after*—"

"It's mainly Western cultures like ours that've been slowest to adopt entomophagy," Ranger broke in, shooting me a pleading glance that I read as, "Can it, please!"

So I did.

"Why do you think that is?" Grayson asked, picking a remnant cicada exoskeleton leg from the tip of his tongue.

Whitey sighed. "According to the Food and Ag folks, the main obstacle to insect ingestion in America is consumer disgust."

No shit, Sherlock.

"What's going on here?" a woman's voice rang out in a high-pitched screech even shriller than the cicada chorus around us.

I looked up the small hill and saw a boney, hard-faced country woman scramble down the pontoon boat porch steps, then make a beeline for us.

"Nut'n honey," Rusty hollered, then turned back to face us, his face pinched in horror. "Y'all don't get her riled up now, okay?"

"What was that?" the woman demanded as she hustled up to us, her plain, angular face flushed, her hair stacked atop her head in a rat's-nest bun. She squinted at each of us for a second, then her face relaxed a notch. "Oh. It's just you bug huntin' guys."

"For y'all that don't know it, this here's my new girlfriend, Bonnie," Rusty said. "But friends has taken to callin' her Bondo, on account of Rusty and Bondo. Get it?"

I didn't need to take another glance at the vehicular graveyard encircling us to "get it." I smiled and offered the woman a hand to shake.

"Hi. I'm Bobbie."

"Bonnie," she said, then pursed her lips into a white pucker. She punched her fists onto her hips and glared at the coffee can half full of cicada exoskeletons in Grayson's hand.

"What're y'all fellas doing with those nasty thangs?" she screeched. "Rusty, you know darn well even the chickens won't eat 'em!"

"We're just planning our annual barbeque, honey," Rusty said.

"With them filthy bug hulls?" she bellowed. "No way!"

"Naw, hon. Regular bugs. We do it every year."

"Ugh!" Bondo Bonnie said, not bothering to hide her disgust. She eyed each of us suspiciously, then blew out a martyred sigh.

"Well, all right. But you guys better not tromp mud in my house or I'll come out here and bust your trucks up!"

"Yes, ma'am," the four men promised solemnly.

She eyed them sourly. "So, you doing it today, then?"

I blanched.

Gawd, I hope not!

"Uh ... we can't today," I piped up. "We've uh ... got to find a place to camp." I shot Grayson a look. "Besides, it's Taco Tuesday, remember?"

"Oh. Right," Grayson said. "What about tomorrow?" he asked, throwing me under the bus.

The guys shrugged and nodded amongst themselves.

"Yeah. I guess that'd work," Rusty said, "That all right with you, Bonnie?"

She rolled her eyes. "I guess. Let's get it over with."

Ranger turned to Whitey. "That enough time to gather up sufficient cicadas to put on a feast?"

The old man nodded. "Weather's supposed to be good tomorrow. If we all get here early in the morning, we should be able to collect up a mess of tender juicy ones before noon."

Lamar elbowed me and shot me a beady-eyed leer. "You know you got to eat 'em the day you catch 'em, right? Or they turn to flies."

Bondo shook her head until her messy bun came undone. "Flies. God-a-mighty, we're eatin' flies."

"Awe, come on, hun," Rusty whined. "It'll be fun. And how about this? I promise to fix the toilet today so it flushes right and everything."

Bondo's puckered face softened a notch. "Fine," she hissed, then turned to Ranger. "But no maggots, you hear? And no beer!"

Chapter Ten

I shot a parting glance at Rusty's conga line of campervans and sighed with relief. At least there wouldn't be heaps of garbage or junk campers in Torreya State Park.

I hope.

"Torreya. Is that the name of the guy who founded the park?" I asked Ranger as we walked past the LBH gang's trucks parked along the edge of the narrow dirt road.

"Well, not exactly," Ranger said.

"What do you mean?" I asked, and glanced over at Grayson. He was a few steps ahead of us, scanning the treetops as we headed back to the RV. What Grayson was looking for was anybody's guess. My money was on a side dish for tomorrow's barbeque.

Tree-frog satay, anyone?

"Torreya is the name of the trees that grow at the park," Ranger said. "*Torreya taxifolia*, to be exact. Commonly known as the Florida Torreya. It was discovered in 1835 by a botanist called Croom. He named the trees after Dr. John Torrey, a scientist of some renown back in the day."

The sound of Latin being spoken lured Grayson our way like a fully-charged bug zapper. Following the courting call of the *Americanus nerdamongus*, he cocked his fedora-topped head and marched toward us, his moustache twitching like a cheesy scene from a *Cheech & Chong* flick.

"*Torreya taxifolia*, you say?" Grayson said.

"Yes," Ranger said. "Known commonly as Florida nutmeg or stinking cedar, because it gives off a strong odor when cut or bruised."

Ranger stooped and plucked a green pine straw from the dirt road, crushed it in his palm, sniffed it, then handed it to Grayson.

Grayson also took a sniff. "Pinus tadae?"

"Pinus echinada," Ranger replied.

Ugh! Either these guys love Latin or they're about to become Latin lovers.

"Loblolly Pine. That was a good guess," Ranger said to Grayson. "But the scent you just inhaled belongs to the Shortleaf Pine. It only grows in a small area of the panhandle, from the Aucilla River west to Okaloosa County."

"Ha. You got me," Grayson said, then handed the crushed pine needles to me.

I took a sniff. It smelled like that Christmas tree air freshener thingy my cousin Earl hung on his rearview mirror. I would've said so, but I didn't know the Latin term for it.

Vehiculara thingamajigus.

"Hmm," Grayson said, glancing around at the thick forest edging both sides of the road. "You said the *Florida* Torreya. Are Torreyas indigenous only to this state?"

Ranger sighed. "Yes. Like the Shortleaf Pine, the Torreya's home range has shrunk to an extremely limited area. Nowadays, it can only be found in the odd bluffs and ravines here in Liberty County and neighboring Gadsden County. In fact, the Torreya's been classified as one of the rarest trees in the world."

"Intriguing," Grayson said, raising a Spock eyebrow. "Bluffs and ravines seem like unusual terrain for a tree to choose to thrive in."

"The Torreya is an unusual tree," Ranger countered. "That's why it was such a shame that sinkhole took out a whole patch of them."

I flinched. "Uh ... I thought you said the park was safe from sinkholes."

"It *is*, as far as I know," Ranger replied. "I was talking about the sinkhole we passed by over at the cemetery."

"Oh."

"Don't worry," Ranger said. "No sinkholes have been reported in the park, proper. But, I mean, it's not like I can *guarantee* such a thing."

"Great," I muttered.

Ranger touched my arm. "You know, if you care to, I could give you and your uh ... *partner* a tour of the park, if you like?"

I glanced into his eyes. His sky-blue peepers seemed to be asking a question, so I answered it.

"Grayson and I are just friends."

Ranger smiled. "I had a feeling."

I returned his smile, earning a wink for my effort.

"How about you ride with me to the park?" Ranger offered. "I'll take you on a tour and point out the best campsites."

"Sounds great," I said.

"What about me?" Grayson said.

I smirked. "You can drop us off at Ranger's vehicle, then follow us to the park."

Grayson eyed me suspiciously.

"I'd like to fill her in on some of the local history," Ranger said.

"Right," I said coyly. "There's no point in wasting the ride time, right Grayson?"

Grayson studied me for a moment. "Fine. But I didn't realize you considered riding with me a waste of time."

"YOU MADE QUITE AN IMPRESSION back at the restaurant," Ranger said as I left Grayson behind and climbed into his forest-green Ford F-150.

"Really?" I asked, stealing a glance at his muscled forearms as I fastened my seatbelt.

"Yes, really." Ranger shot me a smile that made my heart ping. "Someone like you is a real rarity in these parts. Are you...you know, single?"

My heart pinged again. "Very."

Ranger's eyebrow shot up.

I winced. "I...I don't know why I said that. You make me nervous, I guess."

"Well, Pat didn't seem to make you too jittery."

"Pat?" I asked.

"The waitress at breakfast. She's my sister. She's also part owner of the restaurant. She was quite taken by you. She asked me to see if you might be interested."

"In what?" I asked.

Ranger shot me a funny look.

"Oh. Well, no. Nothing personal. I'm just ... straight."

Ranger blushed. "Sorry. It's ... well. Your haircut. Those clothes. I just assumed—"

I stared at his handsome face as it morphed into a donkey's rear-end before my very eyes.

So much for my hot, sexy mama theory.

Ranger grimaced. "I ... I don't know what to say. Sorry."

I blew out a sigh. "No harm, no foul. I just don't play for that team."

"Still friends?" Ranger asked.

"Sure."

Ranger winced. "You look pissed."

"I am. But it's not *you* I'm mad at."

"Then who?"

Good question.

"Nobody," I said. "Let's go."

Chapter Eleven

After an excruciatingly awkward ride to Torreya State Park with Ranger, I was chomping at the bit to see Grayson again. I couldn't believe I'd managed to zero-in on the only man with even less dating game than my exoskeleton-chomping partner.

"Uh ... that's the Gregory Mansion up there," Ranger said as we passed through the park gates. He nodded toward a mammoth, two-story house to our right. "Want me to pull over?"

"Absolutely," I answered, already reaching for my seatbelt.

I recognized the antebellum home from Bristol's webpage. It'd been the only thing that seemed worth seeing in the whole area. But as I stared at it, I realized it wasn't even part of the town.

Geez. Bristol's even more pathetic than I thought.

"What's the story behind the Gregory Mansion?" I asked, opening the Ford's passenger door and slipping a leg out.

"I'll give you and your partner the nickel tour, if you want."

"Sure."

I hopped out of the truck, relieved to see Grayson's old Winnebago pulling into the parking lot two spaces away.

As Grayson turned to face me through the driver's side window, I shot him a megawatt smile that made him flinch.

I dialed it back a notch as I walked over.

"Uh ... Ranger offered to tell us about that big house over there," I said to him as nonchalantly as I could muster.

Grayson's left eyebrow flat-lined. He eyed me coolly for a second, then glanced over my head at Ranger. "So, what's the story?"

A tinge of guilt made me wince. Had I hurt Grayson's feelings by riding with Ranger? Did he *have* actual feelings?

"That's the Gregory House," Ranger said, then cleared his throat. "It was built in 1849 by a plantation owner named Jason Gregory."

"You don't say," Grayson said dully.

"During the Civil War, victims of the gunboat C.S.S. Chattahoochee were brought to the mansion after the ship exploded. They rehabbed there until they could be carried further up river to a hospital in Georgia."

"Up river?" Grayson asked. "Where's the river?"

"The house originally stood on the west bank of the Apalachicola River at a place called Ocheesee Landing. But, like a lot of these old mansions, the Gregory family fell on hard times and couldn't keep care of it. The Neal Lumber Company took it over. They donated it to us in the 1930s, shortly after Torreya State Park was founded."

"How'd they get it here?" I asked.

"The house was taken apart piece by piece," Ranger said. "Then it was floated across the river and reassembled right down to the original wooden pegs that held it together. And here it sits today. Restored to its former glory."

"That must've been some feat," I said, admiring the four columns gracing the front of the impressive white mansion. "It appears to be no worse for wear."

"The mansion's been restored to its former glory," Ranger said. "Too bad we can't say the same thing about the Torreya tree."

"What do you mean?" I asked.

He nodded to his left. "Those are almost all that's left of the once-mighty Torreya forests."

I glanced around, trying to spot one of the stately trees. All I saw were a handful of short, scraggly, pathetic-looking pines that looked like rejects from a Charlie Brown Christmas Tree competition.

"Where are they?" I asked.

"Right there." Ranger pointed to the same row of anemic pines lining the brick walkway up to the mansion. "You're looking at the last stand of a once-majestic dinosaur."

My nose crinkled. "Seriously?"

Ranger walked over to one of the trees and winced in empathy. He bent down and picked up a handful of pine straw from underneath it, then came back, holding it out for our perusal.

I took a quick courtesy glance at the handful of dead plant material. Out of Southern politeness, I offered up the only thing I could think of. "Well, bless its heart."

"Why do you call the Torreya a 'dinosaur'?" Grayson asked, sounding genuinely interested.

Ranger let the pine straw fall from his hand, then brushed his palm on the thigh of his jeans. "Two reasons, I suppose. First, the Torreya's one of the oldest known species of tree on earth. Second, it's a species on the brink of extinction."

"Why? What happened to it?" I asked.

"A perfect storm, that's what," Ranger said. "Back in the early 1800s, there were over half a million Torreya trees thriving along the Apalachicola River Valley. But the first European settlers saw the Torreya as a godsend. They used it for fence posts, firewood, shingles—even riverboat fuel. By the time anyone thought about preserving the species, it had dwindled down to less than a thousand trees."

I shrugged. "That's too bad. But it's just a tree."

"And we're just a primate," Grayson said.

Ranger frowned at me, then gave Grayson a nod. "Exactly."

"How many are left?" Grayson asked, eyeing a flimsy, four-foot-tall specimen sporting a half a dozen measly, sagging branches.

"Not enough," Ranger said. "When the US Fish and Wildlife Service declared it endangered in 1984, there were only the twenty trees you see here at the Gregory House, a couple in Columbus, Georgia, and a dozen at Maclay Gardens in Tallahassee. Plus maybe a hundred or so growing in the wild."

Grayson whistled. "That doesn't sound like much of a viable breeding population."

"Funny thing is," Ranger said, "the Torreya was actually making a comeback until the blights."

My nose crinkled. "Blights?"

"Fungal attacks," Ranger said. "Twelve in all. The latest in 2010. Some strange, canker-type fungus we'd never seen before. Then, to top it off, Hurricane Michael blew through here and tore down the canopy trees protecting the few remaining specimens."

"Geez, that's some bad luck," I said.

Ranger shook his head. "It almost seems like God himself wants to rid the world of the Torreya. Which is really ironic if you think about it."

My brow furrowed. "Ironic?"

"Yes." Ranger glanced at the ground. "The early pioneers settled here because they thought this area was the location of the original Garden of Eden."

"In *Bristol?*" I squeaked.

Ranger shot me a bit of side-eye. "Yes. In Bristol. In fact, until around forty years ago, there used to be a tourist attraction nearby called, *The Garden of Eden.*"

"In *Bristol?*" I squeaked again.

Ranger's face soured. "Yes. Back then, folks believed the Torreya was the Biblical 'gopher wood' Noah used to build the ark."

Grayson's eyebrow shot up. "Intriguing."

I crinkled my nose at one of the scabby little pines. "How can that be? These things are too scrawny to make decent firewood, much less a boat."

"*Now*, yes," Ranger said. "But the original trees used to grow to twenty feet or more. These are just the stragglers. The remnants of a once mighty forest."

"You said Hurricane Michael took out the trees protecting them," Grayson said. "This seems like quite a ways inland for a hurricane to hit."

"That's another reason why I wonder if God has it in for the Torreya," Ranger said. "Michael was a highly unusual hurricane. One of those once-in-a-lifetime beasts that didn't slow down when it hit land. By the time it reached Bristol, it was still packing winds of over a hundred miles an hour. Not only did it destroy most of the protective canopy trees—as those trees fell, they smashed quite a few of the remaining Torreyas on their way down."

"Putting the species on the brink," Grayson said.

"Exactly," Ranger said. "And, as we all know, extinction is forever."

Grayson shrugged. "Unless you're able to rejuvenate viable DNA."

Chapter Twelve

"There she is," Ranger said. "My favorite campsite. Lucky number twenty-two."

He nodded out the window of the Ford toward a small patch of ground surrounded by pines. The clearing was about twice the width of Grayson's RV. The whole site, including a rough-hewn wooden picnic table and a bulletproof barbeque grill, were covered in a thin blanket of reddish-brown pine needles, compliments of the trees encircling it.

"Why's that site lucky?" I asked.

Ranger blushed and shifted into park. "Uh ..."

I stifled a grimace and unhooked my seatbelt.

"Never mind," I said, and scrambled out of the truck.

"A tight fit, but otherwise, it looks ideal," Grayson called out from the RV's driver's side window. "I read that cicadas favor pines."

Ranger nodded. "Some do."

"They must," I said, raising my voice enough to be heard above the shrill calls emanating from the woods around us. "Geez. Sounds like the bugs are holding a rave or something."

Ranger's head cocked slightly. "Hmm. From the pitch, I'd bet they're periodical cicadas."

I winced at the din. "Does that mean they'll only make this blasted noise periodically?"

Ranger smirked. "You wish." He glanced over my shoulder. "Hmm."

"What?" I asked.

"That looks like Darryl's Dodge parked over there. I'm going to check it out."

"Drex!" Grayson called out the RV window. "Help guide me into the spot."

Before I could answer, the RV's back lights flared. Grayson was already backing up.

"Hold on!" I yelled, and scrambled over to help him.

While Ranger ambled across the road to check out the tan-and-white pickup, I directed Grayson into the campsite using hand signals I'd seen airport ground techs use in movies.

"A little more to the left," I said, scissoring both arms as I guided the old Minnie Winnie a little further into the shade of the pines.

"Good luck with that!" a man's voice rang out from the direction of the road.

I glanced over to see a stranger hollering from the window of a black SUV. A pull-behind camper was hitched to its rear. He was stopped in the middle of the road, waiting for Grayson to clear out of the way,

I gave the guy a wave. "Don't worry. We're old pros at this."

"I meant with the bugs," the man yelled. "If the mosquitoes don't drive you crazy, the damned cicadas will."

He reached a hand out the window and dangled a piece of paper in his fist. "We're paid up for the rest of the week. Campsite twenty-three. It's yours if you want it."

"Uh ... thanks," I called back. "But we just paid."

"Too bad. Well, if you've got any enemies out there, be sure to invite 'em on over. We're outta here."

He let go of the slip of paper and hit the gas. I watched the receipt swirl in the wake made by his camper, then flutter to the asphalt.

A sickening *crunch* made me spin around.

Shit!

I ran toward the RV. The back end had just taken a serious notch out of a sizeable pine.

"Drex!" Grayson yelled. "I thought you were watching!"

I winced and sprinted up to the driver's window. "Sorry! But at least it wasn't a Torreya pine."

Grayson glared at me. Something he rarely did. "The damages are coming out of your paycheck, cadet."

I sighed. "I guess that's fair."

I picked up the campsite placard Grayson had run over as well.

Lucky twenty-two my butthole.

AFTER A QUICK INSPECTION, Grayson and I ascertained that the damage to the RV was nothing a little duct tape couldn't handle, so we patched it up and crossed the street to where Ranger was still inspecting the old Dodge pickup.

"Hmm," Ranger grunted absently as we walked up. "This is odd. It's not like Darryl and Dale to miss a meeting of the LBH."

"Maybe they're helping search for Virgil Stubbs," I offered.

Ranger rubbed his chin. "Maybe. But if they are, neither one said anything to their wives about it. I just called them." He peered in the driver's side window and chewed his lip. "They're probably just out for a hike. Nothing looks out of place."

"What about this?" Grayson said, pointing to a sizeable dent in the tailgate.

Ranger sucked his teeth. "I suspect he got that the same way you just got yours."

I cringed. "Sorry about that."

Ranger shrugged. "It happens. I guess you two will want to be settling in. I'll let you get to it." He turned to go. "See you bright and early at Rusty's tomorrow. We've got some serious cicada hunt-

ing ahead of us if we're going to put on a good spread for the barbeque."

"Looking forward to it," Grayson said. "What time should we be
there?"

"I'd say about six o'clock, right before they emerge at daybreak."

Dung beetles at dawn. Awesome.

Ranger smiled. "And bring some large plastic garbage bags with
you, if you've got some."

"Why?" I asked.

Ranger climbed into his truck. "You'll find out tomorrow."

"Are they for catching cicadas?" I asked as he closed the Ford
F-150's door and cranked the ignition.

I thought he hadn't heard me above the rumble of the engine.
But he rolled down the window and winked. "Like I said. You'll find
out tomorrow."

As we watched him drive off, I asked Grayson, "So, what do we
do now?"

Grayson cocked his head at me. "I thought I'd made that clear.
It's twelve-thirty. Time for Taco Tuesday at Appaloosa Diner."

My gut gurgled. "If you don't mind, I think I'll pass."

Grayson eyed me curiously. "Saving your appetite for tomorrow?"

"What? Oh. Right. No. I'm not that hungry. Besides, I want to
catch up with Earl."

Grayson's eyebrow raised an inch. "Are you ill?"

I frowned. "No."

His green eyes studied me as if I were a lab rat. "How's your
head? Any problems?"

"No," I said. "Nothing like that. I just want to invite Earl to join
us, that's all."

Grayson grabbed me by both arms, sending a mild electric shock
cascading through my entire body.

"What's going on, Drex? I thought you couldn't stand Earl."

"Nothing!" I said, breaking free of his grasp. "I don't hate Earl. He just annoys the hell out of me sometimes."

"*Sometimes?*"

"Well, okay, most of the time."

Grayson shook his head. "Then why invite him here if he's just going to bug you?"

"Is that supposed to be some kind of pun?"

Grayson's bushy eyebrows met. "Not that I'm aware of. Your behavior doesn't make sense. I'm afraid you could be experiencing side effects from the vestigial twin lodged in your brain. I'm going to take you to get an MRI."

"No, Grayson! I'm fine. I swear! Can we just drop this, please?"

"On one condition. Tell me why you're inviting Earl up here."

"As a *joke*, okay?"

Grayson blanched. "A joke?"

"Yes. I'd explain it to you, but that's one synaptic activity you don't seem to fully comprehend."

Chapter Thirteen

G rayson was gone. He'd driven off without me on his solo date with the Appaloosa Diner Taco-Tuesday Buffet.

I'd opted out for a mug of chicken noodle soup and a guilty conscience.

I brushed the pine needles from one end of the campsite's rickety picnic table and sat down. The mug of soup I'd nuked in the microwave was still too hot to eat, so I stirred it and watched the steam rise from it, white and thick as cigar smoke in the crisp, calm air.

I stared into the vapor and recalled Grayson's expression when I'd told him, in a scientifically roundabout way, that he had no sense of humor.

If I'd read his stoic face right, he'd been hurt by my remark—as if I'd kicked him when he was down.

Maybe I had. But there was a method to my meanness.

I was pretty sure Grayson had been resentful that I'd ridden with Ranger instead of him. When I'd doubled down and called him humorless, I thought I saw a chink in his armor.

Normally, Grayson had the emotional vulnerability of a Teflon android. If there was ever to be a future between us, I needed to break through that somehow.

The expression I'd seen on his face... Was it possible that he was—dare I even think it—jealous of Ranger and me? Or was he merely suppressing a fart?

I shook my head and blew out a jaded laugh. If he *was* jealous, Grayson had nothing to worry about. Ranger had made that perfectly clear when he'd offered to hook me up with his sister.

Still, Grayson didn't need to know that. Not yet, anyway.

I took a sip of soup and scorched my tongue.

"Ow!"

I guess I deserved that.

Still, toying with Grayson's feelings wasn't something I was doing to punish him. Just the opposite. I figured it was the only way I could find out how *he* felt about *me*.

Was I potential girlfriend material? Or was the vestigial twin in my brain the real object of his desire? Was I merely of scientific appeal to him as a medical curiosity? Or was I something more?

Grayson had been by my side when I'd found out about the mass lodged against my pineal gland in the center of my brain. Without me asking, he'd paid for my medical bills and obtained my MRI scans. Had he done it out of concern for me, or merely the desire to examine my brain condition in all its gory details?

I blew out a sigh. The ambiguity of Grayson's actions had left his feelings for me an enigma.

Hell. Who am I kidding? So are my *feelings for* him.

To be brutally honest, the guy was so odd at times I questioned if he was even human. Then he'd go do something so totally human it took my breath away.

My mind went back to the day Grayson had shown up at my auto garage in Point Paradise. He'd been coy and mysterious. Then he'd collapsed, unconscious, into my cousin Earl's arms. I'd stayed up monitoring him through the night, not sure if he was going to make it. Then, one time as I'd changed the cloth on his fevered brow, he'd grabbed me and kissed me hard on the mouth.

Recalling that moment caused me to sit up and suck in a breath. It had been one hell of a kiss.

Back then, I didn't know if the stranger in my grandma's bed had just given me a disease that would do me in, or a kiss to build a dream on.

I still wasn't sure.

All I knew for certain was that Grayson had changed my life forever. There was no going back to normal. Pathetically, the closest thing I had left to "normal" was my cousin Earl.

I slurped some more soup, then set the mug down on the picnic table. I picked up my cellphone and punched Earl's number. He picked up on the first ring.

I grinned.

This shouldn't take long.

"Hey, Earl. How's things at the garage?"

"Purty busy right now."

Translation: he's watching an episode of Pimp My Ride.

"Me, too," I said.

"Oh, yeah? What *you* up to, Bobbie?"

I faked a yawn. "Aww, nothing really. Just a new case with Grayson."

Earl chuckled. "That so? I thought you two was on your honeymoon."

"Har har. For the millionth time, Grayson and I are just work partners. When are you gonna get that through your thick skull?"

"All right. Just funnin'. Don't get your panties in a wad. So, what's your case about?"

I dangled a dollop of sure-fire Earl bait. "Two-headed turtles."

"Nuh-uh," he grunted. "I ain't fallin' for that again, Bobbie. You must think I'm dumb or something."

"Just joking. Truth is, we're not sure yet. But something weird's going on up here at Ocheesee Landing. People keep catching record-breaking bass and bream."

I paused. I could almost hear Earl salivate.

"They do?" he asked, smacking his lips.

"Yeah. We think it may be something in the water. You know, something that makes things grow bigger."

"Like what happened to Godzilla?"

"Exactly. Now listen. Don't tell anybody, but I was at this fish-fry last night, and I'd swear you could've sunk your arm clear up to your elbow in the mouths of the bass they were gutting and scaling. Made your dad's prize-winning lunker look like a minnow."

Earl grunted painfully. "You think they was over twelve pounds?"

"Fifteen. Minimum."

Earl let out a whimper. "So, you and Grayson chasing some kind a monster fish?"

"I can't say, Earl. It's confidential."

"Awe, come on, Bobbie. You can tell me. I'm part of the team!"

"Grayson told me not to. Besides, you're not here. You can't help from down there in Point Paradise."

I heard the sound of rusty gears grinding. Whether it was something Earl was working on in the garage or his brain cells turning over, I guess I'd never know.

"But ... what if I was to just show up, Bobbie?" Earl asked.

"Gee. I don't know ..."

"There wouldn't be no harm in that, would there?"

"Uh ... I guess not."

"Good! So, where you at?"

"I'm not sure I should—"

"Aww, come on, Bobbie!"

"Okay. We're at Torreya State Park. Site twenty-two. But remember, you didn't hear a word of this from me."

"You got it, boss man."

I envisioned Earl saluting, which he probably was.

"When you heading out?" I asked.

"Grabbin' my fishing gear and I'm gone."

The phone went dead.

I smirked like an evil genius.

Ever since we were kids, Earl had made it his mission in life to pester the living stew out of me. For over thirty years we'd traded pranks and insults like some kids swapped baseball cards.

But in all the years I'd known my annoying cousin, there was only one thing I'd ever seen make Earl Shankles scream like a little girl.

And that, oh yes, was a bunch of flying cicadas.

Chapter Fourteen

M y cousin Earl had come about his irrational fear of cicadas the old-fashioned way—through early childhood trauma.

I took a chug of chicken noodle soup from my mug and smiled nostalgically, recalling that fateful day. I'd been a gullible five-year-old at the time. Earl was a boisterous pest two years my senior.

My memory of the event was so vivid I could smell the aroma associated with it. It was an odd combination of cardboard, wet wool, and flop sweat...

I WAS TERRIFIED, HUNCHED down inside a cardboard box with my best friend Mooky. He was a dirty, worn-out, one-eared monkey made from an old pair of grandpa's wool socks.

According to Earl, unless we both did as he told, Mooky and I were doomed to the dustbin of history.

"You hear that noise?" Earl said, then cupped a grimy hand around his even grimier ear.

"Yes," I whispered.

He cocked his head toward the shrill screeches reverberating from the woods. "That there's the scream of a wild bugaboo, Bobbie!"

I gasped. "A bugaboo? What's that?"

"He's an ugly old rascally-type monster. Likes to eat him up little girls for dinner. And monkeys for dessert."

I cringed. "I'm telling my daddy!"

"Ain't got time for that. Stay put in this here box and shush up. Don't make a peep till I go chase that critter away."

I turned to Mooky for support. His dull, embroidered black eyes seemed to say he didn't think we should take any chances. So I stared faithfully up at Earl as he closed the lid on the box and left us to await our fate alone in the dark.

Of course, unbeknownst to me at the time, Earl had no plans of vanquishing bugaboos for my benefit. Instead, he found himself an old Mason jar and collected up a dozen or so of the screeching culprits—creepy-crawly cicadas as big as my five-year-old fist. Earl's plan was to dump the hideous brown bugs in the box with me and Mooky, then sit on the lid and laugh while we hollered our lungs out.

But things didn't go quite to my cousin's evil plan. When Earl returned and tapped on the top of the box, it scared the daylights out of me. I sprang up out of that cardboard coffin like a Jack-in-the-box on PCP.

I guess I was quicker than Earl had counted on. He was still unscrewing the lid on that jarful of bugs when I had one leg out, straddling the side of the box.

"Hold on!" He yelled, and pushed me back in.

I landed flat on my butt, squashing Mooky underneath me.

I looked up. Earl was dangling the jar over my head, chanting, *"The bubagoos is gonna get you, Bobbie!"*

I flinched in horror. But just as Earl tipped the jar to dump the cicadas on me, they flew out—and headed straight for Earl's head, dive-bombing him like kamikaze pilots.

Shocked speechless, I sat and stared as one of those nasty things had the audacity to crawl right up his nose!

That's when it happened.

Earl let out a scream that could be heard two counties over. He dropped that Mason jar and hightailed it for the house like a chicken in a hailstorm.

As for me, I fell onto my back in that box and laughed until I peed my pants—which, of course, I later blamed on Mooky.

"AH," I SIGHED, SETTING my empty mug on the picnic table. That still ranked among the top ten best moments of my life.

I glanced around at the forest surrounding the campsite. Somehow, the shrill droning of the cicadas in the trees didn't seem quite so annoying.

That day over thirty years ago had been a turning point of sorts for me. It had been the first time I'd seen my pest of a cousin get his just desserts. And it had been the first time I'd truly believed that somebody "up there" was rooting for me.

As we'd gotten older, the pranks and jabs Earl and I pulled on each other had grown fewer and further between. Whether it was because we'd gotten tired of the game or we were running out of ideas, I couldn't say. But we'd never fully given up the duel.

I checked my cellphone for messages. Then looked up at the sky and grinned. Luring Earl to Bristol for a face-to-face smack-down with his arch enemies was a stroke of genius.

This was going to be my masterpiece—and his Waterloo.

And, best of all, like the prize-winning lunker that'd earned Earl's daddy a bass boat and that stupid Red Man chewing tobacco cap that never left my cousin's head, I'd caught Earl fair and square—hook, line and sinker.

Chapter Fifteen

It was just after 3 p.m. when Grayson finally came driving up in the RV. I hustled off the picnic bench to greet him, hoping to mend fences.

"So, how were the tacos?" I asked a bit too cheerfully.

Grayson rolled down the driver's window and thumped his chest with his fist. "Deep fried."

"Seriously?"

"Have you ever eaten fried cheese?"

I grimaced. "This is the South, you know. Geez. I hope they don't fry everything at the barbeque tomorrow."

Grayson leaned over and fished a roll of antacids out of the glove box. "You get in touch with Earl?"

"Yes."

"He coming?"

"Oh, yeah. My guess is he'll be here before midnight."

Grayson tossed a chalky tablet into his mouth and chewed it.

"Listen, Grayson, I asked him to come because—"

He shook his head. "You don't have to explain."

"I want to."

He eyed me blankly. "Even though I probably won't get it?"

"Earl's afraid of cicadas."

Grayson stared at me for a moment. "Remind me not to get on your bad side."

I winced.

Then, to my surprise, Grayson's moustache began to twitch. Suddenly, he burst out laughing, draped himself over the steering wheel, and kept on laughing until the whole RV shook.

I've come to believe that if there really is any magic on Earth, it's got to be laughter. It has the power to pave over a multitude of hurts. I was especially grateful for its magic at that moment, because when Grayson finally gained control of his faculties, he gave me half a smile and asked me to join him in the RV.

"Why?" I asked.

"I want to show you something," was all he said by way of an explanation.

Not wanting to jinx the tentative truce between us, I nodded and hauled myself up into the passenger seat.

"Lamar was at Appaloosa Diner," Grayson said as I strapped in. "He was waiting for me, anxious to tell me the rest of the story about Hacksaw Hattie."

Oh, crap. Here we go.

I wanted to groan, but I nodded enthusiastically instead.

"What did the old geezer have to say?"

"Quite a lot, actually."

As Grayson backed out and shifted into drive, I fished around in my purse for a Tootsie Pop. I found a green one and handed it to Grayson. I pulled out a blue one for me.

"Gimme the highlights," I said, unwrapping the sucker.

"Well, basically, Hattie Stubbs cut off her drunk husband's head with a saw. She ran away, but was rounded up by the villagers and strung up to be hung. But as they put the noose around her neck, Hattie vowed to come back from the grave and get her revenge on Virgil's kinfolk. They're the ones who hung her on the tree."

"He told us most of that this morning," I said. "And to be honest, I'm surprised you're interested. I didn't think you were into ghosts."

"Not *every* ghost, Drex. But a few rare cases do pose intriguing scientific postulations."

I smirked. "Well, since there's *postulations* involved, please. Fill me in."

Grayson glanced over at me. One side of his mouth curled upward. "That was a joke, wasn't it?"

"Sarcasm."

His right cheek dimpled. "Okay. What Lamar *didn't* say this morning was the location of the tree where they hanged Hattie."

"And?" I said as Grayson stared at me. "You just gonna leave me here hanging?"

Grayson's lips twitched. Then his left cheek dimpled. He'd gotten my joke. But honestly, how could he not? It'd been as blunt as a battleax.

"Well, where is it?" I asked.

"Nowhere," Grayson said.

"The tree vanished?"

"No. It was chopped down to make room for I-10. Lamar said it used to stand on the exact spot the truck jackknifed."

I nearly choked on my Tootsie Pop. "No way!"

"Yes, way. And here's where it gets even more interesting. Virgil Stubbs' accident not only occurred on the exact same spot as Hattie's hanging, but exactly one hundred years later, to the very day."

I felt a knot form in my stomach. "Wow. I know you don't believe in coincidences, Grayson. So what's your scientific postulation thingy say about all this?"

Grayson chewed his lip. "Throughout history, there have been innumerable recorded incidences of irregularities in the interdimensional timeline."

"Huh?"

"Ghost sightings," Grayson said. "That's the semi-scientific explanation for them."

I shook my head. "Say what? Are you saying ghosts are real?"

"Not exactly. However, it has been theorized that souls who experience severe psychic trauma can become caught in a purgatory-like state, hung up in a loop in the time-line continuum, doomed to repeat their tragic experiences over and over again until the cycle can be broken."

"What's online dating got to do with any of this?"

Grayson cocked his head and stared at me, then turned back to face the road ahead. "I was referring to unexplained phenomena such as the spirit-forms of Civil War soldiers seen fairly frequently by tourists at infamous battle sites like Gettysburg."

My nose crinkled. "How does *that* work?"

"The sudden, unexpected jerking of the soul from the body is purported to leave some souls in a dimensional limbo state, apparently unaware that they're dead. Perhaps what we have here is a case of a Civil War soldier who died at Gregory House. The sawing off of limbs was a common occurrence at field hospitals. He could be seeking revenge."

"You believe that's possible?"

"As a physicist, I believe in the theoretical possibility of parallel dimensions."

"As in parallel lives running side by side?"

"Quantum theory is producing new evidence supporting not just the existence of three dimensions, but perhaps as many as eleven. What we call 'time' and 'space' are proving not only to be intertwined, but actually the same thing."

"And your point is?"

Grayson shrugged. "Who's to say our ethereal essences can't split their time between more than one dimension? Perhaps even simultaneously?"

I thought of Carl Blanders, the guy who dumped me last year, and cringed.

Does that mean that in some alternate dimension, Carl can see me now? That he knows how far I've dumpster-dived into the loony bin of life?

"Some neuroscientists postulate that's what we do when we dream," Grayson said.

"We travel to other dimensions? That's pretty out there."

"Perhaps. But if it's true, one could hypothesize that when we're no longer bound by our limiting, flesh bodies, we become free to explore alternate dimensions at will."

"Like the Civil War soldier, or Hacksaw Hattie, you mean?"

"Precisely. Speaking of which, I want to document Hattie's tombstone." Grayson hit the brakes. "Lamar said I could find it out here."

I looked out the window and blanched. Across the road, too close for comfort, stood a dozen or so tilting headstones, teetering on the edge of a raw, red-clay abyss.

"Grayson, this is that giant sinkhole near Rusty's place!"

His eyebrow shot up. "Really? How observant of you."

I shot him a sideways look. "Was that an attempt at humor?"

He shrugged. "Depends. Was it funny?"

"I'll have to get back to you on that."

"You two looking for something?" a throaty voice asked from somewhere outside Grayson's window. Suddenly, an old woman in a black poncho stepped into view. She was standing a mere foot or two from the RV.

"Oh," I said, startled. I hadn't noticed her as we'd driven up.

"Yes," Grayson said to her. "We were wondering which one of those headstones belongs to Hattie Stubbs."

"None of them," she replied. "Not anymore, anyway. Hattie fell into the sinkhole with the rest of them on St. Paddy's Day." She cackled out a small laugh. "I guess it was only fitting."

"Fitting?" I asked. "On account of it being ... uh ... the anniversary of her ... you know?"

The woman shrugged. "Yeah, I guess that could work, too. But I was thinking it was funny on account of Hattie being Irish, through-and-through."

"Irish?" Grayson asked.

"She was born Hattie O'Malley. She was a good classmate of my mother's," the old woman said. "They grew up together. Mom said they used to love pulling tricks on each other. It nearly killed my mom when Hattie got hanged. She never believed it was Hattie who cut her husband's head off."

"Who did she think did it?" Grayson asked.

"Mom never said. Took that secret with her to the grave. She died last year."

"I'm sorry," I said.

The old woman leaned in and looked at me. "Thanks. You know, from the picture Mom showed me, you look a lot like Hattie."

"Really?" I said, trying to take looking like a psychotic murderer as a compliment.

"Yeah," she said. "Same face shape. Same red hair, too. Except Hattie's hair was long and fell nearly to her waist."

Chapter Sixteen

"What a nutcase," I said as soon as we were out of earshot of the old woman in the black shawl.

"Why do you say that?" Grayson asked, rolling up his window with one hand, steering the RV with the other.

My eyebrows met my hairline. "Why? Don't tell me you believe that nonsense she said about Virgil Stubbs' bloated, sawed-off head roaming the woods around here for the last hundred years, searching for his body."

Grayson shrugged. "Why not? It worked for Washington Irving."

"What?"

"His book, *The Legend of Sleepy Hollow*. It features a headless horseman who terrorizes a real-life village in New York. You've heard of it, no doubt."

My lip hooked skyward. "Yeah. So?"

"Irving wrote the book two hundred years ago, and yet his story lives on. How do you explain that?"

I smirked. "Human gullibility?"

"Fair point. But many believe Irving's book was based on a true event."

I winced. "What event?"

"An actual soldier who was decapitated by a cannonball during the Battle of White Plains in 1776."

"Gross."

Grayson shook his head. "Not gross. *Intriguing.* You know, Drex, since I began these investigations I've learned that the vast majority of local myths and legends are anchored in reality."

That's rich coming from a guy whose idea of "reality" includes Mothman and alien parasite remover.

"Whatever you say, Grayson."

He chewed his bottom lip. "The only thing I can't quite figure out is the mode of locomotion."

"I'm not following you."

"How can a head alone transport itself? Without a body, I mean. It certainly couldn't ride a horse. How would it hold onto the reins?"

My face puckered. "*That's* your problem with that old lady's story?"

"At the moment, yes. Do you have a working theory?"

"Sure. This is *Florida,* Grayson. Nothing has to follow the normal rules of logic here."

TAP. TAP. TAP.

It was the middle of the night. I was lying on my couch-bed in the main cabin of the RV. A second ago, I'd been blissfully asleep.

I cracked open a groggy eye. The room was so dark I couldn't tell if my eye was open or if I was dreaming. I drifted back off to sleep...

Tap. Tap. Tap.

Crud.

I cracked open my eye again.

Tap. Tap. Tap.

Something was definitely tapping on the window above my sofa-bed. I had a pretty good idea who the culprit was.

I shifted up onto my knees and peeked out the blinds.

Yep. It was my big lunk of a cousin. Earl tapped his fishing rod on the glass pane again and waved. I glanced over at the clock above the stove and groaned. It was 3:47 a.m.

Awesome.

I hauled myself up off the couch and shuffled to the side door.

"Let's get a move on, Bobbie!" Earl whispered excitedly, barraging me with his unwanted enthusiasm the second I opened the door. As usual, my huge bear of a cousin had managed to instantly annoy the living crap out of me.

"What are you talking about?" I grunted.

"Ocheesee Landing! Ain't we going fishin'?"

"Oh. Well..."

He grinned, making me want to knock his teeth out with a hammer.

"The big 'uns bite best right before sunrise!"

I scratched a mosquito bite on the back of my neck. "Can't. Not this morning."

Earl's eyebrows scrunched together below his shaggy, black bangs. "Why not?"

"Because we've got other plans, that's why."

"What plans?" Earl asked, barging past me into the main cabin.

I trailed behind him like a limp dishrag. "Grayson and I are catching something else this morning."

Earl studied me for a second in all my sweatpants and T-shirt glory. He then shot me a knowing grin. "Oh. I *see.*"

"Not *that*," I grumbled.

"Uh-huh," he grunted, setting down his fishing rod. "Your plans got somethin' to do with that secret case you're working on?"

My nose crinkled. "What secre—" I caught myself. "Oh. Yeah. It's our secret plan."

"Cool!" Earl glanced over at the stove. "So, you gonna make us some coffee or what?"

"Yeah," I said sourly. "Right after I decide whether or not to punch you in the face. Why the heck did you get me up so early?"

He grinned and wedged himself into the banquette. "'Cause I missed you."

"Yeah, right." I turned to the kitchen counter and grabbed a can of coffee. "When did you get in last night?"

"Right about midnight. Saw your lights were out. Didn't want to disturb you two love birds, so I just laid down in the front seat of Bessie and zonked out."

I shook my head. "I swear, you can sleep anywhere."

"How was your trip?" Grayson's voice sounded behind me.

I turned to find him standing in the doorframe of the short hall leading to his bedroom. He was already fully dressed in his signature black jeans and black T-shirt.

"Hey, Mr. G!" Earl nearly shouted. "I caught me a few good Z's, thanks for askin'. Looks like you're up and at 'em this morning, too. Got big plans for today?" Then the big lug turned and winked at me with the subtlety of Chuckles the Clown.

"Yes," Grayson said. "We're going on a culinary expedition. Soon we'll be up to our elbows in cic—"

"Sick fishing!" I said, cutting Grayson off. "But that's not until tomorrow, Grayson."

Grayson eyed me strangely, like a robot fed information that didn't compute.

"Watch the coffee," I said to Earl. Then I walked over to Grayson, tugged his arm and whispered, "Follow me."

"What's going on?" he asked after I'd dragged him into his bedroom.

"Do me a favor," I said. "Don't mention cicadas to Earl. Or any other kind of bug, insect, or arthropod, okay?"

Grayson's green eyes studied me. "Why?"

"I don't want to ruin the surprise."

"Surprise?"

"The *prank,* okay? I don't have time to explain. Just ... well, just do this and I'll owe you big time."

Grayson's cheek dimpled. "Owe me what?"

"You name it."

"Deal."

Grayson stuck his hand out to shake. The look on his face made me regret my offer. After all, this was a lot to wager for a stupid joke on Earl. But then an image popped into my mind of brat-boy Earl lifting the lid on that cardboard box, a Mason jar full of creepy-crawlies in his hand...

"Deal," I said, and shook Grayson's hand.

I padded back to the kitchen. Earl had already poured himself a cup of coffee and was inspecting three large trash bags I'd set out on the table.

"What's these bags for?" he asked.

"You'll find out this morning." I knew he wouldn't let it go at that, so I leaned across the table and whispered, "I'd tell you, but I need you to act surprised in front of Grayson. You're part of our secret plan now. Remember, you didn't hear a word about this case from me."

Earl's face grew taught. He nodded solemnly. "You got it, Cuz. Now, where's the Pop-Tarts?"

Chapter Seventeen

"Good lord, would you look at that heap of garbage!" Earl hollered.

"Shh!" I said, elbowing him in the gut. "That's Rusty's *home*!"

"I meant all them blasted old VWs welded together, Bobbie."

I cringed. "So did *I*."

"I see you all brought your plastic bags," Ranger said as Grayson, Earl and I climbed out of my cousin's black, tank-sized monster truck he affectionately called "Bessie."

"Yes sir," Earl said. "I'm Earl, Bobbie's older, smarter, better-looking cousin."

Ranger laughed. "That's some truck you've got there."

"Yeah," I said. "That's Earl's younger, smarter, better-looking girlfriend, Bessie."

"Four-wheel drive?" Ranger asked, admiring the truck's tractor-sized tires.

Earl beamed with pride. "A 'course."

"What's she packing under the hood?"

"A 540-horsepower Hemi."

Ranger whistled. "That'll work."

Earl grinned. "You know it. You need me to haul some of this junk away?"

"Well, uh..." Ranger stuttered.

I elbowed Earl again, and nodded toward the top of the hill, where Rusty had emerged from his camper-van caterpillar house.

"Shh!" I said. "Like I told you, this isn't a junkyard. It's that guy over there's place."

Earl glanced up at Rusty and his cobbled together, conga-line abode. "Whoa. Well, you gotta give the feller credit for ingenuity."

Grayson smirked. "Absolutely."

"Morning," Ranger called out to Rusty.

Rusty waved a freckled hand back at us.

"Bobbie and Grayson are here to get started," Ranger yelled at his LBH comrade. "Brought along a cousin to help." He glanced back at us. "Earl, right?"

My cousin nodded. "Yessir. Earl Shankles, at your service."

Ranger smiled. "Hey Rusty, why don't you come over and show them the ropes?"

Rusty grinned—a row of bi-colored corn teeth missing a back-forty kernel. "My pleasure. Y'all grab your bags and follow me."

We trudged halfway up the hill Rusty's odd VW house sat upon, then over to the left and across a small field. Finally, Rusty led us to a tall, freshly leafed-out maple with a ladder leaned up against its trunk.

Rusty turned to Earl. "You're a big feller. Why don't you climb up that ladder and do the shaking." Nodding to me and Grayson, Rusty said, "You two stand under him and hold your bags open."

Grayson cocked his fedora-topped head. "I don't see what—"

"You'll see," Ranger said. "Around here, we've got a unique system worked out."

"Sure do," Rusty said, holding the ladder. "Now Earl, you climb up there far as you can go. Then you grab ahold of a limb and shake it like a jackhammer."

Earl saluted. "You got it, chief."

As Earl plodded up the ladder, Grayson and I were shuffled into position by Ranger.

"That looks good," Ranger said. "Now hold your bags open wide."

Grayson and I did as we were told.

"Now look up!" Ranger yelled.

A second later, Rusty hollered, "Shake it, Earl!"

Before I could focus on the tree above, a swarm of walnut-sized cicadas took off out of the maple tree. Caught in a brown-green hailstorm, I was bombarded by the bugs us as they blew past us.

"Geez, guys!" I yelled, but I couldn't hear my own words. They'd been obliterated by a shrill call unlike anything I'd heard before—except once when I was five.

For the second time in his life, Earl was screaming like a little girl.

"Aaarrgh!" he screeched, then fell face-first out of the tree.

"Good grief!" I yelled as Earl tumbled to the ground, missing Grayson and me by mere inches. He hit the pine straw at our feet like a catapulted sack of potatoes.

"Earl!" I yelled. "Are you okay?"

He didn't move.

"Quick," Grayson said. "Help me turn him over!"

It took all three men, but they finally wrestled Earl onto his back. My cousin's face looked like a comic strip drawing—an open mouth full of dirt and pine straw, two eyes as big as boiled eggs.

I would've laughed my ass off except for one thing.

Earl wasn't breathing.

Chapter Eighteen

"Quick! Help me haul him up to sitting," Grayson said, taking charge of the disaster.

Ranger and Rusty grunted as they pushed and pulled, wrestling to prop up Earl's floppy, extra-large torso. Once they had Earl slumped over his knees, Grayson pulled his flannel shirt up in the back, took aim, and thumped my cousin hard with his fist.

Earl's chest reverberated like a half-filled drum.

"Nothing!" I squealed.

Grayson pounded Earl's back again. This time, air whooshed back into his lungs like a freshly opened can of Pringles.

"He'll be all right now," Grayson said. "He just got the wind knocked out of him."

Earl sucked in another giant breath and spit out some straw, but his wide-open eyes remained glazed and unfocused.

"Looks like he's gone into shock," Whitey said, running up to us. He turned to me. "Was he in the military?"

"Uh ... no," I said, anxiously chewing my lip. "Why?"

"Does he suffer from PTSD?"

Only if that stands for post-traumatic stupidity disorder.

"No," I said. "But he *did* have ... uh ... kind of a *shock* when he was a kid."

"A shock?" Whitey asked.

"Yeah," I said feeling like a heel. "It's a long story. Basically, a cicada went up his nose and totally freaked him out. And well, he just experienced a repeat performance."

"That'll do it," Whitey said, kneeling and rubbing Earl's hand.

I stared at Earl's ashen face.

"He just blinked!" I said.

Whitey nodded. "That's good! I think he's coming around."

Grayson's green eyes locked onto mine. "Childhood trauma can manifest itself in unforeseen ways, including trust issues and overly controlling natures."

I winced. "Why are you looking at *me* when you say that?"

Grayson shrugged. "I'm simply wondering if you had the same kind of childhood experiences as Earl, that's all."

"Are you kidding? Earl *was* my childhood experience."

"Bobbie?" Earl muttered. "Is that you?"

I glanced down at my cousin. His eyes had lost some of their vacant look.

"Yes. I'm here, Earl," I said. I knelt beside him and gazed apologetically into his half-empty eyes. Guilt overwhelmed me. "You're gonna be okay."

I looked up at Grayson and asked, "He *is*, isn't he?"

Whitey shook his head. "Reliving a childhood trauma can set someone's mental and social growth back decades."

I grimaced. "What should we do?"

Whitey shrugged. "I *could* hypnotize him to reduce the trauma."

I nearly choked. "What are you talking about?"

Whitey straightened his shoulders. "I have a PhD in early childhood psychology."

My mouth fell open. It stayed ajar until Earl began to speak.

"No, Bobbie," he groaned. "Don't let that fella there turn me into no dad-burned chicken or somethin'!"

I stared into Earl's pupils. Basic intelligence had returned to his eyes. In other words, he'd made a full recovery.

"I won't," I said, and patted Earl's hand. Then I glanced up at Whitey and Grayson. "You heard him, guys. Looks like hypnosis is out of the question."

"Then we'll go with plan B," Whitey said. "Let's get him on his feet."

"Plan B?" I asked as the four men tugged a woozy Earl to standing.

"Yes," Whitey said. "Revenge."

I blanched. "Revenge?"

Whitey nodded his cotton head and licked his papery lips. "That's right. And, if you ask me, revenge is a dish best served with honey barbeque sauce."

Chapter Nineteen

Lamar laughed so hard his beard waggled when I, Grayson, and a slightly dazed Earl shuffled up to the picnic table at Rusty's place, dragging our empty plastic bags along beside us like three down-and-out trick-or-treaters.

"Heard you all fell for our little club initiation," Lamar said, then laughed. "Climb a tree and get you some cicadas. Ha ha! They fall for it every time!" He slapped his knee and doubled over.

"Real funny," I hissed. "Earl nearly died!"

"Did not," Earl said. He turned to me and grinned weakly. "Admit it, Bobbie. We been had good. Just like that time you and me made our city-slicker cousin Jimmy tote that thirty-foot ladder half a mile to go pick peanuts."

I cringed, then let out a little laugh. "You're right. I guess what goes around comes around."

"I'm glad to see you're okay," Ranger said. He handed both Earl and me a small, plastic pail. "Now we're going to show you how to *really* catch cicadas."

Earl let out a groan and sat down on the picnic bench. "'Scuze me, y'all. But I think I'm gonna have to sit this one out."

"WHAT ARE WE LOOKING for, exactly?" I asked Whitey as I crouched in the bushes beside the round-bellied old psychologist.

"Nymphs," Whitey said. "That's bug-speak for baby cicadas."

"I know *that*. I mean, *where* do we look? And what do they look like?"

"Well, mostly they'll be on the twigs and leaves about a foot off the ground, cracking open from their exoskeletons."

A case of the willies made my back shiver. "They don't *bite*, do they?"

"Naw. In the nymph stage, they're as helpless as a bunch of ... well, baby cicadas. They're nothing but white blobs."

"*Squishy* white blobs," Rusty said.

My nose crinkled. "Gross."

"Not at all!" Whitey countered, holding up what looked like an overinflated maggot. "See this here? It's the crème de la crème of cicada bites!"

"You've got to be kidding."

"Got one!" Rusty hollered. He held up an inch-long albino grub, then tossed it to Whitey.

Whitey beamed and pinched it lightly between his fingers. "See what I mean?" he said, shoving it in my face. "This little guy's exoskeleton hasn't hardened yet, so he'll require minimal cooking."

Yum. Lucky us.

Whitey plinked the cicada nymph into his pail. The tiny, dull thud it made as it hit the bottom made my gut drop four inches with dread.

"Let's get a move on," Rusty said. "In a couple of hours, these little guys' wings'll fill out. Then they'll fly off and out of our reach."

If only I could do the same...

Chapter Twenty

"No need to de-wing or de-leg them, unless those parts freak you out," Ranger said as he handed me a bowl of squirming white nymphs.

I picked up a wiggly white blob and started to de-wing and de-leg it—until *that* freaked me out even more than the idea of eating it whole.

"Uh ... I don't think I can do this," I said, and set the bowl back on the picnic table.

I'd opted to stay outside and help, instead of going into Rusty's camper-van kitchen. I'd argued that too many cooks spoiled the broth. Now I realized the broth they were cooking up didn't need any help spoiling.

Ranger got a kick out of my disgusted expression. "Come on, now," he chuckled. "Cicada nymphs are purported to have been one of Aristotle's favorite foods."

I turned my nose up. "The ancient Greeks also used crocodile dung for eye shadow, but I don't see that becoming the new normal, either."

Ranger stared at me, eyebrows raised. "How do you know that?"

"Tread carefully," Grayson said, walking up to us, Whitey by his side. "Drex has a degree in Art Appreciation."

Ranger gave me an appreciative glance. "You don't say."

Whitey elbowed me and glanced down at my bowlful of grubs. "Here's a pro tip for you. The females are better eating."

He plucked a fat, pulsing larva from the bowl and held it an inch from my face. "See?" He gently squeezed the swollen grub between his thumb and forefinger. I grimaced and prayed to all that was holy that it wouldn't pop.

"Females stay plumper and juicer during cooking because their abdomens are full of eggs," Whitey said, sailing deep into too-much-information territory. "The males tend to shrivel up in the heat."

"That kind of shrinkage would prove disadvantageous for the annual penis-parade day," Grayson said.

"The *what*?" Ranger asked.

All eyes turned to Grayson. He shrugged.

"The annual festival of Dionysus," he said, nonplussed. "I thought we were discussing ancient Greece, or did I miss something?"

You missed something all right. What, I'm still trying to figure out.

"Uh ..." Ranger grunted. But it was too late. Grayson was on a roll.

"You see, at the historic, annual festival of Dionysus, it was tradition for the men and women to drink copious amounts of wine as they marched around carrying giant phalluses."

Whitey cringed. "Giant what?"

My face collapsed. I shook my head and closed my eyes.

Here we go...

"It was a tribute to Dionysus, the god of wine, of course," Grayson said.

"You're making that up," Whitey said.

"Not at all. In fact, your cicada-grub connoisseur Aristotle himself attributed the parade with the origin of comedy."

"Huh?" Ranger mumbled absently.

"Comedy," Grayson repeated. "You see, as the citizens marched around intoxicated, they hurled jokes and insults at each other, like a traveling stand-up routine. Think about it. If your buddy Aristotle's right, comic theater was most likely begun by a bunch of drunk Greeks toting gigantic dildos."

Whitey and Ranger stared, dumbfounded. Boy, could I relate.

"So, how are you planning on cooking the cicadas?" Grayson asked matter-of-factly, as if his query were the most natural progression for the conversation at hand.

"Uh ... we'll pan fry a few for taste samples," Whitey said, scratching his head in the center of his pelt-like white hair.

"That's good," Ranger said. "Because I think sautéing them makes them taste like old patent-leather shoes."

While frying them makes them taste like new *patent-leather shoes...*

"What will you do with the rest?" Grayson asked.

"Roast 'em," Whitey said. "Rusty's up at his place popping them in the oven as we speak. We'll toss some of those into the pasta, and use the rest for the appetizer."

"Appetizer?" Grayson asked.

"Yes. A savory snack mix we call 'crunchy cicada corn.'"

"Sounds delicious," Grayson said. "Oh! Here's an interesting aside. Did you know that in some South American countries, movie theater concession stands sell roasted ants instead of popcorn?"

I shook my head.

Did you know one more comment like that and I'm urping on your shoes?

I nodded at Grayson. "I want to check on Earl. Have you seen him?"

"Yes. He's up at the centipede hut with Rusty."

"I think I'll go up there for a bit." I shoved the bowl of wriggling nymphs into his chest. "Have fun pulling some more legs."

"Aha!" Lamar said. "So everything he just said about the Greeks *was* a joke!"

I wish.

AS I CLIMBED THE STEPS up to the pontoon-boat porch, Rusty's girlfriend Bondo opened the door and slipped outside.

"I wouldn't go in there if I were you," she said, patting her messy bun with both hands.

"Why not? Is everything okay with Earl?"

"That big hairy guy?" she asked. "He's fine. But take it from me, no gal should ever see a baking sheet full of squirming larvae get shoved into an oven. It'll put you off your feed for a week."

I laughed. "So, you don't eat bugs?"

Her penciled on eyebrows formed McDonald's arches. "Heavens no!"

"But ... how do you get out of it?"

Bondo smiled coyly. "Easy. I'm Jewish."

My head cocked like a puppy's. "Jewish?"

"Yeah. Straight outta the Jersey Shore," she said, letting her native dialect escape its hiding place. "Listen to this voice, would ya? I got the only accent worse than redneck. But don't tell Rusty I told ya that."

"Wow," I said, totally impressed. "How'd you end up *here?*"

Her eyes darted back toward the kitchen window. "Don't ask."

"Okay. So, tell me. Do Jews have a law protecting them from having to eating bugs, or what?"

Bondo laughed. "Kinda. Turns out the locust is the only kosher insect. My people got no stipulations on their slaughter, but the Torah says only four types can be eaten." She winked at me. "It's just a cryin' shame none of 'em are native to the US."

I shook my head in admiration. "Damn. Is there a temple anywhere nearby I can join?"

Bondo laughed again. "Not enough time for that, I'm afraid. I recommend a nice chardonnay, instead."

My nose crinkled. "To go with the cicadas?"

She blanched. "Ack! Absolutely not!"

A movement on my left caught my eye. Ranger and Grayson were emerging from woods, dragging a mangled palm tree behind them like two cave men who'd just jabbed a brontosaurus to death with spears.

I shook my head. "*Now* what?"

Bondo smirked. "Looks like you're in for the works, toots."

"The *works*?"

"Yeah."

Bondo hooked her arm in mine. "Come with me. We ain't got much time."

Chapter Twenty-One

Rusty's tough-talking Jersey gal had banned the guys from having beer at their bug buffet. But she apparently had no similar qualms about wine—for herself and me, at any rate.

While the men busied themselves turning cicadas into unspeakable inedibles, Bondo and I snuck down the hill behind the welded-together camper-van house like a two-woman SWAT team.

"Shh! Wait here," Bondo said as we reached the cover of a mangled stove. Hunched over, she ran like Quasimodo to the safety of a rusted-out washer-dryer stackable unit. Once behind it, she stood upright and motioned me over.

"What's the big secret?" I asked, joining her and pressing my back against the abandoned washer/dryer.

"You'll see."

Bondo took off again. This time she disappeared behind a Buick chassis leaned up on one side like the victim of a homicidal used-car salesman.

I hesitated for a moment. What the hell was I doing? But then the thought of my other option—joining the guys for cicada stew—compelled me forward. I dashed behind the Buick with her.

"Here we go," Bondo said, then tugged the chrome lock on the vintage deep freezer that was keeping the Buick propped up. She opened the freezer and motioned for me to peek inside.

The faint smell of dead fish hit my nose. I hesitated as a chill ran up my spine.

Shit! Is Bondo Hacksaw Hattie? Is Virgil Stubbs in that freezer? Am I next?

I forced a smile. With one wary eye trained on the Jersey chick, I took a quick glance into the bowels of the deep freeze.

I was totally shocked.

The bottom of the freezer was lined with bottles. Not Grayson-style weird-concoction bottles.

Wine bottles.

"You like a buttery chardonnay, or more of a citrus flavor?" Bondo asked. "Me, I'm all about the butter."

She leaned over into the freezer and yanked out a bottle, pulled the cork out with her bare teeth, and took a giant swig.

"Your turn," she said, wiping her mouth with the back of her hand.

"Is that supposed to make the bugs go down better?" I asked.

"Hell, no," she said, shoving the bottle at me. "It's supposed to make you not give a damn."

I grabbed the bottle from her hand. "Excellent strategy. I'm in."

Chapter Twenty-Two

By the time Bondo and I sat down to the guys' at-one-time-moveable feast, I was already three sheets to the wind. In my impaired state, I was too slow to stop lecherous Lamar from sitting down next to me again.

Crap.

Rusty helped Ranger drag an old Barcalounger up to the end of the picnic table. Ranger sat down on his hobo throne and said, "Shall we bless the food?"

I giggled. "You bet your ass. It's gonna need it."

"Ain't that the truth, Cuz," Earl said, eyeing a bowl of dark-brown, deep-fried nuggets that looked suspiciously like a pile of cat turds.

"I'll make it short and sweet," Ranger said. "Dear Lord, we are thankful for thy bounty of which we are about to receive. Amen."

I hiccoughed, crossed my fingers under the table, and said, "Amen."

Bondo, sitting to my left at the end of the bench, nudged me and winked. She smiled conspiratorially, then her eyes darted downward. I followed her gaze to a small, metal flask in her hand. I let out another giggle.

"Shh," she said, raising a finger toward her red-painted lips. Her finger missed and landed on her cheek, making us both snicker.

"Who wants to be the first to try my award-winning cicada cacciatore?" Whitey asked.

"Not me," I whispered to Bondo, and grabbed the flask. I turned away from the table and took a gulp. White stars shot around before my eyes. Then the world went all soft and glassy like peering out a cracked window on a rainy day.

"Pass the cicada corn!" one of the idiots hollered.

"Here you go," Lamar said, handing me the bowl.

I looked down. It was the cat turds swimming in a glassy sea of stars. I glanced around the table. All eyes were on me.

Crap.

I grimaced, popped one of the turds into my mouth, and bit down.

It was that exact moment that I realized Bondo had lied to me. There wasn't enough booze *in the world* to make me not give a damn about eating a bug.

"Ugh! This tastes like crap nuggets!" I hollered, and spit the disgusting mess into a napkin.

"Hold on," Ranger said. "Try it with some of this." He picked up a small bottle and poured a dark, amber liquid over another cat turd he'd put on my plate.

"Whaa's that crap?" I slurred. "Beetlejuice?"

Bondo hooted, slapped a palm on the table, and burst out laughing. She shook so hard she dropped the flask and fell off the bench.

"Oops!" she said, then passed out in a fetal position, butt up in the air, one side of her face pressed into the ground.

Lucky duck.

"Ain't anybody gonna help her?" Earl asked.

Rusty shot a glance at his girlfriend. "Nah. She's fine. Still breathin.'"

Ranger gave me a *what'cha gonna do* shrug and carried on as if Bondo biting the dust was an everyday occurrence.

Maybe it was.

"I know cicadas aren't to everybody's taste," Ranger said, holding up the bottle of gooey gunk he'd poured onto my roasted turd fritter.

"But this syrup should help. It's made from sabal palm flowers. It tastes like honey. Try it."

I grimaced and plucked the sticky fried cicada from the syrupy heap. I closed my eyes, popped it in my mouth, and chewed.

"Well," Ranger said. "Remind you of anything?"

I opened my eyes. "Honey-coated crap nuggets?"

The optimistic expressions on the Liberty Bug Hunter bunch dissipated like spit on a hot stove.

Whitey shook his head at me, then turned his attention to Earl. He picked up a fried cicada fritter and held it up to my cousin's face. "How about you, big guy? You ready to exact revenge on your nemesis?"

"Nematodes?" Earl said, baring his bottom teeth. "I thought they were cicadas."

"Nemesis," Whitey repeated. "Your childhood enemy."

Earl stared at him blankly.

"You know," Whitey said. "Now's your chance to get even with the bugs that ... uh ... bugged you as a kid." He placed the brown bug fritter on Earl's plate and reached for a bottle filled with orange-colored stuff. "I guarantee you my honey-barbeque sauce will do the trick."

"I guarantee you it won't," Earl said, holding up a palm. "No offence, but ain't enough barbeque sauce in the world to make me put a gaul-dang bug in my mouth."

Whitey wilted. Ranger grabbed up a bowl of pale-green slaw. "Swamp cabbage, anyone? I made it myself."

"What are you?" I heard my drunk ass say. "Some kind of redneck Euell Gibbons?"

Ranger blanched, then went on the defensive. "Excuse me, but this is not some common country side dish. It's a rare delicacy made from the Sabal Palm."

"So?"

Ranger looked as if he'd just been slapped. "The Sabal Palm is the state tree of Florida, for crying out loud!"

"Excuse me," Grayson said, rising to his feet. "But what you just said to my partner makes no sense."

I perked up a little. I'd been right! Grayson *was* jealous of the attention Ranger was showing me. He was actually standing up for me! He cared!

"Thank you, Grayson!" I said, my head wobbling with righteous—albeit tipsy—indignation.

"I beg your pardon?" Ranger said, his face pinking up.

"You heard me," Grayson said. "Technically, the Sabal Palm can't be Florida's state tree because it isn't actually a tree. It's an overgrown bundle of grass."

I slumped over the table. My knight in shining armor wasn't defending *me*. He was standing up for a botanical technicality.

Lamar cleared his throat. "Excuse me," he said, then smoothed his scraggly, chest-length beard. "Um ... how about we just call this a truce and skip over to dessert?"

"Now you're talkin'," Earl said.

"Sounds good to me," Rusty said.

"Me, too," Ranger said.

Grayson nodded. "Fine."

"Good," Lamar said. "'Cause have I got a treat for you all." He grinned, then reached into a small cooler beside him and pulled out a half-gallon plastic tub. He peeled off the lid to reveal a batch of homemade ice cream.

"Hoo-boy!" Earl said, rubbing his beefy hands together. "Now that's the ticket!" He grabbed the container from Lamar, stuck a big spoon into it, then shoved a heaping spoonful of ice cream into his open maw.

"Boy, that's first rate," Earl said. "Rum raisin?"

Lamar laughed. "Well, you got the rum part right."

Whitey patted Earl on the back and winked. "Well, son, looks like you got your revenge after all."

It took a moment, but the lightbulb finally went on inside Earl's dim noggin.

"What?" he hacked, choking on the ice cream. "Ugh!" he bellowed, and jumped off the picnic bench like it was spring-loaded. "Lawd, help me! I think I swallowed one a them thangs whole!"

"I think you're overreacting," Whitey said.

Earl spit on the ground. "This ain't no act, mister!" He turned to Grayson. "What's that critter gonna do to me, Mr. G?"

"Odds are, nothing," Grayson said. "You see, the real danger from eating arthropods isn't usually from the insects themselves, but the parasites and plagues they carry in their saliva and blood. The cooking process destroys those, for the most part."

"What about the rest of the parts?" Earl asked, wild-eyed. "Would Listerine finish 'em off?"

Grayson sighed. "More than likely."

"Hurry! Anybody got a bottle handy?" Earl asked, wiping his tongue on his sleeve.

Ranger blew out an exasperated breath. "I keep some in my tool kit in the back of my truck—"

Earl was already making a mad dash for the Ford F-150.

"Help yourself," Ranger said to no one in particular.

We all watched as Earl flipped down the tailgate, revealing what was left of the cabbage palm lying hacked up in the bed. He flipped open a storage bin, grabbed the bottle of Listerine and guzzled it like a hobo with the DT's.

"Woo! That's better," he said after swigging down half the bottle. He set the Listerine down and leaned back into the truck. He picked up a long, tan-colored object the size of a basketball player's leg.

"What's this thing?" he asked, dragging it to the edge of the tail-gate. It was hollow and curled like an overgrown cannoli, except one end came to a sharp point.

"That's a spathe," Ranger said, getting up from the table. "It's the sheath that covers a palm's flower stalks until they're ready to bloom."

"Spathe?" Earl said. "Dang. I was hoping you were gonna say it was a giant tongue scraper."

Ranger's face puckered. "I suppose it could be. At the risk of boring you all, the native peoples of this land made all kinds of things out of spathes."

"Why?" Earl asked.

I smirked. "Because Dollar General wasn't invented yet."

"Spathes are versatile," Ranger said, walking over to the truck. "Let me show you." He grabbed the palm spathe and carried it to the table.

Oh, goody. Dinner and *a show.*

Ranger rested the wide, hollow end of the spathe on the table.

"Spathes are sturdy, waterproof, and they float," he explained. "That's why the indigenous people of the area often used them as bowls and containers to carry everything from water to game to household goods."

"It doesn't look that sturdy to me," Grayson said.

"Oh, believe me, it is." Ranger angled the spathe a little higher for us to admire its elegant design. "Go ahead. Give it a whack. It's as sturdy as wood."

Grayson reached out and thumped the spathe with his fist. The impact nearly knocked the spathe from Ranger's grasp.

As Ranger struggled to regain his grip, an odd, sucking sound echoed from within the spathe.

Suddenly, something tumbled out of the dark recesses of the spathe's hollow end. It rolled across the table with a lopsided gait, then fell off the edge. I watched it land with a sickening thud next to Jersey gal Bondo, who was still passed out drunk on the ground.

That one glance rendered me instantly sober.

The sight of a severed human head can do that to a gal.

Chapter Twenty-Three

The decapitated head fell off the picnic table with a thud, then came to rest nearly nose-to-nose with Jersey gal Bondo, who was passed out on the ground. Its bloated, grey tongue flopped toward her face like a necromantic French kiss.

"Holy shit!" I gasped, bile rising in my throat.

With one side of her face pressed into the dirt, Bondo opened a mascara-encrusted eye and grumbled, "Get away from me, you pervert."

"By golly, she's right!" Rusty said. "That's Virgil Stubbs!"

"Let me see," Ranger said, jumping from the dilapidated Barcalounger for a better view. "Damn. Sure is."

Grayson's eyebrow arched upward. "You weren't kidding about the dirty blond ponytail. I don't think I've ever seen anything so filthy."

"That's not dirt," Ranger said, leaning over the head for a closer look. "It's dried blood."

"Think he got that big gash across his scalp from the windshield?" Whitey asked.

Lamar took a sideways, one-eyed peep and squealed, "Lord-a-mercy! Hacksaw Hattie's done got Virgil!"

Tendons sprouted above Ranger's crisp collar. "I don't make assumptions, Lamar, and neither should you."

"But who else could a done it?" Lamar asked. "His head's been cut clean off, just like the legend said!"

"Enough!" Ranger yelled, giving each of us a serious once-over. "Everybody stay calm. Whitey, you keep watch over Virgil while I call the Sherriff's Department. Nobody touch him, you hear?"

Uh ... no problem there.

Ranger scurried over to his Ford F-150 and climbed into the cab. As he talked on the phone, Grayson took the opportunity to photograph poor Virgil's dearly departed head.

"Geez," I said, swallowing hard. "I sure didn't see that one coming, did you, Earl?"

Earl didn't answer.

I turned around to face him. Earl was slouched over the table, his face in the bucket of ice cream. The big baby had fainted dead away.

WHITEY HAD JUST FINISHED covering Virgil's head with paper napkins when Ranger returned.

"Where's Rusty?" he asked.

"He took Bondo up to the house," Whitey said. "What'd the Sheriff's Department say?"

"They're sending somebody out," Ranger answered, tucking his cellphone into his breast pocket. He glanced over at me.

I was sitting at the picnic table next to Earl, wiping ice cream from his face while Grayson held him up. I grabbed a bottle labeled *cicada-kimchi vinaigrette* and stuck the greenish-brown liquid under Earl's nose. He came to life like a wet cat in a bathtub.

"Whaa...what happened?" he asked, grabbing my arm.

"Don't ask."

Cool, calm and collected, Grayson asked, "How can we be of service, Ranger?"

The overgrown Boy Scout pursed his lips. "Unless any of you have an idea about who did this to Virgil, I suggest you head on out of here. Otherwise, you could get hung up in the Sheriff's investigation. You'd be stuck in Bristol until they're through with you."

Dear gawd. Anything but that.

"Thanks for the professional consideration," Grayson said, gathering his fedora and a handful of cat-turd cicada corn. "Just one quick question before we go. Where'd you find that palm spathe?"

Ranger's left eyebrow flat-lined. "Well, that's a matter for the official Sheriff's Department investigation."

"I understand," Grayson said. "But remember, we're—"

"I *know*. Private eyes." Ranger's back stiffened. "But I'm the one who knows how things work around here. The big guys won't appreciate anybody going to the scene and tampering with evidence."

"Of course not," I said, shooting Grayson a silent *can-it* plea. "We wouldn't dream of interfering."

Ranger's face softened. "Good. I appreciate that. And since you're here and you saw what you saw, I'll tell you this much. Be sure and lock your RV up tight tonight."

My gut flopped. "Are you saying you found that palm spathe inside Torreya State Park?"

Ranger gave a single, nearly imperceptible nod. "You didn't hear that from me."

Chapter Twenty-Four

"**I** don't get it," I said. "Weren't you *with* Ranger when he found the spathe with the head in it?" We were walking away from Rusty's place—the scene of the unspeakable horror we'd just gone through, and also where we discovered Virgil's head.

"No," Grayson answered absently.

As the three of us slowly walked along the narrow dirt lane, I noticed the furrow crossing Grayson's brow below his fedora. Was he holding back something?

"But I *saw* you and Ranger dragging that palm tree together before the barbeque started," I said.

"Bobbie's right. I seen you, too, Mr. G.," Earl said, then kicked a pine cone further down the rutted, orange-clay road.

"Well, yes," Grayson admitted. "I helped Ranger load the palm tree trunk back into the bed of his truck. He'd already cut it apart to get to the cabbage heart. The spathe wasn't part of that."

My left eyebrow went up. "He didn't use a *hacksaw*, did he?"

Grayson shook his head. "Machete."

My eyebrow sank back down. "Even so, do you think Ranger might be involved in this?"

"With dismembering Virgil Stubbs?" Grayson frowned. "If he is, he didn't use that machete to do it."

"How do you know that?" I asked.

Grayson pulled his phone from his pocket and scrolled through it. "See this?" he said, shoving the screen at my nose.

A picture of Virgil's severed head glared at me, inches from my face. "Geez, Grayson!"

"What?" he asked. "See the cut line on the neck?"

"Uh ... yeah."

"It's impressively straight. But the actual edges are somewhat ragged."

I winced at the image. "So?"

"The dismemberment was definitely performed with a rigid blade serrated with small teeth."

I frowned. "Are you saying it was a hacksaw?"

Grayson clicked off the image. "In my opinion, yes."

I shook my head. "Please don't say you think it was Hacksaw Hattie."

Grayson shrugged. "Fine. I won't. It may be a moot point, anyway."

I blanched. "Why do you say that?"

"If our ghostly culprit has already gotten the man she was after, chances are we won't be hearing from her again."

"You can't be serious, Grayson."

"It's a plausible theory," he said. "For *dark* souls, revenge could be the equivalent of when *good* souls are led back to the light."

"You believe in good and evil?"

"The Universe does love its equal-and-opposing forces."

Earl grunted. "Y'all, I been thinkin' about it. You might be on to somethin' with that teeth idea, Grayson. 'Cause it looked to me like some nasty old critter gnawed that poor feller's head clean off."

"Hmm," Grayson said, slipping his phone back into his pocket. "A carnivorous cryptid as the culprit. It's a possibility. Did you know that Torreya State Park is a well-known Sasquatch hotspot?"

"Come on, Grayson!" I argued. "We've been through this!"

He held up a slim hand. "I said *Sasquatch*, not Skunk Ape. Many researchers of the bipedal creature believe there are several different species. Therefore they would be capable of entirely different behaviors."

I blew out an angry breath. "Really? Well, here's another equally crazy theory. How about a freaking walking stick?"

Earl's face puckered. "I don't think that'd work Bobbie. Not unless it was some kinda souped-up James Bond cane. You know, one with a secret chainsaw that popped outta the end of it."

He picked up a stick and jabbed one end at me. "Buzzzz!"

I groaned and slapped the stick out of his hand. "Not *that* kind of walking stick, you doofus! I meant a *praying mantis*!"

Earl's eyebrows disappeared into his shaggy bangs. "Huh?"

I rolled my eyes. "You know. After mating? The female bites the head off the male?"

Earl's upper lip hooked skyward. "No wonder you don't get no dates, Bobbie."

My molars clamped together. "It was a *joke*! Geez, Earl."

"Wait a minute," Grayson said, stopping in his tracks. He cocked a narrowed eye at me. "Are you saying you think Virgil's *wife* did this?"

"Huh?" I grunted in exasperation. "It was a *joke*. Good grief. You guys wouldn't know a joke if it jumped out of the bushes and... You know what? Sure, Grayson. Virgil's *wife* did it. That's *exactly* what I'm saying."

"Hmm." Grayson swiped a thumb and forefinger across his moustache. "I was hoping for a less pedestrian answer."

Earl nodded. "Me, too, Mr. G. I'd much rather ride than walk."

Chapter Twenty-Five

"That was mighty nice of you, Bobbie. Gettin' me my own campsite and all," Earl said.

"No problem. I figured big ol' Bessie would never fit next to our RV. These campsites are too tight."

Plus, you snore like a congested wildebeest...

We were back at our campsite in Torreya State Park. Earl was by the grill. I was by the picnic table, preparing an alfresco supper from the provisions we'd picked up on the way home at Dan's Discounts & Dents, just outside beautiful downtown Bristol.

"Wiener?" Earl asked, tipping up the brim of his red-and-white Redman Chewing Tobacco ball cap.

"Uh ... sure."

He grinned. "You got it, Cuz!"

Earl jabbed another scarily red hot dog onto the Y-shaped stick in his meaty paw. Then he dangled the branch over the barbeque grill like a double-ended fishing pole.

Judging by the height of the flames shooting up between the grilles, I figured my gourmet tube-steak would come delicately seasoned with a hint of both charcoal *and* lighter fluid.

"Think we can go fishin' at Ocheesee Landing tomorrow?" Earl asked, twirling the stick like a redneck rotisserie. "I sure would like to hook into one a those monster-fish you was tellin' me about."

"Well, maybe. Let me check with Grayson."

I set down the pack of day-old hotdog buns and stuck my head in the side door of the RV. I called out to Grayson, who was at the banquette table, busily tapping away on his laptop.

114

"You think it's safe?" I asked.

Grayson looked up from his screen. "Is *what* safe?"

"Fishing at Ocheesee Landing."

He shrugged. "How should I know?"

I scowled. "Weiner."

Grayson's back straightened. "Excuse me?"

I smirked. "I said, you want a hot dog?"

"Oh. Yes. With ketchup and relish."

"I'm your private-eye intern, Grayson. Not your personal slave. Come fix it yourself."

"Fine."

Grayson closed his laptop and joined us outside. He picked up the open package of hotdogs and frowned. "Do you know what the term 'meat byproducts' actually means?"

"No," I said. "And in an effort to lead a normal life, I don't want to know."

He read the package anyway. "Blood, bones, hair, brains, spleen—"

"I get it," I barked over him.

He shook his head. "How can you eat this stuff?"

I let out a sarcastic laugh. "That's rich coming from a man who just ate bugs for lunch. Compared to that creepy-crawly buffet, these hotdogs are filet mignon."

Grayson shrugged. "That's *your* opinion."

I blew out a laugh. "It sure *is*. Cicada cacciatore? Pickled palm cabbage? Blech! And that coffee made out of roasted palm-date kernels? Geez! That crap tasted like something you'd find pooling on the floor of a post-apocalyptic Walmart."

Grayson shook his head. "It wasn't *that* bad."

"Yes it *was*!" I argued. "Sheesh. I was waiting for them to break out the freaking *toadsicles* for dessert."

Grayson perked up. "You know, there actually *is* a species of toad that can survive being frozen and thawed, winter after winter."

"Like a Claxton fruitcake?" Earl asked.

"Yes," Grayson said. "Exactly like that."

"Well, that ice cream I tried wasn't half bad," Earl said. His face soured. "Until I found out them dang raisins was roaches."

I glanced at my mystery meat hotdog.

Ugh. There goes what was left of my appetite.

"They weren't roaches," Grayson said. "They were *cicadas*. I helped boil and marinate them in rum myself."

"Eeeyuch!" Earl bellowed. He shivered his whole body like a bear shaking its fur dry.

Grayson laughed.

Earl stopped his dance of disgust. "You makin' fun of me, Mr.G.?"

"Not as far as you know. But I understand your fear of bugs. It's justifiable, if misplaced."

"Misplaced?" Earl shook his head. "Nope. I'm pretty sure I still got it."

Grayson's eyes met mine for a second before shifting back to my cousin. "What I meant was, there are thousands of harmful bugs we *should* be concerned about, but cicadas aren't one of them."

Earl appeared unconvinced. "You sure about that?"

Grayson gave one deep nod, like a mustachioed Buddha. "Absolutely. You're much more likely to be killed by ticks, fleas and mosquitoes."

"Sure," I said. "Malaria, Lyme Disease, yada yada. But whatever took Virgil's head off was no tick or flea."

"Agreed," Grayson said. "But make no mistake. Insects are capable of incredibly macabre acts—acts that would make murder by decapitation seem like a *favor*."

Earl's lips slid into an upside down U. I shot my cousin a pleading look.

Don't ask, Earl! Don't ask!

"Like what?" Earl asked.

Crap!

"Glad you asked," Grayson said.

I plopped onto the bench, took a savage bite of hotdog, and settled in for Mr. Science Nerd's evening lesson plan.

"Let me tell you about a favorite insect predator of mine," Grayson said. "*Ampulex compressa*, the emerald jewel wasp."

"Sounds purty," Earl said.

"Beautiful and deadly," Grayson said.

"There ain't none a them around here, is there?" Earl asked, scanning the air around him.

"No. And even if there were, you'd be safe. The female's preferred food source for her young is the common cockroach."

"Oh," I said, pleasantly surprised. "Well, then. You go, girl."

"Yes," tutted Grayson. "The problem is, the average cockroach is two or three times larger than the jewel wasp. And, generally speaking, not in the mood to die for her cause."

"So, what's this little wasp do, Mr. G.?" Earl asked, then shoved a spoonful of baked beans into his mouth.

"She evens the odds by fighting dirty," Grayson replied.

Earl stopped chewing. "Dirty?"

"Yes. She launches a surprise attack on the unsuspecting roach. Then she employs her long stinger to penetrate its exoskeleton and inject an anesthetic that paralyzes the front half of the roach's body."

My nose crinkled.

What the hell?

I shrugged. In for a penny, in for a pound. "Why only the *front* half of its body?"

"Two reasons," Grayson said, then smiled as if he'd masterminded the wasp's ingenious strategy himself.

"First, she can now take her time and carefully inject more venom directly into the roach's brain, blocking the specific neurotransmitter receptors that activate the roach's fight-or-flight response."

"Huh?" Earl grunted, dislodging a piece of masticated bun.

Grayson dumbed it down for us. "Basically, the wasp gives the roach a full-frontal lobotomy, turning it into a zombie that she can control as she sees fit."

I nearly choked.

Dang! Is that what Grayson's doing to me *with his EEG machine?*

"Take control of a roach?" Earl asked. "Why would a wasp wanna do that?"

"For the same reason she didn't paralyze the back half of its body. So she can lead the hapless roach to her burrow *under its own steam.*"

I grimaced. "I'm not sure I like where this is going."

"I bet that roach don't neither," Earl said.

"You're right about that." Grayson's green eyes danced with delight. "Because once the wasp herds the roach into her burrow, she lays a single egg on top of it. Then she celebrates by biting off the roach's antennae and drinking the blood from them."

I stared at the ruby-red wiener I'd just bitten into. "Gross."

"Not gross," Grayson said. "*Ingenious.* Now, with her energy replenished, the wasp covers the burrow entrance with pebbles and flies off. Mission accomplished."

Earl shook his head. "That's a fine how-do-you do. What happens to the poor ol' cock-a-roach?"

Grayson shrugged. "After a few days, the egg hatches. Then, in the course of a week or so, the larva slowly consumes it alive from the inside out."

Earl winced. "Lord help! That's plum nasty!"

"It's natural," Grayson said matter-of-factly.

Unlike the mystery meat I just ate...

Grayson opened the package and pulled out a hotdog bun. "After it's eaten its full, the larva spins a cocoon, transforms into a wasp, and emerges from the dead roach's husk. Then it digs out of the burrow and flies off to follow in its mother's footsteps."

My stomach gurgled. "Geez, Grayson. I gotta hand it to you. I never thought I'd feel sorry for a freaking *cockroach*."

Earl chewed his lip. "Mr. G? Is there wasps that can do that kinda stuff to us *humans?*"

Grayson rubbed his chin. "Not that I'm aware of. But there are plenty of equally impressive parasites that target human prey. Take, for instance, the filarial worm that causes Elephantiasis. Or the guinea worm that—"

"Enough, already," I said, swallowing against the rising mutiny taking place in my stomach. "Look. It's getting late. If we're going fishing in the morning, we'd better get some shut eye."

Earl shoved the rest of a hotdog into his maw and mumbled, "Right, Cuz. And after that bedtime story, I'm glad I brought along my trusty old Mossberg."

I laughed. "You brought your rifle? Why? You think a giant wasp is gonna swoop down and get you?"

Earl shot me a look. "Can you guarantee me a hundred percent it won't?"

I glanced over at Grayson. "Well, Brother Grimm, can you?"

"We exist in an infinite universe," Grayson said, squirting mustard on his hotdog. "Therefore, given an infinite sample space, the probability of zero, by itself, doesn't imply an event is impossible to occur. It merely implies that it will almost never happen."

I shot Grayson a look. "It's late. *English*, please?"

Grayson shrugged. "Fine. No matter how extreme the unlikelihood, the probability of any event occurring is never zero."

My cousin grunted. "What'd he say, Bobbie?"

I swallowed hard. "According to Grayson, it could happen."

Chapter Twenty-Six

I awoke to what sounded like three cats yowling at each other—*underwater.*

"What the?"

Lying on my sofa-bed, I hiked myself up onto one elbow.

The odd, burble-squeal-wail sounded again. This time, I realized it was coming from my intestines.

My stomach was swollen with enough gas to fill the Hindenburg. *Damned meat byproducts.*

I scooted off the edge of the bed and fumbled over to the kitchen. By the light of the moon filtering in through the tiny window over the sink, I fished through the garbage bin. I pulled out the mustard-caked hotdog package and checked the expiration date.

I did the math on my fingers. Eight days past their sell-by date.

Crap. I should've known better than to let Earl take charge of acquiring provisions.

Before I teamed up with Grayson, Earl and I'd worked together at my family's floundering auto garage business. We'd spent nearly a year struggling along on a shoestring budget. Thanks to Grayson, money was no longer the dire issue it used to be for either of us. But once you've been stabbed half to death by poverty, removing the skinflint blade from your psyche didn't always come easy.

I tossed the hotdog package back into the garbage and noticed the family-sized can of pork and beans was dented. Badly.

Great.

There was no telling whether it was the beans or the franks to blame for my gastric distress. But the crime itself was easy enough to figure out. Some rogue gang of bacteria had entered my gut, and was now launching a full-scale assault on my colonic regions.

ON MY WAY BACK FROM my fourth trip to the toilet, I heard another odd sound. A light scratching on the window above my bed.

I checked the clock. It was quarter to three. My jaw clamped down like a rusty vice.

If that's Earl, I'm gonna shove his stupid fishing pole so far up his redneck butthole that he'll taste worms.

"Argh," I grumbled as I stomped over to the couch-bed, marched across the flimsy mattress on my knees, then jabbed open a peephole in the blinds.

I stuck my eye to the dark pane for a peek at the jerk scratching on my window.

Suddenly, the world went all woozy.

My pulse thrummed like bongo drums in my ears.

Right in front of me, suspended in midair, a disembodied, bloated head floated in the darkness. Its thick, grey tongue hung loose in its jaws, flopping and twitching like a dying slug.

My knees buckled.

I fell backward.

The world as I knew it faded to black.

Chapter Twenty-Seven

"**D**rex!"
    I heard my name through a fog. Pain seared my left cheek.

"Wake up, Drex!"

My eyes opened. The world came flooding back.

But instead of a grey, floppy tongue, the head floating above me had wild, green eyes. An upraised hand hung beside the face, poised and ready to strike me again.

"You're conscious!" Grayson said, lowering his hand. "What happened?"

"I ... I..."

He grabbed me by the shoulders and shook me gently. "Are you okay?"

"Virgil," I managed to mutter.

"No. It's *me. Grayson.*"

A jolt of annoyance surged within me, fueling my quick recovery.

"Ugh! I know that!" I said, trying to sit up. "I saw Virgil! I mean ... I saw his head! It's outside!"

Grayson's eyes locked on mine, diving deep without so much as a blink. "Are you sure?"

"Yes," I nodded, half whimpering.

After a moment, Grayson let go of my shoulders and propped me up on some pillows. Then he sprinted down the hallway to his bedroom and returned a moment later, brandishing his Glock.

"I'll be back in a minute," he said. "Stay here."

I nodded, then grabbed a pillow and curled into a fetal position on the bed. I was about to suck my thumb when Grayson came flying back inside.

"Earl's in trouble!" he yelled.

"Crap!" I squealed. "Don't tell me that head-thing got him!"

Grayson grabbed my hand and tugged. "Get up! I need your help getting him into the RV. We've got to get Earl to a hospital—and fast!"

Chapter Twenty-Eight

I stared at my huge lunk of a cousin and let out a gasp.

Earl was splayed out on my sofa-bed like a monstrous, pasty-faced grub in a black sweat suit. His cheeks were bloated and pale. His tongue was gray, so badly swollen it no longer fit inside his big mouth.

A thought too terrible to contemplate sent shivers down my spine.

Whatever happened to Virgil is now happening to As if Florida weren't Weird Enough Already ...

Bobbie Drex wants to be a private investigator, not a contestant on The Freak is Right. *But when a sketchy stranger falls face-first at her feet, little does she realize she's the one about to suffer the mother of all hangovers.*

A pistol? A fake ID? A cheesy moustache and fedora? What's up with this guy, Nick Grayson? And why, oh why, does he have the body of George Clooney but the mind of Bill Nye, the science guy?

Talk about a freakshow!

Things get even weirder when Bobbie learns Grayson is a rogue physicist on the hunt for Mothman. Yes, Mothman.

And they say there are no good men left.

If she weren't itching to escape a dead-end job working with her annoying cousin Earl, Bobbie would ditch this dude in a heartbeat. But with Grayson the only catfish swimming around in her dating pool, will Bobbie take the bait or not?

Earl.

Was this the true curse of Hacksaw Hattie? Some kind of biological warfare? Was Earl doomed to have his head explode off his swollen neck like a human bottle-rocket?

"Ungh," Earl moaned.

I grabbed his hand. It felt like a balloon full of sand.

"I'm here Earl," I whispered.

I couldn't tell if he knew it was me or not. His eyes had nearly disappeared behind his swollen cheeks.

"How's he looking?" Grayson called out from the front of the RV as we sped down the road in search of medical help.

"Not good," I called back. "What's wrong with him?"

"I'm not sure," Grayson yelled from the cab. "I only hope it's not contagious."

Earl coughed. A speck of his spittle landed on my lip.

My gut lurched.

Oh, dear lord. This is sooo not good...

Chapter Twenty-Nine

"**D**amn!" Grayson yelled from the driver's seat of the RV.

I glanced up from the edge of the sofa-bed where I was tending Earl, my alarm bells ringing even louder.

Grayson almost never swore.

"What is it?" I yelled back at Grayson, my voice cracking with unshed tears.

"The road is blocked."

"*What*?" I screeched.

I got up and sprinted toward the cab to see what was going on. Grayson chose that moment to stomp the brakes. The RV lurched to a stop, and I careened forward between the seats like a stray bullet. As my face neared the windshield, I managed to break my momentum with a two-handed push off the dash. By some miraculous ricochet effect, I landed with a flounce in the passenger seat.

"Geez, Grayson!" I grumbled. "You need to—"

Flashing red-and-blue lights stole the words from my lips.

"Holy crap!" I whispered. "What's going on?"

Grayson's eyes locked on mine. "Given Earl's condition and the police response, I'd say a deadly chemical spill. Or biological warfare."

I pressed my back against the chair. "Oh, geez!"

A tap on the driver's side window gave us both a start. A man in an official-looking uniform signaled with his hand for Grayson to roll down his window.

Grayson reached for the knob. I grabbed his hand. Contact with him sent electric tingles through my body. I jerked my hand away.

"What about the biological warfare stuff?" I asked. "Open the window and we're exposed."

Grayson shook his head. "If that were the case, these guys would probably all look like Earl by now."

From the back of the RV, Earl groaned. I nodded. "Okay. I hope you're right."

Grayson rolled down the grimy window halfway. The man's face and badge came into better view. He was a Florida state trooper. His badge read, *R. Snyder*.

"What's going on here, Officer Snyder?" Grayson asked.

"Where are you two coming from?" Snyder asked.

"Torreya State Park. We're in a bit of a hurry."

The trooper's eyes narrowed. "Are you, now? Why would that be?"

"It's my cousin, sir," I blurted. "He's ... hurt!"

The officer studied Grayson a moment. "I don't see any wounds. Are you having a heart attack?"

"No! My cousin Earl. He's in the back," I said, and pointed a thumb toward the main cabin. "Please let us through. It's an emergency!"

Snyder eyed us for a moment. "Let me have a look."

I scurried to the main cabin and let the officer in at the side door. One look at Earl and Snyder's eyes nearly popped out of his skull.

"Good lord!" he said. "What happened to him?"

"That's what we're trying to ascertain," Grayson said. "He either needs an exorcist or immediate medical attention."

"I can't help you on either of those scores," Snyder said. "But there's an EMT around here somewhere. Let me get on the horn."

"WHAT'S HAPPENING TO him?" I asked Grayson as we stood beside the sofa-bed, waiting anxiously for the EMT to arrive.

Earl groaned. His lips were as big as sausages.

I winced. "Could it be alien parasites?"

Grayson blanched. "What would make you think that?"

"I dunno," I said, panic rising inside me. "I saw the bottle in your cabinet. I just thought..."

Grayson rubbed his chin. "It's not alien parasites."

I grabbed Grayson by the shoulders. "We've got to do *something*! You told me you're a homeopathic doctor. Isn't there anything in your bag of tricks we can try?"

Grayson shook his head. "Not that I'm aware of."

I looked down at the floor. A tear trickled down my cheek.

"Wait a minute," Grayson said, hovering over Earl. "I think I've got an idea. Help me turn him onto his stomach and pull down his pants."

I cringed. "It's not an alien butt-worm, is it?"

"No," Grayson said. "If it were, his fingernails would be blue."

Chapter Thirty

"That ought to do it," the EMT said, administering a shot into Earl's right buttock. "Thanks for getting him prepped for me. In cases like this, every second counts."

"Exactly my thought," Grayson said.

"What is it?" I asked.

"This?" the EMT asked, holding up the needle. "It's a hypodermic."

Everybody on earth's a freaking smartass!

"I meant, what's the *diagnosis*?" I said, trying not to screech. "What's wrong with Earl?"

"Oh," the EMT said. "Classic anaphylaxis."

"Anthrax?" I yelped. "Are we all gonna die?"

The EMT tossed the needle into a red bag marked *HAZARDOUS WASTE*. "No. And neither is your buddy here, unless he decides to eat a lobster."

"I ... I don't understand."

The EMT nodded toward Earl. "Your friend here, he's allergic to shellfish."

"I know," I said. "I told Grayson that a few minutes ago. But Earl didn't eat—"

"Insects and shellfish are both in the arthropod family," Grayson said. "If I'd known Earl was allergic, I'd have advised him to skip the bug barbeque entirely."

I glanced over at my cousin. He was already deflating like a road-spiked Michelin Man.

"That shot of epinephrine should have him back on his feet in a few hours," the EMT said.

"Really?" Fresh tears spilled down my cheeks. "Thank you! Thank you so much!"

"Thank your friend here," the EMT said, nodding at Grayson. "He's the one who made the connection."

I mouthed the words to Grayson. "Thank you."

He shrugged, then turned to the EMT. "So, what's going on out there?"

The EMT snapped his medical case closed. "Manhunt. They're looking for a body to go with a head."

Grayson nodded. "Virgil Stubbs."

The EMT shot Grayson a funny look. "No. A guy named Dale something-or-other."

Chapter Thirty-One

The inky night was fading to ash, hinting at the sunrise that was just around the corner. The EMT had stayed by Earl's side for nearly three hours, and had just informed us the danger had passed.

"All Mister Earl needs now is some bedrest and a good dose of over-the-counter antihistamines," the EMT said, stepping out the door. "My work here is done."

"Thanks so much," I said, waving goodbye in the doorframe before turning and shutting the RV door behind me.

Grayson was pulling a plate from the kitchen cabinet. "As it turns out, you really *did* have a good reason to fear bugs," he said to Earl, then handed my hungry cousin a freshly toasted Pop-Tart.

Earl pursed his deflated lips and nodded. "I knowed in my gut them dang critters was up to no good."

He sat up and fluffed the pillows, making my couch-bed groan. "Hey, Bobbie. You know, this here bed thang's purty comfy."

His normally irritating remark found no purchase in my craw. I was too relieved to care. The fact that Earl was getting back to his usual annoying self was a good sign. He was going to be okay. Still, I couldn't resist getting a good jab in.

"Don't get any ideas, Cuz," I quipped. "Your fifteen minutes of caring are almost up."

Earl laughed and shot me a grin. "I always knew you was a softie, Bobbie."

I smirked. "Oh yeah? Well, for your sake, I hope Bessie's softer. Because that's where you're sleeping tonight."

"Hold on a minute," Grayson said. "Given the fact that another head was found in the woods last night, I think it would be prudent if we sheltered as a group together in the RV tonight."

"What?" I said. "Maybe it would be even *more prudent* if Earl drove his butt home today."

"Can't," Earl said, then took another swig from a pink bottle. "Doc said I shouldn't drive till I've drunk up all the Benadryl." He waggled the half-full bottle at me. "Looks like about another twenty-four hours' worth to go."

If only I had twenty-four hours' worth of vodka...

"Maybe we should *all* just get out of here," I said to Grayson. "I can drive Bessie while Earl takes it easy on the sofa-bed, pulverizing my mattress to smithereens."

"And miss out on the paranormal action going on here?" Grayson said. "Not an option. Besides, the trooper who stopped us took down the RV's plates and registration. He informed me we're required to remain here until he drops by to interview us later today."

I crossed my arms and groaned.

Unbelievable. Here I am yet again—caught between a Spock and a lard-face.

GRAYSON HANDED EARL a lunch tray and fluffed his pillows.

I frowned. He'd never done that for *me*.

"I'm intrigued," Grayson said as Earl chomped down on a ham and cheese sandwich. "I don't understand why a cicada, given all its more obvious choices, would choose to crawl up your nose when you were a child."

"Maybe for the boogers," I said sourly. "Oh, wait. You ate them all yourself, didn't you Earl? That's why you were always getting your mouth washed out with soap."

Grayson shook his head "You two make me glad I never repro-duced."

Earl laughed and shot me a wink. "There's still time."

I sneered at Earl. "Speaking of *perverts*, what do you think Rusty meant when he said Virgil Stubbs was one?"

The guys stared at me.

"You heard him," I said. "At the picnic. When Bondo woke up and saw Virgil's head lying next to her. She said, 'Get away from me, pervert.' Then Rusty said, 'She's right.'"

"Hmm," Grayson grunted. "It could've just been a figure of speech."

"The feller's done gone to his maker," Earl said, his brow fur-rowed "It don't bode well to speak ill of the dead, Bobbie."

"I suppose you're right. Especially here in Liberty County."

"SO MUCH FOR YOUR 'HACKSAW Hattie's Revenge' theory," I said to Grayson as he studied his laptop screen.

I'd waited for a private moment when my screwball cousin couldn't hear us to bring up the ghostly topic. Earl was busy napping again, sawing logs and turning my bed into a foam-rubber frittata.

Grayson rubbed his chin. "I'll admit, discovery of a second head does complicate the hundred-year-revenge legend. Still, I'm leaving my mind open to that possibility, among other theories."

I frowned. "Like what? And don't say Sasquatch."

"The culprit responsible *does* have a penchant for removing heads," Grayson said. "Though I'll concede the point that Bigfoot's preferred method of removal is twisting them off, not cutting."

"Exactly," I argued. "When you showed me the pictures you took at the picnic, you said it looked as if Virgil's head had been *sawed* off."

Grayson smoothed his bushy moustache with a thumb and fore-finger, then studied his two digits. "Right. So it was most likely performed by a creature with opposable thumbs." He pinched his thumb and forefinger together. "So that doesn't completely rule out our hairy hominid friend."

I grunted with disgust. "Moving on, isn't there a prison around here?"

"Yes. Liberty Correctional Institution. Which, if you ask me, is a rather humorous oxymoron."

"Yeah, a real laugh riot. So, couldn't the beheadings be the work of an escaped convict? If you ask me, I'd *bet* on it."

Grayson shrugged. "It's possible. But there's no point speculating until we get more details."

A knock sounded at the RV side door. It was Boy Scout Ranger, accompanied by freckle-plagued Rusty.

"Hello there," Ranger said. "Just doing a welfare check."

"We're fine, thanks," I said peering at them through the half-opened door.

"Good," Ranger said. "I also wanted to let you know..." He stopped, pursed his lips, and sighed. "Well, I guess I should just warn you, don't go out alone in the woods."

"They found another head," Rusty said.

Ranger shot Rusty a dirty look.

"We heard," Grayson said.

Ranger's eyebrow raised. "You did? How?"

"From Officer Snyder," I said. "We ran into him last night."

Ranger sighed and looked down. "Dale was a good man."

Rusty followed suit and hung his head as well. "Now we know why him and his brother Darryl didn't make it to the bug barbeque."

Dang it! Death. Another perfect excuse I should've thought of.

"Has Darryl turned up?" Grayson asked.

"No," Ranger said. "His Dodge is still parked right across the parking lot over there." He nodded toward the dented-up tan-and-white pickup. "I just took a look. Nobody's been back to it that I can tell."

"I see," Grayson said. "Ranger, would you describe the brothers' relationship as symbiotic or parasitic?"

Ranger blanched and cocked a narrowed eye at Grayson. "That's an interesting way to put it. If you mean do I think Darryl did his brother in, I'd say no. Those two were like peas in a pod."

"Whatever happened to Dale, you can best believe happened to Darryl, too," Ranger said. "Those two were inseparable."

Unlike poor Dale's head.

"Was the method of removal the same?" Grayson asked.

Ranger nodded. "Pretty much identical. Neatly sawed off. Detached cleanly from the spine, too."

Grayson nodded. "So whoever did it apparently knows how to butcher game."

Ranger sucked his teeth. "Well, sure. But around here, *everybody* does."

Chapter Thirty-Two

After waking from his nap and devouring all but the very last pack of my Pop-Tarts, Earl got busy philosophizing about Hacksaw Hattie.

"You know, this whole thing just don't make no sense to me neither, Bobbie."

"What do you mean?" I asked.

"Well, from them pictures Grayson took and from what you done told me, this don't sound like the work of no haint to me. I mean, why would a ghost like Hacksaw Hattie go to the trouble of cuttin' a feller's head clean off his body like that, when she could'a just scared the bejeebers outta him instead?"

"Good point." I turned to smirk at Grayson. "How can you argue that kind of logic? Believe it or not, I agree with Earl. Dale's head makes it a bust."

"Hmm," Grayson said. "Technically, for it to have been a bust, Dale's remains would've had to include not just his head and neck, but a variable portion of his chest and shoulders as well."

"Huh?" Earl and grunted.

I shook my head at Grayson. "I meant the theory of *Hacksaw Hattie* was a bust. Not Dale's head."

"Oh." Grayson nodded nonchalantly. "I admit the evidence is pointing more to a solid, three-dimensional culprit. But then again, there exist no hard and fast rules for what an interdimensional being is capable of. At least, none that I'm aware of."

"Fine," I said, exasperated. "But why don't we put a pin in the Hacksaw Hattie legend for the moment, and discuss the other options."

"Like aliens?" Earl asked, sitting up in the sofa-bed.

"No," I grumbled. "Not like aliens."

"Bigfoot?" Grayson asked.

"No!" I blew out a breath. "A *human* answer, people! One based in *reality*! Come on, guys! The simplest explanation is usually the correct one."

"Ah." Grayson smiled. "Occam's Razor."

"Exactly," I snarled. "And if you two don't stop talking nonsense, I'm going to use it to slit both of your stupid throats!"

OFFICER SNYDER SLID into the RV's snug banquette and pulled a small notepad from his breast pocket. He bit his bottom lip, then said, "Let me get this straight. You three drove all this way just to watch a bunch of bugs hatch?"

I shot Grayson a *this one's for you* look.

"Not *hatch*, per se," Grayson said. "But *emerge*. You see, this is a mega-year for seasonal and periodical cicada cyclic activity. Simultaneous emergence events like this may not occur again in our lifetimes."

"Pardon me," Snyder said, folding the cover over on his notepad. "But if we don't track down who's killing folks around here, might none of us have much lifetime left."

"Officer Snyder," I said hesitantly, "Liberty Correctional Institution is pretty close by, isn't it?"

His laser blue eyes locked on mine. "Yes."

"Well, have there been any recent ... uh ... prison breaks?"

"Gee, little lady," Snyder said, resting the pad on the banquette table. "Why didn't I think of that?" He shot a smirking glance at Earl and Grayson, then said, "Now, how about you just get me a cup of coffee, huh, darlin'?"

"Certainly," I said. I smiled graciously, thinking about the sketchy creamer Earl had picked up at Dan's Discounts & Dents. "You take cream, Officer Snyder?"

"Nope. Black will do."

Rats.

Snyder tapped his pen on the table. "Now that you mention it, Miss, there *was* a man let out of Liberty a few days back. On St. Paddy's day, as I recall. Released on his own repugnance."

"You mean recognizance," Grayson said.

Snyder shook his head. "Nope."

"Who was it?" I asked, handing him a mug of coffee.

"Roy Stubbs. Virgil's cousin. In for attempted murder."

"Murder!" I gasped.

"Attempted," Snyder said. "Sawed a man's leg off for kicking him in a bar fight with it."

My nose crinkled. "So, are you going to arrest him?"

Snyder shrugged. "On what grounds? Being related to the victim?"

"That, and he's apparently handy with a saw," Grayson said.

"One plus one doesn't always equal two," Snyder said, then took a slurp from his mug.

Grayson's green eyes went wonky, like an android that'd just been asked to calculate pi. "But—"

"I think we get your drift," I said, elbowing Grayson. "Things aren't always what they appear to be. Right Officer Snyder?"

"That's right, young lady. Good coffee, by the way."

I smiled sweetly. "Thanks. It's my secret recipe."

Chapter Thirty-Three

"What are you doing?" I yelled at Earl.
I'd emerged from taking a shower to find my cousin blocking the hallway, a goofy grin on his face.

"Just pokin' around."

"Poking around?" I gasped. "How'd you manage to pick the lock on Grayson's cabinet of secret potions?"

"It weren't hard," he said, turning his back on me to stare at the odd collection of bottles that Grayson kept sealed with a padlock. He shrugged his big shoulders. "I woke up too late in the day to go fishing. I gotta do something to occupy my mind."

"Why don't you try counting to three?" I said, slapping his hand away from the cabinet handle.

"Aw, come on, Bobbie. Ain't you curious 'bout what Nubbin's got all tucked away up in here?"

"Shush!" I closed the door and reset the padlock. "And don't call him Nubbin! If Grayson catches you calling him by that nickname he'll turn you into a toad!"

The whites of Earl's eyes doubled. "He can *do* that?"

I began to roll my eyes, but then stopped, wondering about Grayson's powers myself. "Just move it," I said, shoving him down the hallway a step.

"But I *seen* it, Bobbie."

"Seen ... I mean *saw* what?"

"You *know*," he whispered, glancing around as if ghosts might be listening.

"What?" I grumbled.

"That *nubbin thang* Grayson's momma and daddy had cut off a him when he was a kid." He nodded at the cabinet. "I seen that thang in a jar in there."

"What!" I gasped. I grabbed for the lock and tugged on it frantically "Shit! Open this thing back up, Earl!"

He laughed. "So now I'm your best bud again, huh?"

A sudden creaking sound sent my heart dropping into my ankles. I watched in horror as the handle to the RV's side door twisted...

"Act normal!" I squealed.

I dropped the padlock like it was molten metal, then shoved Earl so hard he tripped and did a stumbling belly flop onto the sofa-bed. The bed squealed painfully, and was still jiggling under Earl's weight when Grayson stepped through the door.

"How was your one-on-one with Officer Snyder?" I asked. My overtly sweet tone made Grayson instantly suspicious.

He gave us both the once over. "Fine. What were you two doing?"

"Thinking," I said. "We thought we'd go for a walk. Earl's got a bit of cabin fever."

"That's right," Earl said, holding up an index finger. "Took my temperature myself."

I closed my eyes and let out a low, soft, desperate breath.

"Is that so," Grayson said, obviously unconvinced.

I forced a weak smile. "To tell the truth, I could use some fresh air."

"In that case," Grayson said, "Snyder told me his crew has already done a cursory sweep of this area. He said it should be okay for us to venture out on the trails, as long as we stick close to the campground and wear orange hunting vests so search crews can spot us."

"I got two vests stowed in Bessie that should fit us," Earl said to Grayson.

I frowned. "What about me?"

Grayson sized me up again with his eyes. "I think we can improvise something."

"IS THAT REALLY NECESSARY?" I asked Grayson as he looped the orange ace bandage between my legs, then wound it around my torso again.

"Adds to the stability," he said.

"You look like an orange mummy," Earl snickered.

I tugged at the bandages haphazardly crisscrossing my body like the work of a deranged crossing guard.

Grayson scolded me with his eyes. "You want to go for a walk or not?"

Considering the alternative was to stay in the RV and play "pull my finger" with Earl, the answer was easy.

"Yes."

"Then stop fidgeting." Grayson fastened the end of the ace bandage with a metal clip. "Ready?"

I frowned. "I guess."

"Good. I think I'll use the time to gather more specimens along the way."

My nose crinkled. "Heads?"

"No." Grayson pulled a baggie from his pocket. "I have yet to find an Olympic Scrub Cicada for my collection."

I sighed.

And I *have yet to find a* life.

HOT ON THE TRAIL OF *Diceroprocta olympusa*, Grayson wandered ahead and off-trail like an absent-minded butterfly collector working without a net. I tried to keep an eye on him, but I also wanted some distance between us. I was dying to get a moment alone with Earl.

"So, what did it look like?" I whispered, tugging Earl by the sleeve of his flannel shirt.

"What did what look like?"

"The nubbin!"

"Oh. Gimme a Tootsie Pop and I'll tell ya."

I reached in my pocket and pulled out a red one.

"Nope. I'll have that chocolate one," he said.

I handed it over. "Fine. Now spill the beans!"

Earl unwrapped the sucker and shoved it in his mouth. "Mmm."

"Come on!" I said, glancing around to make sure Grayson was still out of earshot.

"Don't go getting' your panties in a bunch, Cuz." He looked up at the sky, as if the info hung over his head. "Well, let's see. It was kinda dark and pointy. Tell the truth, I couldn't get a good look at it 'cause it was way in the back. But it looked to me kinda like some nasty ol' overgrown scorpion tail."

A weird chill skated down my spine. "That's ridiculous!"

Earl waggled his noggin like a bobble-head. "Fine. Don't believe me. Don't matter none to me."

I chewed my lip.

A scorpion tail? Seriously?

"Earl, are you sure that whatever you saw was actually Grayson's ... nubbin thing?"

"Yep."

"How?"

Earl shot me a *you're dumb as dirt* look. "'Cause it said so right on the label, Bobbie. I can read, you know. It said N-U-B-I-N plain as day."

A tinge of horror shot through me. "Geez Louise."

"Got one!" Grayson yelled, nearly startling the piss out of me.

He emerged from the underbrush and back onto the trail. Above his head, Grayson held up a greenish-brown bug the size of a half-smoked cigar. It buzzed and flailed, trapped inside the mad scientist's sandwich baggie of death.

My stomach flopped. If Earl's intel about the nubbin was correct, Grayson's infatuation with insects could be *familial*—as in, he was a member of the arthropod family himself.

"Want a close-up look?" Grayson asked, shoving the bug baggie at me.

"No. I'm good," I said, feeling suddenly sick to my stomach. "Can we go home now? I need to pee."

"Then you're in luck," Grayson said. "There's a port-a-potty right up the trail."

My nose crinkled. "Awesome."

Grayson led us thirty feet up the narrow trail to a beige, one-man portable toilet. It looked just like the one I'd seen upturned on Bristol's webpage. The way my gut was feeling, I was worried I might soon warrant my own ominously comical caption.

Serial diarrhea bomber strikes again.

I only hoped the walls would hold.

"Gimme some space, would you?" I said to the guys.

Both of them took a step back.

"You got it," Earl said as I opened the port-a-john door.

The overwhelming stench inside hit me in the face like a turd-cream pie.

"Ugh! Smells like a pine tree crapped itself and died," I grumbled. Then I turned my head, took a deep breath, ran inside, and slammed the door shut.

I was in a race to avoid inhaling.

Like Houdini himself, I scrambled to unwind the ace bandage twirled around my torso. I had to get it off enough to get at the part looping over my crotch. That done, I pulled down my pants. Unable to bend at the hips, I decided the quickest route to relieving my bursting bladder was to stand on the toilet rim and let her rip.

With that mission in mind, I heaved myself up and straddled the stainless steel bowl. With a victory wad of toilet tissue in one hand, I was ready to roll—but then I made one critical mistake.

I looked down into the pit.

Suddenly, my bowels turned to ice. Every orifice I had went slack.

Swimming amidst the smelly sea of blueish-green water and used toilet tissue, a man's dull eyed head stared blankly up at me—until I let him have it with both ends of my barrels.

Chapter Thirty-Four

"Which one of you found the head in the toilet?" Officer Snyder asked, whipping out his trusty notepad.

I raised a sheepish finger. "Me."

His sharp blue eyes studied me for a moment. "How'd you get that shiner?"

I cringed and touched the bruise encircling the lower half of my right eye.

"Uh ... she was injured in the escape, Officer," Earl said.

Snyder's back straightened. "Escape?"

I blew out a sigh. "I hit my face on the edge of the port-a-john door as I was leaving, okay?"

"Leavin'?" Earl hooted. "Bobbie shot out of there faster'n' a greased turd from a greyhound's sphincter hole."

Grayson sighed. "Thanks for that imagery."

"So, whose head is it swimming in the turd tank, Officer?" Earl asked.

Snyder pursed his lips. "We don't know yet. My guess is it belongs to Darryl. He's the only one still reported missing."

"What about Virgil's brother, Roy?" I asked. "The one who just got out of prison?"

"What about him?" Snyder said tiredly.

I stiffened. "Could he have done this? Or is he the one in the bottom of the ... you know ... johnny pot."

"No point in speculating at this point," Snyder said. "We'll have to fish the head out and clean it up before we can make a proper ID." He shot me a look. "It didn't help matters that you ... that your *con-*

146

tributions sunk him under. Now we're gonna have to either send in a diver or pump the tank empty to find him."

Embarrassment and indignation mud-wrestled on my face. Indignation won.

"Well, *excuse me*," I huffed. "But I tend to lose control of certain bodily functions whenever I happen to see a *severed human head*. Okay?"

"Mmm-hmm," Snyder said, eyeing me with suspicion. "About that. It's interesting how often heads seem to turn up whenever you're around."

I blanched. "What are you implying?"

"Nothing," Snyder said, closing his notepad. "Like I said. Too soon to speculate. But don't you all go making any new travel plans. I'm going to need you to stick around a few more days."

"I CAN'T BELIEVE SNYDER thinks I might be the one killing these guys!" I said, watching him drive off in his patrol car.

I turned to face Ranger, who'd dropped by unexpectedly again. I figured the overgrown Boy Scout was either concerned for our welfare or convinced one of us was the killer.

"Snyder's simply doing his due diligence," Ranger said, waving him goodbye. "He's interviewing everyone in the campground. I'm just sorry you all got caught up in this investigation. Given the seriousness of the situation, this could take a while to get to the bottom of."

"Great," I said, swatting at a mosquito.

"So, what brings *you* here again, Ranger?" Grayson asked, looking at me with an eyebrow raised.

A tiny smile curled my lips.

Did I just detect a hint of jealousy on Grayson's part?

"I'm overseeing the removal of Darryl's truck," Ranger said. "We're impounding his Dodge to check for prints and fiber evidence. They're hooking her up now."

A shiny red tow truck was idling next to the old Dodge. I recognized the freckled face behind the wheel. Rusty gave us a wave.

"We'll be out of your way in a few minutes," Ranger said. "Like I said, I'm really sorry about all this."

I touched his shoulder. "It's not your fault. And it's always nice to see your face."

Ranger smiled. "Hey, what say I come by tomorrow and give you all a proper tour of the park's unique flora?"

I forced a smile, thinking about the dismal little Torreya trees. "Uh ... why don't we leave those poor endangered trees in peace?"

"Oh," Ranger said. "I meant the *other* unique flora of this region. This region is home to twenty-one species of carnivorous plants."

"*Carnivorous* plants?" Grayson asked, shooting me another odd glance.

"Yes," Ranger said. "Most of them are found only in this particular area."

"How did they end up here?" I asked, actually interested for a change.

"Glaciers," Ranger said.

I blanched. "*Glaciers?*"

"Yes," Ranger nodded. "Believe it or not, during the last ice age around ten thousand years ago, the seeds of these plants caught a ride to Florida—frozen inside glacial ice. The glaciers ended right here where these bluffs now stand, and dumped their contents along this area as the ice melted."

"Intriguing," Grayson said. "Well, you can certainly count me in for a tour. It sounds facinating."

"Good," Ranger said. "I'll be by around nine, then?"

"Perfect," I said, shooting him my best smile. "Oh. By the way, Snyder told us not to go anywhere. But it's okay if we leave the park to get dinner, isn't it?"

"Of course," Ranger said. "But if you planned on going by the Appaloosa Diner, you might want to skip it tonight."

"Why?" Earl asked. "Don't tell me they found a head in the tater salad!"

Ranger's mouth opened and closed like a fish out of water. "Uh … nothing like that," he said, finally. "I just thought, considering how allergic you are to shellfish, that you might want to skip the Friday night seafood buffet."

Earl grimaced. "You better believe I do."

"But there are other options," Ranger said. "Bristol's got a pizza place and a Subway sandwich shop. Or you could make your own dinner from stuff at Dan's Dents—"

"Pizza!" I blurted. "My vote's for pizza."

"Sounds good to me," Earl said.

Rusty tooted the tow truck's horn. The Dodge was hooked up and ready to tow. "We better get a move on, Ranger," he hollered. "Supposed to rain like the dickens tonight!"

Ranger's cellphone beeped. "You go on ahead," he called to Rusty. "I'll be right behind you." He turned to us. "Excuse me, folks. It's the Sheriff's Office."

Ranger reached for his beeping phone. "You don't say," he said into the receiver, shaking his head. "Well, that sure puts a new twist on things. Right. I'll do that."

He clicked off his cellphone. The three of us watched him expectantly.

"Well?" I asked.

"You're not gonna believe this," he said.

Earl gasped. "They *did* find a head in the tater salad!"

Ranger's jaw flexed. "No." He turned to me. "The head you found in the port-a-john? It wasn't just a head. It was a whole person."

"Who?" Grayson, Earl and I asked in unison.

Ranger shook his head. "All we know right now is that he was wearing camo."

I winced. "That could be anybody around here."

"Right," Ranger said. "Funny thing, though. As far as they can see, there's not a scratch on him. They think he must've crawled in there on his own, then sometime later succumbed to the fumes."

I cringed. "You don't think that ... when I ... that *I* killed him, do you?"

Earl's lips twisted. "I've smelled your butt muffins, Cuz. I wouldn't rule it out."

"Shut up!" I punched Earl on the arm then turned to Ranger. "I meant, you know, I couldn't have ... er ... *drowned* him, could I?"

"Uh ... no, ma'am," Ranger said, his eyes on the ground. "Based on body temp, the initial assessment is that he died sometime early this morning."

I shook my head. "That doesn't make any sense. Why would someone climb into a pit toilet?"

"On a dare!" Earl said.

We all stared at him.

"What?" he said. "I ate a tree frog once, on a dare."

Ranger tried his best to ignore Earl. "He's right, in a way. Peer pressure can make people do all kinds of crazy things they haven't thought through."

"Sure, but this isn't one of them," I said. "I saw the guy's face. It was frozen in horror, as if he was—"

"About to drown in a cesspool of filth?" Ranger offered.

"Or he could've been under attack," Grayson said.

"By aliens!" Earl yelled. "I knew it!"

"More likely a bear," Ranger said.

"Or another person," I said. "Besides *me*."

"Whatever it was," Grayson said, "it scared the man so badly that diving into a cesspool was better than the alternative."

I winced. "You mean he was forced to do that or *die*?"

Grayson nodded. "Apparently."

My gut flopped. "What could frighten someone *that* badly?"

"That's the question we're working to solve," Ranger said. "Was he trying to escape a *man* or a *beast*?"

Grayson rubbed his chin. "Or something else entirely."

Chapter Thirty-Five

It was late afternoon. Just as Rusty had predicted when he'd pulled away in the tow truck, the rain was coming down in buckets. Tucked safely inside the RV with Earl and Grayson, I thanked the powers that be for two things—Netflix, and the fact that the pizza place in Bristol delivered.

The deluge pounding on the RV's metal roof made a thunderous sound so loud I barely heard it when someone knocked on the side door.

I glanced at my two companions. Being of the male persuasion, they were, naturally, *immune* to hearing anything that would require them to get up off the couch. Instead, their eyes remained obliviously riveted to Grayson's laptop and a rerun of *The X-Files*.

It wasn't worth the effort to argue with them. I grabbed the money off the table and shuffled to the door.

"Who is it?" I asked.

A muffled voice yelled, "Pizza delivery!"

Wind and rain snuck in as I opened the door. Against the maelstrom, a man in a yellow slicker stood just outside, doing the best impersonation of the Gorton Fisherman in a nor'easter that I'd ever seen.

"How much do I owe you?" I asked.

"Forty-eight bucks." He reached out a leathery hand to take the three twenties I offered.

"Whitey?" I asked as the bills went limp in my hand, instantly soaked by the rain.

His yellow hoodie tipped upward. "Hey, it's you guys!"

"Small world," I said.

He laughed. "Especially around these parts."

"You deliver pizza?" I asked, taking the boxes he handed over. "I thought you were a psychologist."

"*Was*. I'm retired. Now, instead of shrinking heads, I expand waists." He tucked the money in his pocket and fiddled to make change in the downpour.

"Keep it," I said, watching the water rivulets pour off his slicker.

He grinned despite the weather. "Thanks!"

"Hey, why don't you come in?" I said. "Join us for dinner."

Whitey pursed his lips and glanced back at a pair of glowing headlights by the road.

"I would, but I'm training a rookie driver. She's new in town. Doesn't know the route. Plus, I was a little worried about letting her go out here alone, what with all that's been going on lately."

"That's okay," I said. "Invite her, too."

Whitey tucked the money away under his raincoat. "You sure?"

"Yeah. We've got four extra-large pizzas. That ought to be enough. If not, I'll make Earl finish off the Dan's Dents mystery hot dogs."

Whitey grinned. "Well, all right, then. Let me go get her."

"HATTIE CACKLED, 'I'LL be back for my revenge in a hundred years!' then she laughed as the fire ignited her hair into flames the color of fresh-spilt blood," Whitey said.

He sat back and grinned at the stunned-looking young woman sitting across the banquette from him. He shook a boney finger in her face. "And that, Miss Karen, is the legend of Hacksaw Hattie."

"Whoa," Karen said, shaking her head.

The junior pizza-driver apprentice had a shy, bookish appearance. I guessed she was probably in her early twenties. Her plain, milky face was adorned only with a pair of thick, black library glasses and mousy, parted-in-the-middle hair that hung in waves halfway down her back.

"I hate ghost stories," Karen said, shivering. "They scare me something awful."

Earl laughed. "That story gets weirder every time I hear it." He adjusted his position on the folded-up sofa-bed and took a monster-sized bite from a slice of pepperoni pizza.

I'd given my cousin two of the four pizzas I'd ordered and relegated him to the couch on the pretext that he was too big for anyone to fit in the RV banquette seat beside him.

While that was indeed true, the real reason for banishing Earl from the banquette was so that Whitey, Karen, Grayson and I could eat the other two pizzas without it becoming a race to the death. When it came to pizza, Earl was a human Hoover with industrial-strength suction.

"Hacksaw Hattie," Karen said, pushing her thick glasses up on her nose. "I had no idea Bristol was such a weird place. I guess I should've known the second I got here."

"What do you mean?" I asked.

Karen squinted at me through her coke-bottle lenses. "The day I first arrived, I kind of felt like I'd driven into an episode of *The Twilight Zone*."

"Why's that?" Grayson asked.

"Well, I was driving on I-10 and..." She hesitated and glanced at us before continuing. "The first thing I saw after I passed the sign for Bristol was a truck turned over in the road. It was covered in a swarm of bugs like something from a horror movie."

I dropped my pizza slice. "Wait. You saw the tanker truck accident?"

"Not the accident itself," Karen said, shaking her head. "But right afterward, I guess."

"Are you the one who reported seeing a red-haired person running into the woods?" Grayson asked.

Karen shrunk back in her seat. "I thought that was supposed to be confidential."

"Welcome to small-town America," Whitey said. "Nothing you say or do here stays under wraps for long."

"What other details can you give us?" Grayson asked. "This could be important. Lives are at stake."

"Uh ... I don't know," Karen said, cringing at the thought. "Look. I heard about the headless guy they found. I'd like to help, but just thinking about all those bugs makes my mind shut down."

"I know how you feel," Earl said, nodding in sympathy. "They tell me gettin' all scared like that can make your brain go wonky."

You should know. You're living proof.

As I smirked at Earl, he suddenly bolted to his feet. "Hey! I know! Whitey, why don't you hypnotize this poor girl here like you tried to do with me?"

I opened my mouth to tell Earl to can it, but realized he might be onto something.

"What do you think?" I said to Whitey.

The pizza psychologist chewed his bottom lip, then smiled softly at Karen. "It could help you get over your fears."

"Well," she said, chewing a thumbnail. "I don't know—"

"I think it's an excellent notion," Grayson said. "It may also allow you to recall details that could prove helpful in solving the mystery of what's killing people around here."

"Grayson's right," I said, offering her my best smile. "I'll be right beside you the whole time."

Karen sucked in her lower lip. "Well... Okay, I guess. Can I finish my wine first?"

"Sure."

I turned to Earl. He was busy licking sauce from the top of an empty pizza box like a starving hound dog.

"Get up, Rover," I said. "We're gonna need that couch."

Chapter Thirty-Six

Beads of sweat lined Karen's lips, twin pink petals set in a creamy white face that had probably never seen any light stronger than the wattage emanating from her laptop screen.

"You see the overturned truck, the spinning wheel," Whitey coaxed as we hovered around the couch watching and holding our breath.

"Yes," Karen whispered, lying still as a stone on the couch.

"What happened next?" Whitey asked.

"A van," she murmured. "I see a van up ahead. In the road. It's speeding off."

"What kind of van?"

"Don't know," Karen mumbled.

"Describe it," Whitey said softly.

"Far away ... Light-colored. White. Maybe tan. Two surfboards on top."

"Good. Very good," Whitey said. "What else can you tell us about it? What did the license plate look like?"

Karen's head turned feverishly. "Can't ... see. Ah!" she gasped suddenly. "Someone ... running into the woods! Red hair ... bright! The color of fresh-spilt blood!"

"Is it a man or a woman?" Whitey asked.

"Can't tell ... the body. The body ..." Karen blanched, her eyes still closed.

"What about the body?" Whitey coaxed.

"It ... disappeared!"

The hair on the back of my neck stood up. "She's drunk," I said.

"Shhh!" Whitey hissed softly, raising a finger to his lips. He turned back to Karen. "How does the body disappear?"

"Don't know. It was there, then it wasn't. It's just ... gone," Karen mumbled. She writhed in agitation. "Vanished ... into the woods ... like a ghost!"

"It's okay," Whitey said. "You're safe. I'm here with you. Do you want to leave this place?"

Karen nodded. "Yes!"

"Okay. On the count of three, you will wake up and feel calm and serene. This incident will trouble you no more. One, two, three."

Karen's hazel eyes opened. "Wow," she said, rubbing her eyes. "That was relaxing. How'd I do?"

"You did great," Whitey said, helping her sit up.

"I feel great," Karen said, offering us a timid smile. "Is there any more wine?"

"Oh! Oh! I want me a turn now!" Earl said, raising his hand and jumping around like he was on *Let's Make a Deal*. "Please, Mr. Whitey! I don't wanna be scared of them nasty cicadas no more."

Whitey looked at me and shrugged. "Why not. What the hell."

EARL'S EXPRESSION WAS twisted into an angry, red-faced pout. He grimaced and stuck out his tongue.

"What's wrong, Earl?" Whitey asked.

"I hate me the taste of turpentine."

"Why do you taste turpentine?"

"Mama just washed my mouth out with soap."

I sniggered and tiptoed over to the kitchen counter. I grabbed the dish soap and whispered to Whitey. "Come on, just one little squirt?"

Whitey stifled a laugh and shooed me away. "Why did Mama wash your mouth out with soap, Earl?"

"'Cause I called Bobbie Miss Doody Pants."

Grayson snorted. I punched him on the arm.

"How did Mama find out?" Whitey asked.

Earl scowled. "Bobbie ratted on me. But I'm gonna get her back. I'm gonna put her in a box and fill it with bugs!"

"So, you're not afraid of bugs?"

Earl laughed. "No way! But Bobbie is! She's a crybaby."

Whitey turned to us and whispered. "Interesting. This appears to truly be the actual traumatic event that triggered his fear of cicadas." Whitey smiled. "This should be pretty easy to turn around."

The old, white-haired psychologist turned back to Earl, laid out flat on the couch like an oversized mummy. "So you've got your cousin Bobbie in the box now, Earl. And you caught some bugs. What kind?"

"Big ol' June bugs!" Earl sniggered. "Got me a whole Mason jar full. Gonna dump 'em on her and sit on the box so she can't get out. Then I'm gonna listen to her holler!"

"Go ahead and do that now," Whitey said.

Earl licked his lips. A faint smile came over his face. "I'm opening the box now." Suddenly, his expression turned to frustration. "Argh! Get back in there Bobbie! You ain't supposed to jump out like that!" His hand made a small pushing gesture.

"What are you doing now?" Whitey asked.

"I'm opening the dang jar. Gonna dump it on her." Earl let out a small laugh. Then, all of a sudden, he twitched so hard his feet flew up off the couch.

"What's happening?" Whitey asked.

"Bugs!" Earl squealed. "They's on me!" He spat. "In my mouth. Up my nose! Lord help! They's in my ears. My eyes!"

Then Earl sat up like Nosferatu in his coffin and let out that same ear-piercing scream I'd heard thirty years ago.

"Aaaaaaaaarrghh!"

"It's okay, Earl, I'm with you," Whitey said, patting his hand. "I made the bugs go away. They're all gone now."

Earl's body relaxed a notch. "But what if they come back?"

"They can't harm you," Whitey coaxed. "You are a *giant* compared to them. You're big and strong. You can squash them all with your thumb. You have no reason to fear cicadas ever again."

Earl laid back down, smiled a big, dopey grin, and muttered, "I'm a giant."

"Okay, Earl," Whitey said. "On the count of three, you will wake up and feel calm and serene. This incident will trouble you no more. One, two, three."

Earl opened his eyes and glanced around at us.

"I knew it," Earl said, sitting up and grinning slyly at Whitey. "You couldn't hypnotize me, could you?" He pointed at his cranium. "My brain is too powerful."

Earl glanced over at me. "Am I right, Bobbie?"

I smirked. "Whatever you say, Mr. Doody Pants."

Chapter Thirty-Seven

After Whitey and his pizza protégé Karen left, I was ready to hit the hay.

"I'm calling it a day," I announced, hauling myself up from the banquette, where Grayson was busy internet surfing.

As I stood, I suddenly froze.

Where am I going to sleep?

I had to bunk with either Earl or Grayson.

"Uh..." I mumbled.

"Go ahead and use my bed," Grayson said, as if reading my mind. "I've got some things I want to research."

I glanced over at Earl. He was splayed out on the sofa-bed like a pepperoni-stuffed starfish.

"Thanks," I said, then scurried into the bathroom before Grayson could rescind his offer.

AFTER SHOWERING, I tugged on my best T-shirt and sweatpants, then slipped into Grayson's bed. As my head hit the pillow, a random thought sobered me faster than mainlining a shot of espresso.

Any minute now, Grayson will be lying beside me. All night. Just inches away...

My gut flopped with anticipation—until another thought obliterated any idea of romance.

What if Earl was right about that scorpion tail nubbin thing? What if Grayson's really a space creature that turns into a hideous, killer insect at midnight?

As that crazy notion carjacked my brain, Grayson's shadowy silhouette appeared in the bedroom's dimly lit doorframe. I stifled a gasp.

"He's out like a busted headlight," Grayson's darkened form said.

As he turned, I could've sworn I saw an antennae poking from his head. I swallowed hard. "I guess Benadryl and beer will do that to a person."

"So could some hypnotic brainwashing," he said, tugging off his black T-shirt. The yellow glow from the hallway shone on his perfect, six-pack abs.

I let out a nervous laugh.

Grayson slipped out of his black jeans. "I'm glad you're awake. I wanted some time alone with you."

My heart surged with panic. I was certain Grayson's insectoid, x-ray eyes could see my heart pounding underneath my sweatshirt.

"Alone time? Wha ... what for?"

"To discuss what Karen revealed under hypnosis, of course," Grayson said clinically.

My chest sank. "Oh. Right."

"The van she saw with the surfboards on top. It seemed too unusual to be a mere coincidence," he said, his body a grey form clad only in black boxer shorts.

"I don't know about that," I said, trying to keep my eyes above his neckline. "The accident took place early in the morning, remember? Karen's attention may have been drawn to the van because the roads were otherwise empty at that hour."

"Perhaps." Grayson turned and hung his jeans on a hanger, making me feel guilty for the pile of rumpled clothes I'd tossed in the corner.

"You know, Panama City isn't far from here," I said. "I don't think it would be unusual at all for a couple of surfers from Tallahassee to be on their way to the beach to catch some righteous waves."

"Good point. So, what's your take on Karen saying the person leaving the accident scene had hair as bright red as freshly spilt blood?"

I shrugged and pulled the covers up to my neck. "The girl was tipsy. She could've been repeating a subliminal suggestion. After all, Whitey had just told her the legend of Hacksaw Hattie and her blood-red hair."

"Hmm," Grayson said, carefully laying his folded T-shirt over his jeans, then hanging them in the tiny closet. He turned back to face me. "Very good, Drex. That was my thought exactly. But what about Karen's comment that the body disappeared as it reached the woods?"

I pursed my lips. "You got me there."

Grayson shook his head softly. "Something isn't adding up. But it will. Because despite what Snyder says, one plus one *always* equals two."

I held my breath as Grayson lifted the covers and sat down on the edge of the bed.

"Speaking of two, you want a pair of earplugs?" he asked.

"Oh," I said. "Yes, please. Don't say I didn't warn you about letting Earl sleep on the sofa. His snore could end up shaking the rivets loose on your RV."

"Let's hope not." Grayson fetched a pair of earplugs from the nightstand and handed them to me.

"Thanks," I said as he lay his hot, half-naked body down beside me. As I stuck a plug in my ear, I asked, "You're not going to wear any?"

"No need. I've gotten used to the godawful racket."

I sat up on an elbow. "In a couple of *hours*?"

Grayson pulled the covers up to his waist and grinned. "No. I'll admit it took me a couple of months."

"Har har," I said, then flopped on my back and stuck my other earplug in.

When Grayson didn't reply, I turned onto my side facing away from him, and sunk into the covers.

Grayson's lame joke had relieved some of the tension I'd been feeling. But not enough. My heart was still thumping in my throat like a banjo-picking toad-frog.

Good thing I'd stashed a can of Raid under the bed—just in case.

I DREAMT A WARM HAND was pushing gently on my arm.

"Wake up, Drex."

My eyes flew open. It was dark, but this was no dream. Grayson was pressed up against my back, whispering in my ear!

"Drex, wake up."

Is he ... does he want ... are we finally going to—

Suddenly, the RV shook as if it'd been hit by a meteor. I flipped over to face Grayson.

"What was *that*?"

"I don't know," he said, his lips inches from my own. Instead of his usual dry, clinical tone, Grayson's voice sounded calm and reassuring.

I didn't take that as a good sign.

I craned to see in the darkness.

"Earl's stopped snoring," I whispered. "Do you think he fell off the sofa-bed?"

The RV shook violently again, tumbling me up against Grayson. He wrapped his arms around me protectively.

"No," he said, squeezing me to him. "Not unless he just fell off for the third time in a row."

Chapter Thirty-Eight

Last night, I'd begged Grayson not to get up and investigate what had jostled the RV around three times—partly because I didn't want to leave his arms, but mostly for another reason I wasn't quite ready to divulge.

But at the moment I *could* tell him that nothing good would come of him tromping around in the dark by himself in the pouring rain. I'd argued that the conditions would've left him too vulnerable, and that it would be better to wait until morning.

For once, Grayson hadn't put up a fight.

We'd lain side by side, shoulders touching, until it stopped raining at 4:38 a.m.

I knew the exact time because I never went back to sleep. Instead, I'd lain next to Grayson with my eyes wide open, barely able to stand the electric thrill of his energy, but not wanting it to stop, either. When he'd awoken and risen at six o'clock, I'd been both relieved and disappointed.

I'd remained in bed, content to listen as Grayson belted out a tune in the shower. The performance was typical Grayson. In other words, it was godawful. He sounded like a mangy Tom-cat squeezing *Born to be Wild* out his butthole.

I giggled under the covers until Grayson emerged from the bathroom. Then I gave him fifteen minutes to himself before I got up and trudged into the main cabin, no longer able to resist the lure of fresh-brewed coffee.

"Mornin' guys," I said as I shuffled into the kitchen in pink slippers and sweats.

Grayson was seated at the banquette, clacking away at his laptop. Earl was standing at the kitchen counter, his nose in the carton of Dan's Discount coffee creamer he'd pulled from the fridge.

One sniff made Earl's face pucker. He glanced up at me, his thick black hair standing up like an electrocuted polecat. "Mornin' Cuz," he offered.

"Hey," I said. "Earl, you see or hear anything funny last night?"

He tossed the curdled creamer in the bin and grinned at me. "Nope. But I think I *felt* something."

Grayson looked up from his laptop screen. "What?"

Earl smiled. "Can't say for sure. But like they say, if this RV's rockin', don't come knock—"

"Shut it!" I said, cutting Earl off.

Grayson cleared his throat. "According to earthquaketrack dot com, there was a mild earthquake last night."

"Huh. That could definitely explain it," I said, perking up from my first sip of coffee.

"Possibly," Grayson said. "Still, I'd like to inspect the front end this morning, just to be sure."

I nodded. "Okay. But it's already dinged up so badly it'll be hard to tell if it got damaged last night or not."

Earl shot me a wink. "Aw, don't be so hard on yourself, Bobbie. By now, we've all got us a little wear and tear."

JUST AS I'D PREDICTED, a damage inspection of the RV's front end yielded inconclusive results. Thanks to its age and Grayson's driving, the motorhome's hood and front panels were covered in more pock marks than a pineapple with measles.

Grayson pulled a magnifying glass from the back pocket of his black jeans and studied a rather large dent above the chrome grille.

"The heavy rain last night washed the chassis clean," he said, swiping the pooled water from the deep ding. "Do you recall that dent being there before?"

"No," I said. "I'll have to go check my dent-al records."

Earl laughed.

Grayson's eyebrow rose, then fell, apparently disappointed that I really *didn't* keep a diary of the RV's dents and scratches.

Tires crunched gravel nearby. All three of us turned in the direction of the sound.

"You ready for our field trip?" Ranger called out, driving up in his Ford F-150.

"Packed and ready," I said over-cheerfully. I'd hoped to elicit another hint of jealousy from Grayson. If I did, he didn't let on.

"Did you feel the earthquake last night?" Grayson asked Ranger, walking over to meet him by the road.

"Sure did," Ranger said, climbing out of the Ford and offering a hand to shake.

"I didn't know Florida had earthquakes," I said.

"They're mighty rare in the state," Ranger said. "Limited mainly to the Panhandle area."

"Does Florida have fault lines, then?" I asked.

Ranger shook his head. "No. Florida wasn't formed by volcanic or tectonic activity, Miss Drex. It's actually sitting on a gigantic, fossilized barrier reef."

"Whoa," Earl said. "The more I find out about this here state, the freakier it gets."

Amen to that, cousin.

"So, where are you taking us today?" I asked Ranger.

He grinned. "We're heading south to Sumatra."

"Indonesia?" Grayson said, his eyebrow arching.

"Nope," Ranger said. "We've got our very own Sumatra right here in Liberty County. Just west of Tate's Hell."

"Oh, right. Tate's Hell," I said. "Sounds charming."

Ranger laughed. "Why don't you hop in and ride with me, Miss Drex? I'll tell you all about it on the way."

"Sounds good," I said, and hooked my arm in his. I knew I was being a bit of a tease, but after lying next to Grayson last night, I was desperate to know if my partner had feelings for me beyond mere clinical observation.

"Me and Grayson'll follow you two in Bessie," Earl said. "How far we got to go?"

"A little over thirty miles," Ranger said. "It's nearly a straight shot south from here. Just take County Road 12 to State Road 65, then head toward Sumatra. When you see me pull off the side of the road, we're there."

"That'll work," Earl said, and tipped his Redman ball cap.

"See you soon," I said, and waved at Grayson.

He noticed me, but he didn't wave back.

Chapter Thirty-Nine

As usual, I found myself looking for romance in all the wrong places.

As I climbed into Ranger's F-150, I knew it was no Cinderella's carriage. But I hoped it make Grayson jealous, just the same. I mean, it wasn't as if I wanted the two men to challenge each other to a *duel* over me or anything, but...

Well, maybe that was *exactly what I wanted.*

"So, I promised you a story, didn't I?" Ranger said, turning off the radio and shifting into drive.

"You did," I said, strapping in. "The legend of Tate's Hell, I believe."

I leaned over and gave him a peck on the cheek. Ranger blanched, then laughed nervously.

Geez.

When it came to flirting, Ranger, the overgrown Boy Scout, was turning out to be as big a nerd as Grayson. Maybe *bigger*. In fact, I was beginning to think perhaps the only thing those two *didn't* have in common was Grayson's bushy moustache.

"Uh ... okay. Here goes," Ranger said, punching the gas too hard. We lurched forward like a bad carnival ride. "Sorry," Ranger said, and eased up on the pedal. He laughed nervously again, then stared at the windshield as he spoke.

"It all started right after the Civil War ended. You see, Jebediah Tate was a Civil War veteran. He took advantage of a homestead grant and bought 160 acres of land out here for five whole dollars."

"No way!" I said. "Wow. What a deal. That hardly sounds like hell to me."

"Oh, no. That's not the hell part. Jebediah's hell was the fact that he was *superstitious*. He married a half-Cherokee woman who bore him a son they named Cebe. Together, the three of them farmed the land, kept scrub cattle, and gathered pine oil to eke out a living."

My nose crinkled. "Now *that's* starting to sound more like hell."

"You best believe it. Those pioneer days were tough going at the best of times. Crop failures. Diseases. Animal attacks. One mistake and you're a goner."

"Sounds lovely."

"Anyway, when Jebediah's wife died of scarlet fever, that was the last straw for him. He sought out a local Native American medicine man and made a pact with him to bring him better fortune. The deal was, as long as Jebediah gave the old medicine man a pig a year and stayed out of his patch of cypress forest, Jebediah'd have good luck."

I smirked. "I think I know where this is going."

Ranger glanced over at me and shot me a shy smile. "Well, as legend has it, for three years Jebediah gave up a pig and things stayed good. Then, in 1874, he decided to deny the medicine man his annual hog. The old man kicked up a fuss and told Jebediah that not only would his family see hard times ahead, but that before it was over, they'd go through hell."

I rubbed my hands together. "It's getting juicy now. Go on."

"Well, that very same year, Jebediah died from malaria. The pine trees nearly quit making any oil. The sugar cane was stunted. And the rangy cows began to disappear."

"Tough luck for his son Cebe," I said.

"Exactly. The only bright spot for Cebe was those pigs. They multiplied so fast he had to build two new pens to house them."

"Oh," I said, surprised. "So, where's the hell come in?"

"That next spring, Cebe got married."

"Oh." I laughed. "Well, that'll surely do it."

Ranger chuckled. "She was a mail-order bride. A fiery German immigrant who also happened to be Jewish."

I thought of Bondo and smiled. "Jewish, eh?"

"Yes. That meant she didn't eat pork, so all those pigs were useless to her. She took to complaining to Cebe about wanting beef. Finally, Cebe gave in and took off into the woods to find a scrub cow."

"What happened?"

"Well, Cebe set off with a shotgun and his hunting dogs. Long story short, he lost his dogs, his gun, and himself in the bogs around here. After seven days and nights of wandering the swamps, being eaten alive by bugs, Cebe found the stand of cypress trees the old medicine man had warned them to stay out of. Cebe went in anyway, hoping the old man's magic would save him."

"Let me guess. It didn't."

"Right-o," Ranger said. "Instead, Cebe got bitten by a snake. Delirious from the venom and from drinking dirty water, he ran through the swamp until he finally stumbled into a clearing. When he was found, he only lived long enough to say, 'My name is Cebe Tate, and I just came through Hell.'"

"Ah," I said. "And thus, Tate's Hell was born."

Ranger nodded. "That's right. And it's remained a legendary and foreboding swamp to this very day."

I shook my head. "Liberty County is full of surprises."

"Well, actually Tate's Hell is in Franklin County," Ranger corrected. "But believe me, where we're going next is even stranger, if you ask me. But, thankfully, a whole lot less deadly." Ranger glanced over at me and winced. "Or, at least it *used to be*."

Chapter Forty

"There they are," Ranger said, slowing the Ford down and glancing out the driver's window at the grassy median off State Road 65.

I leaned forward and followed his gaze. About thirty feet off the highway, I spotted what appeared to be a whole clutch of cobras swaying with the breeze, their yellow heads poking up above the knee-high grass.

"Whoa!" I gasped. "What are those?"

"*Sarracenia flava*," Ranger said.

"Snakes?" I gulped.

Ranger shot me a funny look, then smiled. "Not snakes. Yellow pitcher plants."

"Oh." I took another glance and sighed with relief. "That's more like it."

"Let's pull over for a better look."

"Sounds good to me."

"They're out early," Ranger said as he pulled the Ford over to the side of the road. "Another bonus of our unusually warm winter, I guess. In another month or so, the whole side of the road will be covered with their dancing yellow heads."

"I bet that's truly something to see," I said, slipping a foot out the car door.

I stepped down. My boot sunk two inches into the squishy soil. "Yuck!" I took a tentative step, slipped, and nearly did a banana split face-first into the muck.

"Aargh!" I yelled, and grabbed onto the Ford's door handle for support.

"Fabulous," I heard Grayson call out.

I turned to see him click a photo of the stand of pitcher plants before elegantly climbing down out of Bessie. Earl shut off the Hemi engine and popped open the driver's door.

"*Sarracenia flava?*" Grayson called out to Ranger.

"Exactly," Ranger said, nearly gleefully. He nodded toward a stand of perhaps fifty tall, lime-green, sausage-like plants, each capped with a lemon-yellow flap that reminded me of the hoodie on Whitey's rain poncho. "The yellow pitchers there are the showiest of our carnivorous plants."

"Excellent," Grayson said.

Ranger beamed with pride. "These unusual beauties are part of what makes this whole region so special." He led us to the closest pitcher plant and pointed out the open gap between the top of its tubular stalk and the yellow, hood-like cap suspended above it.

"Insects are lured in through here," Ranger said. "Then they fall down this pitcher-like throat, where they're digested in a pool of enzymes."

Earl's face puckered. "Bug eatin' plants? How'd that happen? Did these here plants get together one day and say, 'Hey, y'all. Let's eat us some bugs.'"

"Well, yes and no," Ranger said. "The adaptation you see here took eons. Thousands, maybe millions of years."

"Or it happened quickly, with a freak genetic mutation," Grayson said, folding his arms across his chest. "Any mutation that proves wildly advantageous can render the old model obsolete in a matter of one or two generations."

"True," Ranger said, stiffening. "I suppose it can. But whether quick or slow, adaptation is a never-ending process."

Grayson nodded. "Agreed."

"Look over here," Ranger said, pointing to a couple of pitcher plants on the left end of the stand. "You can see new adaptations happening in these plants right now."

"Really?" I asked, intrigued. "Where?"

"Their coloration," Ranger said. "See how most of the plants are yellow-headed with greenish throats?"

"Yes."

"Then there's a few over there that are blotched with red. Like Grayson said, if that red color variant proves to offer survival advantages, it could become the new normal for the species in a few decades."

"That's really interesting," I said. "But ... do these poor plants *have* decades to live? I mean, are they endangered?"

"Not *this particular* species," Ranger said. "But, sadly, it's the only one of the twenty-one species of carnivorous plants in this area that *isn't* endangered. The yellow pitcher is actually a pretty hardy species."

I took another step into the muck for a closer look at the nearest pitcher plant specimen. I was surprised at how large it was. Its yellow head rose nearly to my hip. And the plant's green, tubular throat was so thick and waxy, it appeared to have been made of dense plastic.

"I got a question," Earl said, lifting his Redman cap to scratch his head. "What would make a plant like that decide to start eatin' bugs?"

"Poor soil nutrients," Ranger said. "These plants couldn't get the minerals they needed from the earth, so they decided to supplement their diets by making lures to attract and trap insects."

Earl whistled. "Well if that don't beat all. How many bugs does one a these here fellers eat?"

Ranger grinned and shrugged. "I suppose as many as it can catch."

"I'll be." Earl took a step toward me and sunk up to his shin in the muck. "Whoa!" he hollered, his boot making a sucking sound as he pulled his foot free. "Them pitcher plants like this swampy stuff, eh?"

Ranger nodded. "This particular geographic area is what we call a seepage slope. It's part of the Apalachicola National Forest. And yes, the pitcher plants love this kind of environment."

Earl swiped at the mud on his jeans leg. "How many different kinds a these thangs you got growin' around here?"

"All told, we've got four species of pitcher plants," Ranger said. "Not to mention seventeen types of sundews, butterworts, and bladderworts."

"My granny always told me not to mention nobody's warts," Earl said. He reached over and plucked a beetle from a leaf and mashed it between his thumb and forefinger. "Mind if I give this feller here a snack?"

Ranger smiled. "Be my guest."

Earl waggled his eyebrows and dropped the squashed bug down the greenish-yellow throat of the pitcher plant. "There you go, little guy. Better'n biscuits and gravy."

"So," Grayson said to Ranger, "you say the remaining species of carnivorous plants around here are endangered?"

"Yes. But not as badly as the Torreya pine." Ranger glanced around and sucked in a long breath of moss-scented air. "As you can see, we've still got plenty of bog and swamp to support these pitchers. But the poor Torreya pine is just one wildfire away from extinction."

"Can't they do something to save them?" I asked.

"Sadly, the Torreya doesn't seem to warrant the priority," Ranger said. "It's not like the long-leaf pine. Its decimation impacted gopher tortoises and red-cockaded woodpeckers. But if the Torreya trees disappeared tomorrow, as far as we know, no other creatures would be adversely affected."

He sighed and took a step back toward his truck.

"Maybe it's the last holdout of a vanishing ecosystem," Grayson said, calling after Ranger. "Or perhaps its true purpose has yet to be discovered."

Ranger's shoulders slumped. He stopped and turned around. "Or perhaps it really *doesn't* have a place in this world. Either way, once a species is gone, you can't go back."

The sudden blast of a horn made us all turn to face the road. A truck was heading toward us, fishtailing as its driver slammed on the brakes. A window rolled down, revealing a familiar, bearded face.

"Ranger!" Lamar yelled from the truck. "I need to talk to you!"

"What about?" Ranger called out.

"You seen Rusty? He was supposed to meet me to go fishing over by Tate's Hell."

"No," Ranger said. "You try calling him?"

Lamar tugged his mossy beard with a scrawny brown hand. "Yep. Three times. No answer."

Ranger's brow furrowed. "That's not like Rusty."

"I know," Lamar said. "I sure hope nothin's gone and happened to him."

A horn blasted long and low. It was followed quickly by a siren wail. We all stood frozen in the muck, mouths agape, as first an ambulance blew past, then a firetruck whizzed by—both heading north toward Bristol.

Lamar and Ranger exchanged glances.

"Everybody load up," Ranger barked. "And hurry!"

I took a step toward Ranger's truck. "No," he said, hustling toward his F-150. "You'd better go with your friends. This could get messy."

Chapter Forty-One

I t was like watching the *Wizard of Oz*...
      On PCP.

The last twenty minutes flashed by in a blur of whizzing forest and whining monster-truck tires as we barreled down the backroads of Liberty County, chasing Ranger's F-150 at speeds exceeding ninety miles an hour.

I thought Bessie might blow a gasket before Ranger finally slowed his Ford enough to take a familiar turn off State Road 20.

Trailing ten feet behind him, Earl took the turn on two wheels. Centrifugal force send me sliding sideways for an up-close and personal session with Grayson. As I pushed myself off him, I caught a glimpse out the passenger window and gasped.

"What in God's green tarnation?" Earl said as I stared into the void.

We'd arrived at the place where the old cemetery had stood. But the cemetery headstones were gone. The crumbling building on the corner was gone. The whole field itself was gone—swallowed up by the ravenous sinkhole.

The massive crater's sides had caved in and were eating away at everything in its path. The crumbling edges were quickly inching toward the road itself.

"Holy crap!" I yelled, leaning over Grayson and pressing my nose to the passenger window. "There's nothing left! Not even a gravestone!"

"Steer as far from the hole as you can," Grayson said, the reason in his calm voice wavering slightly. "The edges may be ready to give way."

"You got it, Mr. G," Earl said, maneuvering Bessie into the opposite, oncoming lane.

When we reached the turn-off to Rusty's place, Ranger's Ford had just rounded the corner. As we took the turn, the F-150 ahead of us fishtailed, slinging orange mud as it dug deep into the ruts in the narrow road.

"Back off a bit," I yelled. But it was too late.

A spray of orange mud splatted Bessie's windshield like projectile vomit. Earl slammed on the brakes and hit the wipers. They smeared the slick mud from one end of the windshield to the other.

"Can't see a dang thing!" Earl said, mashing the wiper fluid button. Slowly, the wipers trudged across the muddy windshield until visibility went from muddy to filmy.

When it was finally clear enough to make out the scene in front of us, we couldn't believe our eyes.

Just beyond Ranger and Lamar's vehicles was the type of scene usually found only in a disaster movie. Most of Rusty's junkyard hideaway had vanished. The whole front slope of the hill—along with Rusty's formidable junk car collection—had disappeared into another ravenous, gaping sinkhole.

"Holy smokes," Earl said, pulling up behind Ranger's Ford.

We hopped out and joined Lamar and Ranger, who were staring silently into the raw abyss, mouths agape.

To my surprise, Rusty's odd, camper-van centipede of a house was still intact, perched atop the remaining back half of the small hill. The front half of the hill had been erased by the sinkhole, leaving the makeshift auto-hovel teetering precariously on the edge of a sheer wall of orange clay.

At the center of Rusty's house, the pontoon-boat porch jutted out over the abyss, creaking and groaning as it slowly see-sawed over the edge.

"Would you look at that," Lamar said, shaking his head. "Oops," he said, then stepped back and let out a giant sneeze. "Aaa-choo!"

As the blast echoed across the cavernous sinkhole, the pontoon porch groaned, then broke away from the house and skidded toward the open pit.

"Whoa!" Earl said. "Now *that's* somethin' you don't see every day."

"Stand back!" Ranger said, as the boat splashed into the hole.

But I didn't move. Instead, I stared, mesmerized, as the pontoon boat collided into a mélange of rusty appliances, toppled pines, palm tree parts, and assorted automobile pieces floating in the water at the bottom of the sinkhole. Half submerged, they bobbed and swirled lazily in the dirty water, like bathtub toys waiting their turn to go down a humongous, half-clogged drain.

A hand gripped my upper arm. "Move back," Grayson said.

As I stepped back, a movement amid the debris at the bottom of the pit caught my eye. I gasped.

The top of Rusty's junky Volkswagen beetle burbled as it floated mere inches above the surface. A large bubble of air escaped out one side as the chassis churned in the dirty water. In the filthy orange foam, I thought I saw something move.

"Where are Rusty and Bondo?" I cried out.

"Don't know," Ranger said. "I hope they made it out of here in time."

The Boy Scout stared into the sinkhole, shaking his head. "That heavy rain last night must've washed out the entire substrate around here. We should leave. Immediately."

"You think they could still be up there in the house?" Grayson asked, nodding toward the row of welded-together camper vans.

"I sure hope not," Ranger said.

Suddenly, a large chunk of the hillside collapsed like a calving glacier. The centipede house let out a metallic wail as it broke apart. The front half tumbled into the swirling pit.

"We need to get out of here," Ranger said.

We stared at him blankly.

"I mean *now*!" he said, shoving us toward our vehicles. "This whole area could go any second!"

Chapter Forty-Two

S lowly and cautiously, Earl followed the same ruts Ranger and Lamar made as they left the narrow dirt road leading to what was once Rusty's place. I sat in the middle, keeping an eagle eye on the sliding window behind me and hoping the horrible sinkhole wouldn't swallow us before we could get the hell out of there.

As soon as their tires hit asphalt, Ranger and Lamar gunned their engines and blew past the crumbling road and gutted cemetery. They barely slowed until they pulled into the parking lot at Appaloosa Diner.

"I'm going inside to see if anybody's seen Rusty or Bondo," Ranger said, jumping out of his Ford and making a beeline for the door.

"Wait a minute," I said. "What about the ambulance and fire truck? Do you think he might've been in an accident?"

"No. I heard on the way to Rusty's there was an accident at Bong Chemical. That's where they were headed. I sure hope Rusty got out of there."

"What kind of vehicle does he drive?" I asked.

Ranger stopped. "Usually that rusted out VW of his. Did you see it?"

I gulped. "Maybe. I think I might've seen it disappear into the bottom of that sinkhole."

Ranger locked eyes with me. "You sure about that?"

I chewed my lip. "No. Not a hundred percent. It could've been another one of his junk cars."

Ranger blew out a breath. "Let's hope that's the case."

I nodded solemnly. Ranger patted me on the back. "He'll turn up," he said. "Don't you worry."

But Ranger himself didn't seem too convinced as he turned and headed for the entrance to the Appaloosa Diner. I trailed behind him, replaying what I'd seen at the sinkhole.

Was Rusty in that car? Was Bondo?

Ranger opened the door and held it for me. Like a clumsy ox, I managed to hit my head on the metal awning on the way in.

"You okay?" Grayson asked, taking my arm from behind.

"Uh ... sure," I fumbled. "Just worried."

"No need," Grayson said, eyes locked on Ranger. "I'm here."

"Mmm, boy!" Earl said, sniffing the air scented with bacon and biscuits. "Let's eat us somethin', y'all."

He slid into an empty booth. For once, I wasn't going to argue with him. I left Grayson and Ranger to their pissing match and scooted in opposite Earl. As I did, a waitress walked by carrying two plates heaped high with what I affectionately called UFOs—unidentified fried objects.

"I want me one of them," Earl said.

I shook my head. "No way. Nothing fried for you."

Earl pouted. "Why not?"

I pointed at the daily special on the board—a fried chicken, bacon and shrimp basket. From the description, even the bacon was battered and deep fried.

Geez. Maybe this place really is *the Garden of Eden.*

"Because," I explained to Earl. "They probably use the same grease to fry the bacon that they fry the shrimp in. You want to end up all grey and bloated again, like Virgil's dead head?"

"Hush!" Earl whispered.

"Why?" I followed his darting eyes around. Half the people in the restaurant were staring at us.

I cringed. "Oh. Sorry."

Lamar plopped down beside me, shaking his mangy head. "Did you *see* that cemetery? Completely wiped off the map! It's that dad-burned curse, I tell you! Hacksaw Hattie's gettin' her revenge and takin' everybody straight to Hell with her!"

"Lamar!" Ranger scolded.

"Admit it," Lamar said, staring up at Ranger. "You were thinking it, too."

Ranger's eyes narrowed. "I was not."

Lamar elbowed me. "You know they used to call this place the Garden of Eden, right?"

"Was that before or after they put batter-fried bacon on the menu?" I quipped.

Lamar's beady eyes narrowed. "Not this here restaurant. That area around the cemetery that just went under."

"You don't say," I said dully, keeping my eyes on the menu. If I had to listen to more conspiracy theories, they'd better come with a side of grits and eggs.

Lamar let out a noisy breath. "Yes, I *do* say. I'm tellin' ya, that's the place of *original sin*," he said, his voice growing louder. "That nasty ol' serpent that tempted Adam and Eve lived there."

I sighed and looked up from the menu. "And your point is?"

Lamar's eyes grew wide. "Let those with eyes to see know the truth. That serpent's who Hacksaw Hattie *really* is!"

During Lamar's rant, Ranger had come and stood behind him. Now he pressed his hands on Lamar's shoulders, leaned down, and whispered, "I won't hear any more of this, Lamar. We've got enough bad news to deal with without you blowing it out of Biblical proportion."

"Fine," Lamar grunted, then picked up a menu.

"So what do we do now?" I asked as Grayson returned from the washroom.

Ranger opened his mouth to speak, but his cellphone buzzed. "Order me a fried shrimp and bacon basket," he said, glancing at the phone's display. "I'm going to see what the Sheriff's Office wants, then I'm going to start asking around about Rusty."

Lamar shook his head as Ranger walked away. "I got a bad feeling about this."

"Which part?" Grayson asked.

Lamar's small, dark eyes darted from Earl to me to Grayson. "Bad news is like a hurricane."

"What do you mean?" I asked.

He scratched his scraggly beard and said, "I got a bad feeling about that big ol' sinkhole at Rusty's. If you ask me, it's just the eye of *this* storm."

Chapter Forty-Three

For the third time, I swatted Earl's hand away from Ranger's fried bacon and shrimp basket. "You're allergic!" I hissed. "I'm not telling you again!"

"Dang it," Earl said. He pouted at his own empty basket and took a slurp of Mountain Dew. Then he slumped back into the booth and watched Lamar squirt mustard on his burger.

He set the mustard back with the mountain of condiments and said, "I don't care what Ranger says. It was Hacksaw Hattie's who up and kilt Virgil and Dale."

I blew out a breath.

Here we go again.

Earl read my expression and scowled. "Come on, Bobbie. How else you explain that red-haired ghost woman the pizza girl saw running away from that busted up tanker?"

Lamar stopped chewing a mouthful of burger. "What pizza girl?"

Grayson looked up from his cellphone. "Technically, Karen never said whether the person was a woman or a man."

His words ticked a thought inside my brain. "True, but Karen *did* describe the person's hair as blood red."

Grayson clicked off his phone. "And your point is?"

I chewed my lip. "What if it really *was*?"

"Was *what*?" Grayson asked.

"*Blood.*" I set down my glass of tea. "Think about it. When Virgil's head was found, it had a gash on top, and his ponytail was soaked in dried blood."

"Yes," Grayson acknowledged with a nod.

"Well, what if Virgil's head bled from the cut so badly that it *looked* like he had long red hair? That would make Virgil fit the description of the person Karen saw running into the woods."

"Interesting," Grayson said. "But now we're back to the real mystery. Karen said she saw the head's body disappear right before her eyes. How do you explain that?"

I frowned. "I dunno."

"I know how!" Lamar said, choking on a sip of coffee. "Because what pizza girl saw was a ghost! The ghost of Hacksaw Hattie!"

"Shh!" I hissed. I pursed my lips and glanced around at the restaurant. A man in a brown shirt was leaning up against the paneled wall. A thought fired in my brain like a ricochet bullet.

"I got it!" I blurted.

"Got what?" Earl asked. "Brain damage?"

"No," I sneered. I turned to Lamar. "Did Virgil wear a uniform when he drove for Bong?"

"Naw. Bong was too cheap to spring for something like that."

I locked eyes with Grayson. "What if Virgil was wearing camouflage hunting clothes when he had his accident?"

Grayson frowned. "I'm not following."

I nodded. "Okay, listen. Let's say it *was* Virgil who Karen saw running toward the forest, and that he was wearing camouflage. When he got near the wood line, his clothing would've blended into the background, creating the illusion his body disappeared—*but his bleeding head didn't!*"

Grayson sat up at full attention. "That's highly plausible," he said, his green eyes flashing. "Good work. However, if you're right, that solves one question but creates another."

My nose crinkled. "What's that?"

"If it *was* Virgil who Karen saw, why did he run into the woods instead of seeking help?"

"Huh." I sat back in my chair and crossed my arms. "I don't know."

Earl perked up. "I got it! Maybe ol' Virgil hit his noggin on the windshield and got hisself magnesia!"

"You mean amnesia?" I asked.

Earl shrugged. "I dunno. I forget what it's called."

"What about the hundred-year curse?" Lamar argued. "That can't be no coincidence. And how do you explain the sinkholes swallowing up everybody? Virgil Stubbs couldn't a done that."

"Not everything has to be related," Grayson said.

Lamar's beady eyes slanted. "So you're admitting Hacksaw Hattie could'a still done it."

"Well, I suppose," Grayson said. "It's improbable, but I don't disagree entirely about your legend having a connection here."

"What do you mean?" I asked, choking on a fried shrimp.

Grayson shrugged. "The story of Hacksaw Hattie could be a bastardization of an older—perhaps even ancient—Native American legend."

"Oh!" Earl grunted, raising his hand. "Did them Indian folks make hacksaws outta them palm spathe thangs?"

"I wasn't referring to the method of death," Grayson said. "I merely postulated that the 'omen of death' associated with certain occurrences could have its basis in older mythology."

"Huh?" Lamar grunted.

Grayson rubbed his chin. "From what I've learned on various insect-related websites, most native peoples tend to hold negative perceptions of swarming insects and biting bugs."

"No shit," I said, slurping down some iced tea. "Bugs suck in every language."

"Perhaps," Grayson said. "But for Native Americans, their beliefs go deeper than simple loathing. Quite a few indigenous tribes associate insects not only with disease, but with evil, witchcraft, and bad luck."

Lamar's grey eyebrows met below his furrowed brow. "You saying this Hacksaw Hattie ghost is also a *witch*?"

"Not exactly," Grayson said. "I think she's something even more cryptic than that."

"Cryptic?" Lamar asked.

Grayson nodded. "It means—"

"Earl! Stop it!" I hissed, swatting my cousin's meaty paw away from Ranger's food again. "You have some kind of death wish or something?"

Earl pouted and wrung his stinging hand. "Not that I know of."

I shook my head and turned to Grayson and Lamar. "Look. I say the person running from the scene was Virgil Stubbs. End of story. It just makes the most sense."

"Who's doing the killin' then?" Lamar asked.

"My vote's on Roy Stubbs, Virgil's crazy cousin," I said. "If you can cut somebody's leg off, you can cut heads off, too."

"Sorry that took so long," Ranger said, walking up to our booth. "But I think we can eliminate Roy Stubbs from the equation."

"How so?" I asked as Grayson scooted over to make room for Ranger in the booth.

Ranger slid in, then lowered his head a notch and whispered, "They just ID'ed his body. He's the guy you found in the porta-john."

"Oh." I shrunk back in my seat. "But wait. Couldn't he have killed Virgil before he died?"

"Possibly," Ranger said. "But not likely, at this point."

"Why not?" Grayson asked.

"Because they just found another severed head."

"Where?" Grayson asked.

"Just west of Torreya State Park."

I grimaced. "But Roy could've done it before he died."

Ranger shook his head "No. This one was fresh." He locked eyes with me. "So fresh it was still bleeding."

Chapter Forty-Four

"Who found the severed head?" Grayson asked.

Ranger swallowed hard and twirled the straw in his iced tea. "A couple of hunters out looking for wild boar."

My stomach gurgled. I stared across the booth at Ranger, then at the cold shrimp-and-bacon basket on the table in front of him. "Have they identified who it belongs to?"

"No. Not yet." Ranger poked at his food with a fork, then finally looked up. "This one could take a while."

"Why's that?" I asked.

He grimaced. "Boars got to it first. That's how the hunters found it. One of them shot a boar charging at him. From what I've been told, the boar squealed, fell over, and coughed out a human ear."

I gasped. "An ear? Are you serious?"

"They're omnivores," Ranger said, pushing his food aside.

"Does that mean 'ear eaters' in pig Latin?" Earl asked.

Ranger shot him some side eye, then grimaced. "Well, I guess, technically, yes. It means they're opportunist eaters, eating whatever they can find."

"Kind of like you," I said to Earl, swatting his hand away from Ranger's dinner for the umpteenth time.

Ranger glanced over at me and Grayson. "You're both detectives. With Roy Stubbs now out of the picture, do either of you have any theories as to who's doing this?"

"We discussed it a bit while you were gone," I said, glancing around at Earl, Grayson and Lamar. "I think we can all agree that it wasn't the ghost of Hacksaw Hattie."

Lamar scowled. "Not *all* of us."

Ranger shot Lamar a *give it a rest* look. "So if our killer's not Roy Stubbs or this idiotic ghost, who else can it be?"

"I have an idea," Grayson said.

"Let's hear it," Ranger said.

Grayson rubbed his chin. "I believe we may be looking at a case of iterative evolution."

"Idiot revolution?" Earl asked, his eyes as big as boiled eggs.

I blew out a breath. "Yeah, Earl. The idiot revolution. It's like the Pepsi Generation. And once again, you're part of it."

"Iterative evolution," Ranger said, repeating Grayson's proposed theory. The Boy Scout leaned back in the booth and chewed his lip. "The resurrection of an extinct species."

"That's right," Grayson said.

Ranger locked eyes with Grayson. "Are you serious about this?"

Grayson nodded, his lips pressed into a white line.

"Come on!" I said. "That's crazy—even for *you*, Grayson!"

"No it's not," Ranger said, nodding thoughtfully. "You know, I read about a case of that recently. The Aldabra white-throated rail bird."

"Exactly," Grayson said.

Earl leaned in over the table. "The abracadabra *what*?"

"Aldabra bird," Grayson said. "It's a flightless brown bird that was declared extinct almost a hundred thousand years ago. But recently, it was spotted in its native habitat."

My nose crinkled. "An extinct species that came back to life?"

"Yes." Ranger said. "I read about it, too. It's true."

"But ...," I stuttered, "how is that possible?"

"Through the power of God," Lamar said, his hands clasped in prayer position.

"Hmm," Grayson grunted. "That, and the re-expression of ancient genes."

Earl nodded. "We talkin' Levis or Wrangler, Mr. G?"

Grayson worked his tongue against his cheek for a moment, possibly biting his tongue. Then he held his hands palms-up over his empty plate. "It's simple, really. Let me explain."

Grayson picked up a salt shaker. "Say this is an ancient extinct species." He shook some salt onto the plate.

"Okay," I said.

Grayson picked up a pepper shaker. "And let's say this is the species that evolved from it." He shook black pepper over the salt on the plate. "As you see, the salt species has disappeared, but its genetic material lives on, hidden within the DNA of the newer, pepper generation. It's latent, buried genetic markers like these that revealed we evolved from ancient apes."

"Speak for yourself," Lamar growled. "I ain't no monkey's uncle."

"Fair enough," Grayson said. "But either way, it's been shown that hidden genetic traits can re-emerge when environmental conditions become right for them again. In the case of the Aldabra bird, perhaps the predators that consumed the flightless bird to extinction have disappeared, making it possible for it to re-emerge again and survive in its original habitat."

I sat back in my chair. "So *that's* iterative evolution."

Grayson nodded. "More or less."

Ranger stared at Grayson, absently tapping his knife on the table as he talked. "So, you're saying you think something's changed in the environment around here, and that change has triggered the re-emergence of some kind of prehistoric predator?"

Grayson nodded. "That's precisely what I'm saying."

Stunned, I glanced over at Ranger. He swallowed hard and asked, "Any idea which predator?"

"Yes," Grayson said. "The lost species of *Arthropleura*."

Earl gasped. "The lost city of Atlantis!"

Grayson shot me an *I blame you for this* look, then turned to Earl. "I said, 'the lost *species* of ...'" He shook his head. "Never mind. *Arthropleura* was a prehistoric millipede."

My face puckered. "Another *bug*?"

Grayson raised his chin a notch. "An *arthropod*. In the family of lobsters and scorpions."

Lamar laughed cynically. "You're tellin' me a dad-burned *bug's* been eatin' peoples' heads off around here? Pshaw! What a load of malarkey!"

Grayson sighed. "You can't explain a butterfly to caterpillar people."

Ranger's brow furrowed. "As I recall, *Arthropleura* could grow rather large."

Grayson nodded. "Indeed."

"How big we talkin' about here?" Earl asked. "Watermelon size? Bulldog? Humvee?"

Grayson's left eyebrow shot up. "Impressively large. Up to nine feet. In fact, *Arthropleura* was the largest known land invertebrate to ever roam the Earth. Bigger even than the mega-cockroach."

Earl grimaced, then smashed an insect crawling across the windowsill with his thumb. "Well, *that* one sure ain't gettin' any bigger."

I shook my head and blew out a breath. "Fine, Grayson. I'll entertain your giant bug theory. So, what would this Arthur Murray thing normally eat?"

"*Arthropleura*. It would consume other insects."

Earl's eyes grew wide. "A cannibal bug?"

Grayson sighed. "Actually, that would make it *entomophagous*."

"Whatever," I said. "Either way, it makes no sense. How could a bug as big as a bull gator survive on eating tiny little bugs?"

"It's not unprecedented in nature," Grayson said. "Take the blue whale, the largest animal on the planet. It eats only krill, tiny shrimp not even an inch long."

"That's right," Ranger said, perking up.

"But krill gather up in huge schools," I argued. "That makes it easy for the whale to get a huge mouthful all at once."

"Just like them big ol' swarms of cicadas in that video," Earl said.

I exchanged glances with Grayson and Ranger.

"Oh, my word!" I locked eyes with Grayson. "You're saying this mega-cicada event could be the environmental trigger that brought this thing back to life?"

"Absolutely." He turned to Lamar. "I also think it could be the origin of the Hacksaw Hattie legend."

Lamar cocked his scraggly head and focused his narrow, beady eyes on Grayson. "You saying Hacksaw Hattie's really a gigantic millipede?"

Grayson nodded. "In a matter of speaking, yes."

Lamar shook his head. "I ain't buying it."

"Consider this," Grayson said. "The origin of the legend of headless victims roaming the land could've begun not *one hundred* years ago with Hacksaw Hattie, but *thousands* of years ago—as an actual historic event recounted through the generations by Native American tribes."

Lamar's face puckered. "How can a killer millipede turn into a hacksaw murderer?"

Grayson smiled. "I'm glad you asked. Let's postulate that, over the centuries, the millipede's return occurred with such infrequency—let's say once every hundred years—that no one who lived to witness the creature one time survived long enough to see its return. With no eyewitnesses to keep the actual facts of the story alive, they faded into history, eventually morphing into a simple, cautionary tale that swarms of bugs bring with them evil and death."

"But what about Hacksaw Hattie herself?" Lamar said. "She was *real*. Her body's in the ..." He grimaced. "Her body *was* buried in the cemetery."

"Yes," Grayson said calmly. "For a hundred years. I propose that a century ago was the last time Arthropleura arose. It feasted on mega-year cicadas and also killed Hattie's husband. Superstitious villagers blamed her for his murder, and she became the victim of a vigilante hanging."

My nose crinkled. "But why would a millipede kill *people*?"

"Maybe because its native food is no longer available," Ranger said. "So it was forced to adapt."

"Yeah," Earl said. "Hey, if a little ol' plant can start eatin' bugs, why can't a big ol' bug start eatin' people? Right?"

I frowned. "Okay. But why *here*?"

"Since we're going down this lane, how about this for a theory," Ranger said, leaning back in the booth. "Perhaps *Arthropleura's* ancestors traveled south on the glaciers and were dumped here, just like the seeds of the carnivorous plants were."

Earl chuckled at me. "Kinda like that toadsicle thang you talked about, Bobbie. Freezin' and thawin' every year like a fruitcake."

"This is all horse manure!" Lamar said, slamming his fist on the table. "I got my own theory. Bristol here's the original Garden of Eden. That thing what's killin' people is the devil serpent from the Bible itself!"

"Interesting thought," Grayson said, nodding at Lamar. "He has a point. If this area truly *is* the original birthplace of man, it serves that it could just as easily be the birthplace of all kinds of other species, too."

Chapter Forty-Five

"Let me get this straight," I said to Grayson. "You're saying a giant, prehistoric millipede is on the rampage around here, biting people's heads off?" I dropped a fried shrimp back onto my lunch plate. "Sorry. I'm just not buying it."

"What's your main objection?" Grayson asked, as if I couldn't decide between an electric toothbrush or a manual one.

"My *main* objection? Ugh!" I blew out a breath and glanced around the restaurant. "For one thing, don't you think someone would've noticed a gigantic bug running around here by now?"

"Not necessarily. Arthropods are elusive creatures. For instance, thousands of cockroaches can live in a person's house and they could remain totally unaware."

I grimaced. "Thanks for just ruining my life."

Grayson shook his head. "Regardless of your reservations, Drex, in my opinion an ancient arthropod is the solution that best fits the facts at hand."

My eyebrows met my hairline. "Seriously? And just exactly what *are* these so-called 'facts' of yours?"

Grayson handed the waitress his salt-and-pepper flecked plate, then leaned over the table. "First, we have the precedent set by the Native American legend, which means we're dealing with a creature whose lifespan or regeneration capabilities span hundreds if not thousands of years. Secondly, the timing of its recurrence coincides perfectly with the mega-cicada event taking place right now."

"Well, hold on," Ranger said. "About that timing point... Normally the cicadas don't emerge in March. It's usually more like May and June. This year's early timing is due to the exceptionally warm winter we had."

"Aha!" Grayson said. "Even *more* validation that this constellation of events happens only once a century."

"Fine," I said sourly. "The timing's right. So, what else you got?"

Grayson sat up and straightened his shoulders. "Arthropods are among the most numerous species on the planet. And their ability to adapt to environmental changes is unparalleled."

"That's a good point," Ranger said. "But it makes me wonder if the arthropod in question isn't a millipede, but something else entirely."

Grayson's eyebrow shot up. "Go on."

Ranger chewed his lip. "Well, it makes more sense to me that the arthropod in question would be one whose existence is somehow reliant on the unique elements offered by Liberty County's one-of-a-kind environment."

"Well postulated," Grayson said. "So you're saying the creature in question is dependent on the unique terrain, flora and fauna of the local area to complete its one-hundred-year life cycle."

"Correct," Ranger said. "Taking that into consideration, I propose the creature is most probably a prehistoric ancestor of the *cicada* itself."

Grayson rubbed his chin. "Intriguing, but—"

"Hear me out," Ranger said. "Cicadas spend their nymph stages underground, sucking sap from roots."

"Holy Moses!" Earl said. "If these here bugs you're talkin' about's as big as hippos, they'd sure need them a lot of sap to suck."

"Exactly my point," Ranger said. "I believe they could be reliant on the extra-potent sap found only in the Torreya tree."

"And now those trees are nearly extinct," I said.

"Correct," Ranger said. "And this creature ... this overgrown insect thing ... is on the warpath over it."

"Of course," Grayson said, talking to himself. "The van. The dents. It all makes sense now."

"To *you*, maybe," I said. "What are you talking about, Grayson?"

"The van Karen saw leaving the accident scene," Grayson said, his eyes distant, following the thread of his own thought.

"Van?" Ranger asked.

"Yes," Grayson said. "The one with the two surfboards on top. That could've been an enormous cicada with deformed wings."

"Good lawd," Earl said. He glanced through the window up at the sky outside. "A bug as big as a dang helicopter? Swoopin' down and cuttin' people's heads off?"

"No," Grayson said. "At that enormous size, flight should be a physiological impossibility."

"I agree," Ranger said. "The thing would be reliant on land travel."

"He'd have to have him some big ol' legs," Earl said. "As big as that thing that poor feller's head fell out of at the picnic."

I closed my eyes and took a moment to clear the image of Virgil's head from my mind. I reopened them and glanced over at Ranger. "If you're right about this overgrown insect being reliant on the sap of the Torreya tree to live, this could be its final stand."

"Yes," Grayson said. "And I think he knows it."

"*He*?" I said, turning to stare at Grayson. "You think it's a male?"

"Yes."

"Why?"

"Isn't it obvious?" Grayson said. "The dents in all the vehicles around here? They're the results of rutting behavior."

I nearly choked on my iced tea. "*Rutting behavior*?"

Grayson nodded. "If I'm right, we're looking at the re-emergence of Cicada *Palaeontinidae*, a mega-sized cicada with a mega-sized appetite for mates."

I cringed. "And you think Fords and Chevys float his love boat? Come on!"

"Why not?" Grayson said.

"Because!" I argued. "Don't you think the creature would notice that his partner isn't ... uh ... *playing along?*"

Grayson shrugged. "Not necessarily. The male ladybug has been witnessed mating with a female for four hours before he realized she was dead."

I sat back and shook my head.

Well, that certainly explains a lot.

Chapter Forty-Six

When I came back to the table after using the ladies room at Appaloosa Diner, Lamar appeared to be in the throes of a meltdown.

"I don't care what you say," he yelled, spittle flicking from his lips onto his Spanish moss beard. "There ain't no such thing as a giant, horny, he-devil bug runnin' loose around here!"

I glanced around the restaurant and shriveled to the size of a dung beetle. Every single eye was staring at our booth. Again.

"Shh!" Ranger hissed at Lamar as I slipped into the booth. "It's just a theory. Nobody's saying this thing is *real*."

Grayson opened his mouth. I kicked him in the shin.

"What?" he grumbled at me. I discreetly shook my head.

"But what if it *is* real?" Earl asked, his eyes half wild. "What're we gonna *do* about it?"

"Y'all are ready for the check, aren't you?" the waitress asked, shooting us one of those unreadable sideways glances mastered by seasoned members of the service industry.

Ranger leaned in over the table like a quarterback in a hail-Mary huddle. "Listen. I'd suggest we skip the peach cobbler and get out of here," he whispered. "We've still got a lot of bugs ... er, *issues* to work out with this theory before I dare say a word about it to the Sheriff's Department."

"Yes, about that," Grayson said, then winced again, as the toe of my boot impacted his shin once more.

"Never mind," I said. "Let's go."

THE WHOLE CREW HAD convoyed back to our campsite in Torreya State Park. We were assembled around the picnic table—our official war room—preparing strategies against the threat of a giant, killer-cicada attack.

Grayson emerged from the RV and laid a three-foot square whiteboard down across the top of the picnic table. He whipped three colored markers from the breast pocket of his black shirt, then stared at us solemnly. "Lady and Gentlemen, Mission Cicada *Palaeontinidae* begins."

I sighed. "Okay, Grayson. First off, we need another name for this monstrous bug thing. I'm tired of trying to say cicada polliwog—whatever thingamajig."

Grayson drew himself up, apparently taken aback. "What you just said is harder to say than *Palaeontinidae*."

"Oh!" Earl said, raising his hand. "Since the ol' bug's of the male persuasion, what say we call it Hacksaw Harry?"

I shrugged. "Why not. It's no more absurd than anything else going on here."

Grayson cleared his throat. "Drex, whether you believe in the mission or not, something is killing people around here. And unless you've got a better theory, I would appreciate your support with this one."

I winced. "Just trying to be the voice of reason."

"Well then, I suggest you find a better argument than 'This is dumb.'"

I grimaced. Grayson was right. As both a detective and a counterbalance to his crazy, I was scoring a big fat zero.

"Okay," I said. "Let's get serious. But first, do you have a better suggestion for this creature than Hacksaw Harry?"

"Emmet," Grayson said.

"Emmet?" My eyebrow shot up. "That seems rather random."

"Not at all," Grayson said. "It's a synonym for insect."

My eyebrow rose slightly. "Oh. Well, in that case, it's perfect, right Earl?"

Earl saluted again. "I'm with you fellas. Emmet it is."

I slapped on a serious expression and turned to Grayson. "So, where do we start, commander?"

"Let's take a look at this tactically," he replied, not missing a beat. "Lamar. Earl. You're both hunters. How do you go about tracking your woodland prey?"

"Besides runnin' 'em over with the truck on accident?" Earl asked.

Grayson sighed. "Yes. Besides that."

"First off, you got to know your prey's habits," Lamar said.

Grayson nodded. "Excellent. So what do we know about cicadas' habits?" he asked, writing the word *Habits* on the whiteboard.

"They like to suck tree sap!" Earl said.

Grayson wrote *sap* under the word *Habits*.

"Uh ... they fly," I said, trying to be helpful. "Except this one, of course."

"Not totally accurate," Ranger said. "Cicadas only fly in their final adult stage. Otherwise, they spend their lives mainly underground."

Well excuuuse me.

Still, something Ranger said pinged more than mild irritation in my brain.

"Underground," I fumbled. "Uh ... this is just a wild idea, but ... do you think this thing ... uh, *Emmet*, could be responsible for creating the sinkhole at Rusty's place? You know, by digging out of his burrow, or whatever?"

"Hmm," Ranger said. "Interesting idea. But if that's true, the creature couldn't be responsible for the recent killings. Virgil and

Dale's heads—as well as Roy's body—were all found *before* that sink-hole opened up."

"Okay," I said. "But maybe there's more than one."

"Sinkhole?" Ranger said. "Yes, of course—"

"No," I said. "More than one *giant bug*."

"Hmm," Grayson said. "On what data are you basing your hypothesis?"

"Observation," I replied. "When we were at the sinkhole at Rusty's place, I noticed a lot of palm spathes floating in the water along with the cars and appliances. But thinking about it now, I hadn't noticed any palm trees growing on his property."

I nodded at my cousin. "And like Earl said earlier, those spathes look a lot like oversized legs. Could what I saw actually have been part of a giant, freshly shed exoskeleton?"

"Interesting," Grayson said, rubbing his chin. "The hole at Rusty's could indeed mark the spot of a second emergence."

"Second?" Ranger asked. "And where was the first?"

"I think I know," I said. "There used to be Torreya trees at the cemetery, right Ranger?"

"Well, yes. But the last ones died a few months back."

"Is it possible the trees' roots could've remained viable for a while after they died?" I asked.

Ranger frowned. "I suppose. Why?"

"Because those dying roots could've been the last remaining food source for the giant cicada nymph," Grayson said, picking up my lead. "When its food source finally dried up, it was forced to emerge prematurely, and shed its exoskeleton before it had fully developed."

"Resulting in the malformed wings Karen thought were surfboards," I said, earning me a genuine smile from Grayson.

"Exactly," he said, his green eyes flashing. "Building on that idea, let's postulate that the creature had, over the millennia, adapted its useless flying wings for another purpose. Perhaps to aid in attracting smaller prey-cicadas, or for funneling swarms of them into its awaiting jaws."

"But premature emergence deformed the wings ended that mass-consumption feeding advantage," I said.

"I'm afraid the tanker truck accident didn't help the creature either," Ranger said. "We had to dig a trench as big as an Olympic swimming pool to bury all the cicadas that died there. I bet there were upwards of half a million or more."

I shook my head. "So poor, deformed Emmet turned to the only prey it was fast enough to catch."

"Exactly," Grayson said. "Humans."

Chapter Forty-Seven

Ranger shook his head and let out a low whistle. "It's poetic justice, if you think about it. We killed Nature's Torreya trees and cicadas. Now this freak of Nature is killing *us*."

"I still ain't convinced it's a giant bug to blame," Lamar said. "I mean, why would a big ol' cicada eat a man's body, but not his head?"

"I think I know," Grayson said. "Like mosquitos and ticks, it could be looking for a blood meal. Incising the neck would give it access to the jugular."

"What's a clown got to do with this?" Earl asked.

Lamar shot Earl a look. "But why take the *whole* head off?" he asked, ignoring Earl. "No sir. This here beheadin' business is the work of Hacksaw Hattie, for sure."

"Geez!" Ranger hissed at Lamar. "What's it going to take to convince you there's no such thing as that ridiculous ghost?"

"Hold on," I said, surprising myself with my sudden defending of lecherous Lamar. "It could be that Hacksaw Hattie really *did* kill her husband a hundred years ago, and that this beast Emmet had nothing to do with it."

"Hmm," Grayson said, tipping his fedora at me. "Go on."

"Okay. What if this year is somehow the perfect storm—a double whammy of no Torreya sap, plus no cicadas. This could be the *very first time* this Emmet creature has turned to killing people for its own survival."

"Desperate times call for desperate measures," Ranger said.

"Just like Dan's Discounts & Dents," Earl said, nodding solemnly.

"Interesting deduction," Grayson said. "So, can we agree that Hacksaw Hattie had her day a hundred years ago, but what we're dealing with now is something entirely different?"

Lamar frowned and grunted, "I guess."

"Good," Grayson said. "Let's get back to the plan." He leaned over the picnic table and wrote the word *Prey Items* on the whiteboard. I gave Mr. Sensitivity the stank eye. He wiped the words off and wrote *Casualties*.

"So, we've got four known dead," Grayson said.

"Correct," Ranger said. "Virgil Stubbs, Dale Martin, Roy Stubbs, and now the unidentified head half eaten by boars."

Grayson wrote down, *Virgil, Dale, Roy, Boar's Head.*

I shook my head.

Don't forget the mayo.

"What did all of these casualties have in common?" Grayson asked, tapping his marker on the whiteboard.

"They're all men," I said.

"Hmm." Grayson wrote that on the board.

"They were all found in the woods," Lamar said.

As Grayson scribbled that down, Ranger said, "Don't forget. Darryl Martin's still missing. And now Rusty and Bondo are, too."

Lamar piped up. "But if they fell into that sinkhole like Miss Bobbie said, they weren't killed by that Emmet bug."

"Unless Emmet dug the sinkhole," Grayson said, "and had them for a snack afterward. So, what else do our victims have in common?"

"They were alone," Ranger said.

"But wasn't Dale with Darryl?" Lamar asked.

"They could've become separated," Ranger said.

"Right," Grayson said. "But what I'm *really* after is, why did the bug choose to attack *these* individuals, when there were probably dozens of other viable targets?"

A thought occurred to me that made my gut flop. Still, in the interest of science, I put it out there.

"Uh ... do you think the creature could have seen them as potential ... uh ... *mates*?"

Lamar and Earl snickered. Ranger silenced them.

"She's got a point," Ranger said. "After emerging, the male cicada's role is primarily singing, flying, and mating. Males only live a few weeks at most, and spend that time mating with as many partners as they can find. And since this one doesn't fly, he's got even more time on his hands for singing and mating."

"Precisely," Grayson said, smoothing his moustache with his thumb and forefinger. "So how do we capitalize on this rutting urge?"

I stared at Grayson.

That's the $64,000 question...

"Oh, I know!" Earl said. "We could bring back some a that idiot DNA stuff of yours and make Emmet a girlfriend out of it."

"Yes, I thought about that," Grayson said, making my jaw drop. "Unfortunately, there's not enough time. But I think I've got an alternative idea."

Grayson glanced over at me. Every molecule in my body skipped a beat.

"Hold on," I said, glancing around for an escape route. "If you think I'm gonna pose as a freaking female cicada, you can forget it!"

Chapter Forty-Eight

I flapped around in the inflatable Sumo wrestler suit, trying to look like a sexy Asian cicada and wishing I had a pair of chopsticks to poke both of Grayson's eyes out.

"You're right," Ranger said, turning to Grayson and shaking his head. "She looks more like a stage three larva than an adult cicada."

Geez. Apparently, I can't even attract bugs.

Grayson sighed. "Well, it was worth a shot. Earl, go ahead and get her out of the suit."

"Hold on a second!" I grumbled.

"What?" Earl asked, tugging on the plug on the left cheek of my inflatable backside.

A thought hit me like a warm squirt of bird poop. "Uh ... never mind."

If Grayson was right and Emmet the monster bug had tried doing the nasty with a Dodge pickup and our RV, I was pretty sure the amorous arthropod wasn't that particular when it came to hookup partners. So why not give the Sumo thing a try? I'd been about to say exactly that when I realized I would be throwing myself under the bus.

Duh! Dangling off a wire as a giant cicada's sexy sushi platter was an experience I could definitely live without.

"Looks like it's back to square one," Ranger said.

"Thank you," I muttered as I wrestled with a dying Sumo balloon. Part of me was relieved, and part of me was in abject amazement that Grayson traveled around with an inflatable Sumo suit. I mean, what kind of a nut job does that?

Grayson chewed his lip. "What we need is a lure Cicada *Palaeontinidae* would find irresistible."

I kicked out of the last saggy leg of the deflated diaper warrior and stumbled over to the picnic table to join them. "So what exactly does a recently hatched male cicada do when he's looking for a good time?" I quipped.

Ranger piped up. "He sings to find a mate."

"Okay," I said. "So why don't we just sing back?"

Ranger eyed me as if I'd insulted his mother. "Because the females don't sing."

"Oh." As I sat down at the table, I became aware of how quiet the woods were. Where had all the cicada noise gone?

"Females don't sing, but rival males *do*," Grayson said.

"And your point is?" Ranger asked.

"If we can get Emmet to sing, we could use his own call to *locate* him."

"How do you get a male cicada to sing?" Earl asked.

"By setting up a competition," Ranger said.

My upper lip hooked skyward. "What are we talking about here? A barbershop quartet to the death?"

"No," Ranger said. "Males don't fight for females. They compete for mates by out-singing each other."

"Exactly what I was thinking," Grayson said. "We could use one of Lamar's recordings to mimic a rival male. We could blast it out into the woods and see if we get a response."

"Super," I said. "And if Emmet does respond, what do we do then?

"Run!" Lamar said.

"We lure it into a trap," Grayson said.

I shook my head "How? If it's as big as a Volkswagen, it certainly won't fit inside the door of your monster trap bedroom."

"No," Grayson said. "But we can set up another trap. A type of bug boudoir Emmet will find enticing."

I braced myself. "And how are we going to lure it in?"

"With the one thing it can't resist."

"Change?" I quipped.

"No," Grayson said. "With something that hasn't changed in millions of years—just like that joke."

Chapter Forty-Nine

R anger's cellphone chirped. He glanced at the display.
"I better take this," he said, and got up from the picnic table
and walked toward his truck.

Grayson stood. "I think I have just the thing to attract Cicada
Palaeontinidae," he said, then marched toward the RV.

I started to rise to follow him, but Grayson put his hand up like
a stop sign. "No. Wait here, Drex. I'll be back in a minute."

I sat back down and frowned.

"What do you think he's got in there?" Lamar asked, nodding
toward the RV.

I blew out a sour breath. "You're asking me? The guy just produced an inflatable Sumo suit."

"That ain't the only weird thing he's got hid up in there," Earl said
to Lamar. "Mr. G. keeps a bunch of strange stuff locked up in them
cabinets."

My cousin turned to me. "Hey, Bobbie. I bet it's one of his crazy
potions! Or maybe that nubbin thang—Ow!"

"Shut it, Earl!" I barked as my boot kicked his shin. "That's
Grayson's private business."

"I found it," Grayson announced, emerging from the RV. He
held up an old-fashioned-looking bottle made of brown glass.

I leaned forward, trying to get a peek at the new label Grayson
had surely pasted over the old one. I strained my eyes, expecting to
see something along the lines of;

Hello! My Name Is:
Horny Cicada Attractor

BUT THERE WAS NO NEW label. It was simply an old bottle of household cleaner, unaltered in any way.

"Pine-Solve-It?" I said. "*That's* your secret formula?"

"Yes." Grayson opened the cap and handed it to me. "Take a sniff and pass it around."

I snatched it from his hand, skeptical but grateful he'd said "sniff" instead of "swig."

"Whew!" I winced as the potent odor of pine punched me in the nose.

I handed the bottle to Earl.

"Whew-ee!" he hollered. "That smells just like that soap my mama used to wash my mouth out with."

"I had a hunch about that when you said it tasted like turpentine," Grayson said. "Which leads me to my point."

He's got a point. Thank you, Universe.

"What else do all of the victims have in common?" Grayson asked.

"Uh ... they're all dead?" Earl offered.

A pain shot through my head. Whether it was from Earl's stupid remark or from sniffing the Pine-Solve-It, I couldn't be sure.

Grayson let out a long, low breath. "No. Well, yes. But they also all smelled like pine."

"By golly, I think you're on to something!" Lamar said, taking a tentative sniff from the bottle. "When that tanker spilled, it was carrying Pine-Solve-It wash-water. Virgil could've got hisself covered in it during the crash!"

"And the port-a-john where I found Roy Stubbs," I said. "It was reeking of pine-scented deodorant."

Among other things...

"But what about Dale?" Earl asked.

"I think I know the answer to that," Lamar said. "A lot of us hunters use pine to mask our scent while we're trekking in the woods."

"Excellent," Grayson said. "So we have our common denominator. The scent of pine."

Grayson leaned over the table and scribbled on the whiteboard. "Now, here's how I see this playing out. First, Lamar, you'll play a selection of male cicada mating calls to get Emmet's attention. When the creature calls back, we'll ascertain its location, then lure it out with the scent of pine. Once we've got Cicada *Palaeontinidae* on the move, we lure it into our waiting trap."

Lamar nodded. "Sounds easy enough."

I winced.

Aw, crap, Lamar. Now you've jinxed us for sure.

WHILE GRAYSON, EARL and Lamar talked decoys and trapping ideas, I fixed a pot of coffee, then waited for Ranger to get off the phone. I was anxious to speak with him about something a little more down-to-earth than Grayson's resurrected dinosaur bugs.

"What's the Sheriff's Department say about all this?" I asked as he climbed out of the cab of his Ford F-150.

Ranger shut the door, then cocked his head at me. "You mean about the giant cicada?"

Seriously? You, too?

A dull pain began to throb inside my skull. "No. I meant what do they say about the *murders*."

Ranger's face went stoic. "You don't believe your partner's theory about a killer arthropod?"

I shrugged. "Let's just say I'm keeping my options open."

Ranger studied me for a moment. "I suppose that's what you detectives do, isn't it."

I held my eyebrows steady. "Uh ... yes. So, what does Officer Snyder say about who's behind the killings?"

Ranger looked down and toed the ground with his boot. "I'm not at liberty to say."

"Aw, come on, Ranger. Give me something!"

Ranger's lip curled slightly as his eyes met mine. "He says they're following all possible leads."

I let out a jaded laugh. Then I glanced over at the picnic table. Earl had his hands up over his head, animatedly acting out what appeared to me to be Bigfoot hurling a boulder. Lamar, and Grayson watched from the benches, nodding enthusiastically.

I shook my head. "Obviously not *all* possible leads," I quipped.

Ranger shrugged. "I wish I had more information I could tell you, but the Sheriff's Department is keeping a pretty tight lid on it—and I'm not in the pot."

My nose crinkled. "Why not?"

Ranger's face puckered with resentment. "Either they think I'm too close to their suspects, or they think I might be in on it myself."

"I guess they're right to be cautious."

"What?" Ranger said, bristling at my comment. "Why do you say that?"

I flinched. "Sorry! I didn't mean to imply... Look, I only meant that, at this point, I guess the killer could be anybody."

Ranger let out a sigh. "You're right. I don't mean to get defensive. It's just that Snyder and the others ... they think they know better than I do. To them, I'm just a dumb forest ranger. Well, I know this town and these woods better than any of them. They should be at least consulting me."

I touched him on the arm. "I totally agree."

Ranger studied me for a moment. His narrow eyes softened. "I've got to admit something."

My heart pinged. "What?"

"Honestly, at first I didn't hold much faith in what your partner was talking about."

"Oh. That's normal."

Ranger shook his head. "It sounds crazy. Some Lazarus creature resurrected from the past? But the more I think about it, the more logical it sounds—from a science perspective, anyway."

I put a hand on Ranger's shoulder. "Believe me, I understand how hard it can be to get on board with Grayson's logic sometimes. But since I started working with him, I've had more than one firm belief go as wobbly as Jell-O in a microwave."

"Like *what*?"

"Like Jell-O in a microwave," I repeated over the din of cicadas.

"No," Ranger said. "I meant what *beliefs*."

"Oh. Well ... I'm not sure I should say. As Grayson's intern, I have to maintain strict confidentiality about our work."

I wasn't sure why I'd told Ranger that. It wasn't as if I held some deep, dark secrets about anything. But for some reason, I wanted to impress the overgrown Boy Scout. I guess I wanted him to think of me as an intriguing, mysterious detective—instead of a failed mall cop/mechanic with nothing better to do with her life.

"*You* don't trust *me* either," Ranger said. "I get it."

"What do you get?" Grayson asked, mere inches from my back. Like a ninja warrior, he'd snuck up beside us.

Grayson's green eyes darted from Ranger to me, then back again, flashing in a way I'd never noticed before. Exactly what was going on with my odd partner, I couldn't put my finger on.

Chapter Fifty

It was late afternoon and Grayson had gone full commando. And I didn't mean he'd lost his boxer shorts.

"Lamar," he barked, "Go gather your cicada recordings then report back here, *stat*."

Lamar straightened his shoulders, causing his beard to shrink upward from his navel to his nipples. "Yes, sir!"

Grayson turned to my cousin. "Earl. I'm putting you in charge of constructing the decoy. You have the schematics?"

Earl saluted with the scroll of papers rolled up in his right hand. "No, sir, Mr. G. But I got the drawin' we did right here!"

"Very well," Grayson said. "Move out, men!"

Lamar and Earl scrambled for their trucks. Grayson turned on his heels and marched over to Ranger and me.

"You know the terrain around here, Ranger. Is there a place ... a natural ravine or something ... we could use to funnel the creature into our waiting trap?"

Ranger chewed his lip. "Hmm. Let me think a minute."

While Ranger mulled over the question, Grayson's full attention fell on me. He stared into my eyes. That odd flashing pulsed across his corneas again.

Is this Grayson in combat mode or is something else going on with him?

Earl's words echoed in my throbbing head. His description of the nubbin thing in the jar looking like a scorpion tail made my gut drop.

Holy crap! Is Grayson part insect? *Is that weird look in his eyes some kind of instinctual mating frenzy? Like that Vulcan 'pon farr' thing that drove Spock crazy in* Star Trek?

"I got it," Ranger said.

Grayson broke his scorpion mind-meld eye contact with me. "Let's hear it," he said.

"There's an area not far from here where two bluffs come together. The pioneers used to use it as a natural cattle corral."

"Sounds perfect," Grayson said. "Show me."

"I want to come along," I said.

Grayson shook his head. "No. I need you here."

I frowned. "What for?"

Grayson glanced around. "Tidy up the RV. We may have company."

"What?" I hissed.

But it was too late. Grayson already had Ranger by the arm, hustling him toward his Ford F-150.

I KICKED A PINECONE fifty yards. "Leave me behind to clean up this damned RV like your personal maid? I'll show you," I grumbled to myself, then stomped up the side stairs and into the RV.

Anger had upped the volume in my pounding head. I needed an aspirin. Or something stronger...

A hasty search of the bathroom medicine cabinet yielded nothing but a dried-up throat lozenge and a little baggie of tree bark. I read the label on the bag.

Hello! My Name is:

Willow. Chew for Pain.

YEAH. THAT AIN'T HAPPENING.

I tossed the bag of bark into the bathroom garbage bin. As it hit the bottom of the can, a thought came to me.

What about the cabinet of concoctions Grayson had locked away?

If Grayson had *Alien Parasite Remover*, surely he had something in there to get rid of a blasted headache, too.

And, I'll admit, I was dying to get a look at that nubbin in a jar...

I scurried to the kitchen and scrounged around in a drawer until I found a tiny flat-head screwdriver—the kind my Grandma Selma used to use to fix her old Singer sewing machine. Two seconds later, I had the tiny blade shoved up into the small padlock securing the cabinet. To my surprise, it didn't take much to make the little lock release.

Yes!

As it clicked open, I yanked the lock off the handle and pulled open the cabinet door. It squeaked so loudly I jumped back in surprise.

Crap!

If Grayson was still in the same county, he surely had to have heard it. I needed to work fast. I stepped back up to the cabinet and quickly rummaged through the bottles inside.

Toad Stool Poison.

Toad Stool Antidote.

Toad Stool.

Seriously?

I stood on tiptoe for a better look.

What I saw made me gasp.

There it is! Way in the back like Earl said...

The tall, narrow jar looked like something designed to store dried spaghetti. I tipped the bottle in front of it to the side for a better look. I caught a glimpse of the label.

Hello! My Name Is:
Nub

"DANG IT!" I HISSED.

I leaned a little further on tiptoe. My fingers strained to reach the jar that was obstructing my view...

Suddenly, the RV's side door burst open.

"Aargh!" I squealed. Then I lost my balance, fell backward, and knocked my head against the paneled wall.

"Aha!" Earl said, tromping into the room. "Caught you red handed!"

"Shut up!" I yelled, scrambling to my feet. "I just wanted to see Grayson's nubbin."

Earl laughed. "I thought you already had."

"Ha ha," I said sourly, rubbing my head. "And for your information, no. I haven't."

"Well, Cuz, I hate to inform you, but that ain't where a man typically keeps it."

My face puckered. "You suck, you know that?"

The sharp sound of footfalls on gravel made us both freeze in our tracks.

Earl thawed first, and ran over and peeked out the blinds.

"Woohoo!" he chortled. "The boss man's back, Bobbie. And you're about to get in trouble!"

Chapter Fifty-One

"So, what's for dinner?" Grayson asked as he came through the side door of the RV. "I'm starving."

I scurried away from the freshly relocked hall cabinet, struggling to disguise my guilty expression with one of righteous indignation.

"Excuse me?" I said. "Are you looking at *me*?"

Grayson's green eyes locked onto mine. "Yes. And frankly, I don't like what I see."

Earl blurted, "She didn't mean no harm by it."

"What's that supposed to mean?" Grayson and I both said to each other.

"You first," I said.

"I meant you don't look well," Grayson said. "Are you ill?"

I sagged with relief. Grayson hadn't caught me rummaging in his secret cabinet. "Uh ... I have a headache."

"Your turn," Grayson said. "What did Earl mean when he said you didn't mean any harm by it?"

I shot Earl a *can it* glare, then glanced up at Grayson. "I ... I accidentally used your razor to shave my legs."

"I see." Grayson eyed me skeptically. "Well, like Earl said, no harm done."

"So what we gonna do about some eats?" Earl asked. "I'm starvin'."

"Good idea," I said, a tad too enthusiastically.

"It's late," Grayson said. "We've got a big day ahead of us tomorrow. Why don't we order some sandwiches from Subway and call it a day."

DINNER WAS OVER, AND so was the day. I was in Grayson's bed. Earl was already sawing logs on my sofa-bed down the hall, barely fifteen feet away.

"So, Drex, what did you *really* do?" Grayson asked, slipping into bed beside me.

"What do you mean, what did I really do?"

Under the covers, Grayson's hand gripped my bare kneecap, then rubbed my skin. Electricity shot through me so strong it made eyes bulge.

"Hmm," he said. "Just as I suspected. You obviously didn't use my razor to shave your legs."

I jerked my leg away. "What do you care what I did? I'm nothing but your housekeeper and cook, right?"

"I thought you liked cooking. And after the Night of the Living Beefaroni, you told me never to cook again, remember?"

"Ha ha," I hissed, and pulled the covers up to my neck.

I felt the mattress beside me dip down. In the dim light, I saw Grayson raise himself onto one elbow.

"Seriously," he said into the dimness. "Why do you think I only see you as a housekeeper and cook?"

"Oh, I dunno," I quipped sourly. "Maybe because you told me to stay here and clean up the RV while you ran off and left me out of the investigation? Then you came back and asked what's for dinner? Or did I get that wrong?"

"You got it wrong, Drex. I needed to talk to Ranger. Alone."

"About what?"

"That's on a need to know basis." Grayson laid back down. "So what did you do that made Earl say that you didn't mean any harm by it?"

"Nothing that you need to know."

Grayson sighed. "Fine. I just don't like having secrets between us."

I sat up and laughed out loud. "Are you kidding me? Grayson, all we *have* between us is secrets."

"You mean like the fact that you won't tell me when your head is hurting?"

I frowned. "It's just a headache."

Grayson sat up beside me. "How long have you had it? Did it come on suddenly? Any shooting pain associated with it?"

I bit my lip. "All of the above. Why?"

"You know why."

"You think it's the twin thing in my brain acting up."

"Don't you?"

I winced. "I don't know."

Suddenly, the RV jostled violently. I tumbled sideways into Grayson.

"The creature's back," Grayson said, holding me in his arms.

"Not good."

"Actually, it *is*," he said, gently pushing me upright.

My nose crinkled. "How is that *good*?"

"It means Emmet's still alive. And still in the area."

"Uh ... still not seeing how that's *good*."

Grayson laid back down.

"You're not going after it?" I asked.

"No. I don't want to spook it. We've got the perfect plan to capture it. You'll see tomorrow."

I shook my head and lay down beside him. "How can you be so calm about all this giant killer insect business?"

"Because I have faith, Drex."

My eyes flew open. "Faith? *You*? I didn't think faith was in your scientific wheelhouse."

"Like you said, we both have a lot of secrets."

Grayson sat up on one elbow beside me again. In the greyish-blue light I watched as he reached over and put his hand across my forehead. Electric tingles went clear to my brain.

"No fever," he said.

"That's good."

"Depends on which diagnosis you're looking for. I want to do an EEG on you in the morning."

"Can't it wait? You've already got big plans for the day."

"Nothing bigger than this." His hand slipped from my forehead as he returned to lying on his back. "Let's get some rest and readdress this in the morning."

"Okay."

I fluffed my pillow and pulled the covers back up to my neck. Before I could even say "Goodnight," I heard Grayson breathing low and steady.

He was sleeping by my side.

I smiled, and suddenly realized my headache was gone.

Chapter Fifty-Two

I awoke to an ear-splitting, high-pitched noise. Either giant cicadas had us completely surrounded, or Earl had fallen victim to my latest prank—I'd hotwired my last pouch of Pop-Tarts with a nine-volt battery.

I bolted upright in bed. Grayson was gone. I scrambled into the main cabin in my pajama T-shirt and shorts. Earl was dancing around the kitchen, wringing his hand like he'd touched a hot stove.

I smiled inside. The day was off to a great start.

"What's up?" I asked casually.

"Nothing," Earl said, eyeing me suspiciously. "Why don't you sit down and let me pour you a cup of coffee, Cuz."

I grinned.

Uh ... nope. That ain't happening.

"Thanks, but I'll get it myself," I said.

I poured a cup of joe, then I put on an oven mitt and grabbed the pouch of Pop-Tarts from the shelf, discretely detaching the battery wire clipped to the foil pouch like a mini jumper cable.

"I think there's some Dan's dented yogurt cups in the fridge," I said, then tore open the pouch and popped the pastries in the toaster.

"Right," Earl said, confusion lining his face. "How'd you do that?"

I looked up at him innocently. "Do what?"

He glanced at the cabinet shelf and shook his head. "Well played, Cuz." Then he snickered, poured himself another cup of coffee, and yanked opened the fridge.

WHEN I GOT OUT OF THE shower, Grayson was waiting for me at the banquette. His left hand encircled a coffee cup. His right one was tapping on his laptop keys.

"How are you feeling?" he asked, looking up from the screen.

I smiled. "Fine, actually."

"No headache?"

I shook my head. "Nope. Not a peep."

"Good. I still want to do the EEG, but since you're feeling better, I think it can wait."

"Fine by me. What's on the monster-catching agenda today?"

Grayson scanned my expression. "First, you and I have some projects to complete. We're in charge of delivering the tactical chemical components for capturing Cicada *Palaeontinidae*."

"By that I presume you mean the scent lure," I said, slipping into the booth opposite him. "What about the decoy and the trap?"

"Lamar and Earl are already on it. It'll take a good half-day's work for them to set it all up. In the meantime, we need to gather supplies to prepare the olfactory attractant."

I smirked. "You mean we're gonna need more Pine-Solve-It."

Grayson's chin raised an inch. "Yes. Among other things."

"Like what?"

"We need to concoct an effective stunning solution."

"Wait a minute. *Stunning* solution?"

"Yes. To render the creature harmless once we capture it."

I sat up straighter. "Oh."

"That's right, Drex. It's time for your first lesson in the art of chemical warfare."

My eyes darted to the locked cabinet in the hallway, then back to Grayson. My heart pinged with anticipation. Today was the day I'd finally find out what was in that blasted jar...

"You sure you're okay?" Grayson asked.

"Absolutely," I said, focusing back on him. "Where do we start? Is there something in your cabinet we can use?"

Grayson sighed. "Unfortunately, no. Since we're dealing with a completely new species, the best place to start is by examining the tactics used by its natural predators."

"Makes sense. What are they?"

Grayson flipped his laptop screen around for me to see. A huge, black-and-yellow striped wasp waved its angry antennae at me.

"Whoa!" I said, blanching. "We don't have to catch any of *those, too*, do we?"

"No."

"What *is* that?"

"*Sphecius speciosus*," Grayson said. "Often referred to simply as the cicada killer or cicada hawk. It's a large, solitary digger wasp species in the family Crabron—"

"I get it. So, we need to reproduce its poison, right?"

"Venom."

"Excuse me," I said, stifling an eye roll. "*Venom*."

Grayson sniffed. "The cicada wasp immobilizes its prey by injecting it with venom from its stinger, similarly to how the emerald jewel wasp subdues a cockroach."

"Lovely."

Grayson flipped his screen back around. "There are five species of cicada killer wasps in the Americas. Judging by their natural territorial range, I believe the species we're after is the one I showed you. *Sphecius hogardii*."

"Such a lyrical name," I said. "Rolls right off the tongue, don't you think?"

"Now that you mention it, yes," Grayson said, his cheek dimpling. "I'm glad you're enjoying this task."

He tapped a couple of keys on his computer. "And we're in luck. The formula for its venom is right here online."

He turned the screen back around for me to see, reminding me why I flunked geometry.

"Looks complicated," I said.

"Not exceptionally. All we need now is to gather the proper ingredients. I've already got the willow bark."

Uh oh.

"So, should we get started?" Grayson asked.

"Absolutely. I just need to take a quick trip to the bathroom first."

Chapter Fifty-Three

I was in the Walmart toy department, aiming a lime-green, high-capacity super-soaker water gun at an unsuspecting redneck's ratty beehive hairdo.

I smiled.

Some days this job really does *have its perks...*

I pulled the trigger.

At that exact second, my cellphone rang, startling the crap out of me. For a moment, in some terrible twist of fate I thought I'd actually shot the woman.

Ms. Beehive must've thought the same. She turned around and returned fire with a single-finger salute.

My phone chimed again. I whirled on my heels, shoved the gun back on the shelf, and dug into my purse. Grayson was on the line.

"What?" I hissed.

"Everything okay?" he asked.

I looked around. The woman was gone. "Yeah. What's up?"

"See if they have grain alcohol in half-gallon bottles."

I snorted. "Why? You throwing an after-party?"

"What?"

"Never mind. Anything else?"

"Yes. Earl called. He needs more duct tape. Pink if they've got it."

"Right. I'm on it."

THE NEAREST WALMART to Bristol was thirty-three miles away in a quaint little Main Street town called Marianna. Situated just east of town center, the mega store had been built atop a hill completely flattened to accommodate it. Ironically, from its massive parking lot, customers could enjoy a view of what remained of their once-thriving local businesses.

I shook my head at the irony and crammed the last of my mega-store bags into the bed of Bessie.

My last chore before heading back to Torreya State Park was to bring home dinner for the troops. But as I drove around the town in search of something unique, I thought about Earl and his allergy, and began to worry about what lurked in the grease of the local eateries. To play it safe, I ended up driving back to camp with bags of Burger King.

As I rode along the rural backroads toward Bristol, I glanced in the rearview mirror at Bessie's flapping payload. Her bed was stacked high with cases of Pine-Solve-It and piles of assorted cheap, non-American-made provisions.

I waxed nostalgic for a moment, wondering if we humans were barreling down a path to extinction just as surely as that bug Emmet and those poor Torreya trees. I supposed only time would tell. And from the clock on Bessie's dashboard, I was way past due.

BY THE TIME I GOT BACK to the campground, the sun was hanging midway in the crisp, afternoon sky. The men had already loaded up their pickups—their mysterious contents covered with blue plastic tarps.

"Sorry I'm late," I said as they snatched the Burger King bags from my hands like hungry raccoons.

"I sure hope this ain't our last meal," Lamar said, hefting up a bag.

I blanched. "Are you worried about dying tonight?"

Lamar stared at me with his beady eyes. "Well, I am *now*."

I winced. "Sorry."

"Geez," the scrawny old guy muttered, holding up a Whopper. "I only meant I usually eat me two of these thangs. I'm liable to call that big ol' bug right to me when my empty stomach starts a rumblin'."

"It's statistically improbable the two sounds share a common frequency," Grayson said.

"Huh?" Lamar grunted, and glanced at me.

"It's highly unlikely," I translated.

"Don't let them fancy words a theirs fool ya," Earl said. "I done learned that in this here universe, anything can happen."

I WAS IN THE BACK BED of Bessie, riding a spare tire like a bucking bronco. Earl was at the wheel, Grayson riding shotgun.

As sharp-shooter of the bunch, I'd been designated to shoot Pine-Solve-It out of a toy Uzi onto the road behind us. Lamar was seated beside me, his scrawny butt wedged in the center of another tire. The old man belched, then cranked the volume on the cicada love calls belting out of a ghetto blaster nearly as big as he was.

"I can see why the pioneers liked this place," I yelled to Lamar as we bumped and jogged down a narrow dirt road that bisected the deep ravine. On either side of the road, orange and white clay bluffs rose nearly thirty feet above us, boxing us in.

"Yep," Lamar said, his arms and legs poking out of the tire like someone adrift on an inner-tube. "Them two bluffs meet up ahead in about half a mile. It's a natural corral."

I squeezed the trigger on the toy gun, sending a farty jet of greenish foam onto the ground behind us. "Hand me another bottle of

Pine-Solve-It. I'm out," I hollered over the din of Bessie's engine and the recorded cicada calls.

. Lamar leaned over and fished a plastic bottle out of the cardboard case of twenty-four I'd bought at Walmart.

"Go easy on that stuff," he said, passing the bottle to me like it was a beer. "We're already down to half a case."

"No worries," I yelled. "There's more back at the RV. That stuff was on sale. It's cheaper than bottled water."

Lamar scratched his mangy, bearded cheek. "Yeah. They can't give that crap away no more." He picked up the empty bottle and laughed. "New and improved my ass," he said, then shoved the empty into an open slot in the carton.

Before I could finish reloading the Uzi water gun, Earl suddenly stopped the truck. The back window on Bessie's cab slid open. Grayson's face popped into view. We played a quick game of charades with him until we figured out he was signaling for Lamar to turn down the volume on his cicada boom box chorus.

"We're turning around here," Grayson yelled as the shrill calls abated. He glanced at me. "Be sure and douse this whole area well."

"Got it," I said.

While Earl maneuvered his monster truck through a six-point turnaround on the narrow road, I followed Commander Grayson's orders and super-soaked the piss out of every poor weed that had managed to eke a living out of the hard, bare clay.

While I sprayed, I noticed the ravine walls were striped with undulating waves of white limestone and hard, orange clay. As the truck turned around, I saw how the ravine came to a narrow, pointed dead-end, like a giant crack in the earth.

In sharp contrast to the desolate ravine, the bluffs above us were thick with forest. Pines, scrub oaks, and a mix of wild plums and dogwoods topped them like a living carpet. It was a beautiful, unspoiled area that looked as alien in Florida as a white buffalo.

"What now?" I asked, tapping my Uzi on the back window as Earl finished turning Bessie around.

"We head back to the mouth of the ravine," Grayson said, reappearing in the open center pane. "We'll wait there and deploy the decoy when the time is right."

Grayson slid the window closed. I turned to Lamar, who was already reaching to crank up the volume on his ghetto blaster. "How's the decoy gonna work?"

He grinned. "You'll see."

He turned the cicada calls up to ten million decibels, then reached over and patted the blue tarp in the corner of Bessie's bed. The kitchen-table sized lump hidden under it was being held down by more bungee cords than I could count. Whatever was under there wasn't going anywhere.

"This baby'll follow the natural slope down into the ravine," Lamar said, giving the tarp one last pat. "Once the bug takes the bait, we'll follow it in, where it'll be trapped."

My upper lip hooked skyward. "Then what?"

Lamar opened his mouth, but whatever he said was obliterated by a shrill, whining noise.

"Geez! Turn that crap down!" I yelled.

Lamar's wide-open eyes locked on mine. "That ain't me!"

Suddenly, the crash of breaking branches echoed from atop the ravine. Both of our heads jerked upward for a look.

Something big was rampaging through the woods overhead.

And it was coming our way—fast!

Chapter Fifty-Four

S hit! Emmet is real!

Lamar ducked under the decoy tarp in Bessie's back bed.

I scrambled off the tire and pounded frantically on the back window of the cab. "It's coming, Earl! Gun it!"

Earl must've heard me wrong. He hit the brakes instead.

The back window slid open. Grayson's face appeared in the frame. "Is everything all right?"

"No!" I yelled. "It's coming!"

"What is?"

"The—"

I glanced up.

Out of the corner of my eye, I caught a glimpse of something barreling toward us from the top of the ravine.

As it raced forward, its beige body glimmered faintly in the fading sunset.

It was huge, just like Grayson said it would be.

"Look out!" I yelled.

But it was too late.

Like a lion ambushing its prey, the creature shot out of the forest and leapt off the edge of the bluff over our heads.

"Aaarg!" I screamed, and got off a final shot of Pine-Solve-It.

The thing landed on all fours on the road a few feet from Bessie's tailgate.

I realized my effort to kill the monster was futile.

I hadn't blasted a giant cicada.

I'd nailed a kamikaze daredevil riding a beige dune buggy.

I stared, mouth agape, as the driver jammed the ATV into park and pulled off his head gear.

I gasped. "What are *you* doing here?"

Officer Snyder examined the green goop dripping from his helmet, then stared up at me.

"Funny," he said. "I was about to ask you the same thing."

Chapter Fifty-Five

"There's still no word on Rusty and Bondo?" I asked Officer Snyder, handing him his helmet after wiping off the Pine-Solve-It goop.

"No," he said, resting the helmet on the seat of the dune buggy. "We've been patrolling these woods for days but haven't found anything new."

"So nothing's turned up since the head mangled by boars?" Grayson asked.

Snyder's eyes narrowed. "How'd you know about that?"

"Ranger told us," Earl said.

Snyder shook his head. "And he wonders why we leave him out of the loop. Look, we'll be searching this quadrant until the end of the day tomorrow. Then we're heading over to Torreya State Park. Are you all still camping over there?"

"Yes," Grayson said.

"You packing?" he asked.

"To leave?" I asked.

Snyder shook his head. "No. *Guns.*"

"Oh. Uh ... yes," I answered.

He smirked at me. "I mean *besides* your toy machine gun."

"We have weapons," Grayson said.

Snyder turned to my partner. "You all legal to carry?"

"Yes, sir," Earl said.

"Good. I advise you keep them loaded. And stay sharp."

Snyder climbed back onto his ATV. "And if I were you, I'd consider heading over to Tate's Hell while there's still a few campsites left. We're gonna be clearing everybody out of Torreya day after to-morrow."

"Thanks for the heads up," Grayson said.

Snyder nodded, then winked at me. "And good luck with your bug hunting, darlin'. Though I'd say that Uzi is a bit of an overkill."

Chapter Fifty-Six

"Well, last evening's hunt for Cicada *Palaeontinidae* was a fiasco," Grayson said, helping himself to a cup of coffee from the tiny kitchen stove. "And now we need to clear out of here by tomorrow morning."

"What are you complaining about?" I said sourly. "I'm the one who took one for the team last night. By the way, thanks for telling Snyder you were helping me fulfill my fantasy of being Rambo the Roach Terminator." I shook my head. "The guy must think I'm a complete idiot."

Grayson's cheek dimpled. "Well, you *were* the one who shot him with Pine-Solve-It."

Earl snickered. "He's got a point there, Cuz." My cousin pulled on a pair of oven mitts and reached for a box of Pop-Tarts I'd bought at Walmart yesterday. "'Scuze me, Mr. G."

Grayson shot Earl an odd look, then walked over and slid into the banquette opposite me. "What's up with the oven mitts?" he whispered.

I smirked. "Tin-foil allergy."

A sharp knock sounded on the side door, then it opened before anyone said a word. Ranger poked his head inside. "Everybody decent?"

"That's highly debatable," I said, then bit into my blueberry Pop-Tart.

"Where was you last night, Ranger?" Earl asked, fumbling around like a malfunctioning robot trying to open the Pop-Tart pouch with oven mitts on his hands.

"Official park business," Ranger said, giving Earl a raised eyebrow. He turned to Grayson and me. "The investigation's moving east. We'll be closing the park tomorrow morning."

"We heard," Grayson said.

Ranger scowled. "How?"

"We ran into Officer Snyder last night," Grayson said. "He cut our mission short. But we still have time to try our plan again tonight."

"But not back at the ravine," I said to Grayson. "You heard Snyder. The place is off limits now. They're expanding their search for bodies there today."

"Just as well," Ranger said. "I drove over and checked the ravine road this morning. Didn't see a single sign of activity. Not one lousy animal track out there."

Grayson's lips pursed. "The searchers must've spooked the creature."

"Maybe," I said. "But you know, I don't think the Pine-Solve-It that I sprayed yesterday did anything. Lamar told me it didn't smell right."

"Smell right?" Grayson asked.

"Yeah. It's different somehow. Lamar said the new and improved formula actually bombed with customers. Like when Coca-Cola changed its formula back in 1985."

"Here's an idea," Ranger said, helping himself to a cup of coffee. "Maybe it didn't work because there is no such thing as a giant bug."

"Well, I suppose there's always that remote possibility," I said, smirking at Grayson.

Ranger scooted into the booth beside me. "Besides shutting down the ravine, what else did Snyder have to say?"

"He said they're closing in on some suspects," Grayson said.

Ranger nodded. "It's about time."

"So how we gonna catch that critter now that we can't go back to the ravine?" Earl asked, holding a Pop-Tart between two oven mitts like seal flippers.

Ranger shot Earl a squinty eye, then chewed his bottom lip. "You know, I think I just might have an idea."

Chapter Fifty-Seven

"You ready to go?" Grayson called out, his head stuck sideways in the frame of the RV's side door.

"Just a minute!" I groused. "Geez! I've got to go to the ladies' room."

"Hurry it up. We'll be late."

"I think Emmet can wait another minute," I muttered to myself.

I finished my business and locked up the RV. As I walked toward Earl's monster truck to join him and Grayson, Ranger called to me from his Ford F-150.

"Come ride with me," he said. "It'll be fun."

I walked over to his window. "Thanks, but I've got a couple of things I need to discuss with Grayson."

The handsome Boy Scout shot me a GQ smile. "Nothing that can't wait, I'm sure. And you're a lot better company than Lamar."

Huh. Maybe Ranger's not as nerdy as I thought.

"Okay. What the heck." I waved Earl and Grayson off, then opened the passenger door on Ranger's Ford. "So what special place did you have in mind for trapping Grayson's imaginary monster now?" I asked as I climbed in.

Ranger laughed and shifted into drive. "An old warehouse. It's abandoned now. Used to belong to Bong Chemical."

"An abandoned warehouse. Sounds pretty *Scooby Do*."

Ranger cocked his head. "Yeah, it does, now that you mention it. But it may be just the place to trap these monstrous insects for good."

My brow furrowed. "Insects, *plural*?"

Ranger shrugged. "You said it yourself. There could be more than one."

"Yeah. I guess so."

We pulled out of the campgrounds at Torreya State Park and headed south down County Road 12 in the direction of Sumatra. A few miles down the forest-lined highway, we turned off onto an old asphalt road crumbling with disrepair.

I glanced in the rearview mirror. Earl was right behind us in Bessie, Grayson riding shotgun.

"How long has it been since they last used this place?" I asked as we jostled slowly along the potholed road.

"Going on fifteen years, I guess. There it is," Ranger said, nodding at an abandoned metal building straight ahead.

He shifted into park. "Let's go have a look inside. I want to see if you think it's strong enough to hold this monster bug thing."

"How would I know?" I asked. "I'm no structural engineer." I glanced back and saw Earl's monster truck pull into the clearing behind us. "Better defer that decision to Grayson."

"Won't hurt to have a peek while we wait," Ranger said as we climbed out of the Ford. I followed him along a small, worn trail in the grass that led up to the warehouse. To me, the place looked more like an airplane hangar than a storage facility.

"What did Bong use this building for?" I asked.

"Growing, mostly." Ranger yanked the handle on the massive, garage-style door. It creaked loudly, then rolled up on rusty tracks toward the ceiling about twenty feet over our heads.

"Growing?" I asked, spotting a half-dozen ragged rows of black nursery pots.

"Yes."

Ranger stepped inside the warehouse and tapped one of the five-gallon pots with his boot. It rolled over and dumped its contents—several gallons of dried-up soil and the withered stem of dead plant.

I glanced around at the scattered rows of abandoned pots. In the center of each one a stick poked up like a deformed Popsicle stick. Then I realized that each stick was actually the dried-up skeleton of a small, dead, pine tree.

An odd feeling washed over me.

I turned and looked Ranger in the eye. "Either Bong was the host of a Charlie Brown Christmas Tree Special, or something's rotten in Denmark."

"The latter, I'm afraid," Ranger said. "I knew you'd figured it out, Miss Smarty Pants."

My gut flopped. "Figured what out?"

"Don't play dumb with me," Ranger hissed. "You know what. The new Pine-Solve-It formula is shit without the sap of the Torreya tree."

I shrugged. "So?"

Ranger's eyes narrowed. "Bong's been trying to synthesize the formula for years, but these bastard excuses for trees just won't give up the secret to their unique cedar scent."

He reared back and kicked one of the pots savagely. It skittered halfway across the warehouse.

My jaw dropped. I swallowed hard and locked eyes with Ranger. "You're helping Bong harvest the rest of them, aren't you?"

Ranger scowled. "We tried to culture the damned things, but the stinking cedar wouldn't grow no matter what conditions we tried. The stupid trees left us no choice."

I reached for my purse.

"I wouldn't do that if I were you," Ranger said. I glanced up and froze. Ranger, the overgrown Boy Scout, had gone rogue.

He was pointing a Ruger at me.

Suddenly, Earl and Grayson appeared in the warehouse door.

"Watch out!" I cried.

But my warning had come way too late. As they stepped inside, I saw Earl and Grayson weren't alone. Rusty was at Grayson's side, a gun pointed in my partner's ribcage. Whitey had a shotgun pointed at Earl's side.

"Walk 'em on in, boys," Ranger said.

Slowly, Earl and Grayson inched forward, egged on by pokes from the gun barrels.

I gasped. "What the hell is going on? What have we got to do with any of this?"

"Like everything in life, it's a matter of natural balance," Ranger said. "And you and your pals here just crossed the line from assets to liabilities."

Chapter Fifty-Eight

R anger pointed his Ruger at my ribcage and laughed. "You all served as a good distraction for the folks around here, chasing your imaginary bug monsters around," he said. "Great work keeping the likes of Lamar and the other superstitious kooks around here focused on that stupid Hacksaw Hattie legend."

I scowled at Ranger. "What are you going to do with us?"

"Same as everyone else who turns into a liability," Whitey said.

Rusty laughed, his missing molar now adding a sinister flair to his freckled face. "You're about to meet your maker, Miss. Just like Dale and Darryl."

"That's right," Ranger said. "Pity about those two. They were doing a good job tailing the census agent the U.S. Forest Service sent here last fall to inventory the remaining Torreya trees. He was like a prize birddog, finding and tagging them for us. Hell, most people couldn't tell a Torreya from Tarzan."

"That's how you found the trees," I said.

"Exactly," Ranger said. "Why do the hard work when the government does it for you? And once that agent ID'd the Torreyas, Dale and Darryl would take off the yellow tags and put them on some nearby sickly looking little pine sapling. Then they'd harvest the puny little Torreya trees with their trusty hacksaws."

"But they're endangered!" I said.

"So what?" Ranger bellowed, his face growing red. "It's not like anybody cares about the species. The Torreya is doomed. What the storms and habitat destruction haven't gotten yet, the fungus blights will. What's the harm in capitalizing on the miserable little tree before it becomes extinct?"

"Like Dale and Darryl, you mean?" Grayson asked.

Ranger flinched. "That was a mistake."

"What happened to them?" I asked.

"Roy Stubbs, that's what," Rusty said.

Ranger sighed. "He's Bong's unofficial 'headhunter,' if you know what I mean. They sent him out to dispose of the Forest Service guy, who was getting wise to our plan. Best we can tell, Roy apparently enjoyed the job so much he did in Dale and Darryl, too—for sport. With their own hacksaws, I might add."

I winced. "What about Lamar? Is he in on this, too?"

Ranger laughed. "In a way, I suppose. I couldn't hope for a more convenient stooge to go spreading gossip about the legend of Hacksaw Hattie. He was an even better distraction than you three were."

"What about Virgil Stubbs, the truck driver," I said. "Surely Roy didn't do in his own cousin!"

"Nope. That one we took care of ourselves," Ranger said.

"But why?" I asked.

Ranger spat at one of the dried-up saplings. "Because we'd worked our asses off for nothing! That's why!"

He kicked another dead tree. The pot went flying. "We'd spent months harvesting and extracting the last batch of Torreya sap we could squeeze out of the remaining trees. Then that idiot Virgil goes and wrecks the rig as he's hauling it to Bong!"

"I thought it was wash-water," Grayson said.

"So did everybody else," Ranger said.

"Virgil spilled our future on the ground," Whitey said. "So we took his future in return."

"I don't understand," I said. "How was that Torreya sap going to be your future?"

"It was worth its weight in gold to Bong," Ranger said. "They were going to lock the last samples away until their lab techs could figure out how to synthesize it. Like I said, the new and improved formula is crap, and everybody knows it. They're losing millions in sales every month."

"But what about Roy Stubbs?" I asked. "He was found in the pit toilet—"

"Roy Stubbs?" Ranger laughed. "What do I care about that crazy old convict. Maybe he got his just desserts and the Ty-D-Bol guy did him in."

"But—" I stuttered.

"Enough of your questions," Ranger barked. He turned to his partners in crime. "You fellows have your hacksaws ready?"

"Yep," Whitey said.

"Sure do," Rusty said.

Ranger smiled. "Good. Then let's get these three liabilities over to the burial grounds, pronto."

Chapter Fifty-Nine

To say things weren't looking good would've been a gross understatement.

Earl was tied up and lying in the bed of his monster truck, right next to whatever he and Lamar had concocted and stored underneath that blue plastic tarp. Rusty was at Bessie's helm. Whitey rode shotgun, keeping an eye on Grayson, who was tied up and wedged between them on the front bench seat.

I'd been relegated to riding along with Ranger in his Ford, my hands cuffed to the passenger door handle. From that angle, I could see Grayson's face behind us in the rearview mirror. His expression was unreadable.

"Too bad you and my sister couldn't be friends," Ranger said. "I think Pat really liked you."

"I don't get it," I said, craning my neck to face him. "What's in this for *you*, Ranger? Money?"

Ranger shook his head. "Something more important. *Respect.*"

"Respect?"

Ranger glanced down at the forest ranger badge pinned to his breast pocket and flicked it with his finger.

"This lousy piece of tin might as well be fake," he said. "The local yahoos around here don't give me the time of day. To them, I'm nothing but an ape in a uniform, running around chasing butterflies. They don't think I've got what it takes to do their job. But they'll be kissing my ass when I'm mayor, by God."

I nearly choked. "*Mayor?*"

"That's right. *Mayor*. In a couple of months I'll be running for the position. And with the backing of Gerold Bong, I'll most likely be running unopposed."

"Bong of Bong Chemical, I assume."

"CEO. He already owns Liberty County. Soon I'll get to run it for him. And no more tromping around in the mud. I'll be sitting pretty in a cushy office in that nice new town hall he just built and paid for."

I shook my head. "What did your sister Pat get out of the deal?"

Ranger's reaction made me think my question had surprised him.

"Well, nothing," he said. "Unless you count the new awning on the Appaloosa Diner. That was a surprise gift from Mr. Bong. He had his construction crew fashion it out of the leftover metal roofing from the town hall building."

"You don't say," I said.

"See? Gerold Bong's not such a bad guy."

I frowned. "What does Bong get out of making *you* mayor?"

Ranger grinned. "When I'm in charge, I'll be the naturalist overseeing the management of the rest of the Torreya trees."

I blew out a breath. "I guess the world can kiss the poor Torreya goodbye."

Ranger glanced over at me. "Too bad you won't be able to do the same with your boyfriend."

Seriously?

"Grayson's *not* my boyfriend. He's my partner."

"You sure about that?"

"Yes."

"Hmm," Ranger said, taking delight in teasing me. "What was it that he said to me the other day? Oh, yeah. Grayson told me to back off, that you don't need your heart broken again. Now if you ask me, that doesn't exactly sound like someone who doesn't give a crap about you."

My heart sunk. I glared at Ranger. "Why are you telling me this?"

He shrugged, his blue eyes twinkling. "I don't know. Maybe on the hope that it might add to your pain when you watch him die."

Chapter Sixty

R anger shifted the Ford into park. Lost in thought, I glanced out the passenger window and realized I recognized the place.

Ironically, we were back at the spot where this whole fiasco had begun. We were deep in the woods behind the interstate, where Ranger and the Liberty Bug Hunter crew had buried the piles of cicadas that had died during the tanker-truck spill.

A shiny new backhoe stood at the ready beside a freshly dug hole. I recognized the machine, too. It belonged to Rusty. It had been the only thing of any value I'd spotted at the dumpsite he called home base.

The thought of being buried alive six-feet deep in bugs made me shiver. I hoped they killed me first.

"Let's go," Ranger said, un-cuffing me from the Ford's door handle. "Try anything and your boyfriend gets it first." He got out and walked around to the passenger door, opened it, and hustled me out with encouragement from his Ruger.

Behind us, Whitey and Rusty were busy herding Grayson and Earl out of Bessie. They marched them up to where we stood, about six feet away from the edge of the freshly dug hole. My stomach flopped as I saw a hacksaw in Whitey's free hand.

"We doing the heads now or what?" he asked Ranger, his eyes gleaming.

Why is it always the psychologists who turn out to be the nut jobs?

I shook my head in dismay. A rancid, rotten odor lingered around the place, making me want to hurl.

"You've been burying the bodies with the cicadas," Grayson said.

"Wow," Ranger deadpanned. "Aren't you the clever detective."

"You need to bury them deeper to avoid odorous vapors," Grayson said.

"I know that," Ranger hissed, suddenly angry. "Something keeps digging up the corpses." He nodded toward several mounds of orange clay strewn about the burial site. "Rusty, looks like whatever it is has been at it again. And it's not buzzards or bears."

While the two men spoke, Grayson's eyes met mine. For the first time, I detected something in them that made my blood turn cold. My partner's usually calm, determined expression was tinged with an unreadable wildness. Was he actually *afraid*?

If he wasn't, he was even crazier than I thought.

"You!" Ranger said, sticking his chin up at Grayson. "I was hoping your crazy scheme to catch that ridiculous super-bug would uncover what's been digging up body parts. But it looks like that plan has just run out of time."

Ranger motioned to Rusty. "March them up to the hole. We'll do them first, then her."

"Wait," Grayson said. "I can do it."

Ranger eyed him sideways. "*You* want to kill her?"

Grayson appeared confused. "No. I can synthesize the formula—for the original Pine-Solve-It."

Ranger laughed sourly. "Right. You can do what the Bong scientists can't." He aimed his Ruger at the hole. "Go on. Let's get this over with."

Whitey shoved Earl closer to the edge. His mouth had been duct taped. I shot my cousin a tearful goodbye glance.

"Look, I'm a world-renowned scientist," Grayson said as Rusty jerked him by the arm. "I can prove it. Come on, Ranger. What have you got to lose?"

"Hold up," Ranger said. "Prove it, then."

Grayson grimaced. "I have credentials back at my RV. Let Drex and Earl go and I'll show you."

Ranger laughed. "You think I'm a fool, just like the rest, don't you? Well, let me assure you, I'm not."

"Of course you're not," Grayson said. "Give me two hours. That's all I ask. If I can synthesize the formula, it could change your life and theirs."

Ranger cocked his head and smiled sadistically "What exactly is it you think you can accomplish in two hours?"

"Everything," Grayson said. "Give me access to a tablespoon of Torreya sap and my lab back at my RV. That's all I need to replicate the formula there. I do things like this all the time."

"Yeah, sure you do," Ranger said.

"I can prove it," Grayson said. "I recreated the venom of the cicada-killer wasp to subdue the Cicada *Palaeontinidae* after we caught it. I've got a syringe full of it in the truck."

Ranger's nose crinkled. "You're shitting me."

"No," Grayson said. "I shit you not."

"Okay, I'll call your bluff," Ranger said. "Rusty, take him over to the truck. Keep your gun on him." He stuck his Ruger in my ribcage. "Any funny stuff and Miss Marple here gets it."

Miss Marple? I'm not that old!

I felt the poke of the Ruger in my side while Rusty hustled Grayson over to Earl's truck and back again. When they returned, Rusty was carrying Grayson's backpack.

"Open it," Ranger said.

Rusty unzipped the bag.

"Careful," Grayson said. "You don't want to get stuck with what's inside."

"Ack!" Rusty said, and dropped the pack like a hot rock. "*You* do it," Rusty said to Grayson.

"Fine. But I'll need my hands free."

Ranger nodded. Rusty untied Grayson's wrists. He knelt on the ground, opened the backpack, and pulled out a syringe as big as a turkey baster.

"Whoa," Ranger said.

"There's enough here to stop a charging elephant," Grayson said.

Ranger shoved me toward Grayson. "Inject her with it."

My eyes met Grayson's. His green eyes remained cool and cat-like as he shoved me back toward Ranger.

"I would," Grayson said, "but she could just fake a reaction to fool you."

Ranger straightened his stance a bit. "Okay. Then give Whitey a dose."

"Gladly." Grayson stabbed the old man's arm and mashed the plunger.

Whitey's eyes nearly popped out of his head. The shock of white hair on his head stood straight up. He smiled weakly, then crumpled and fell, face first, onto the ground. A second later, he was snoring like a broken band saw.

"Impressive," Ranger said. "But still, no deal."

"You're in complete control here," Grayson said. "Think about what's at stake. If I can't replicate the formula, you've lost nothing but a couple of hours. But if my formula *works,* you'll be holding all the cards with Bong Chemical. You'll be *king of Liberty County.* You can write your own ticket."

Ranger's chin rose an inch. A fractured smile curled his lips. "Okay. You've got your two hours."

"And they walk out of here unharmed," Grayson said, extending a hand to shake. "Deal?"

"Hmm," Ranger grunted, keeping his hand at his side. "Let's take this thing one step at a time."

Chapter Sixty-One

Grayson had been gone for an hour and forty-five minutes, and I no longer had any fingernails.

Pretty soon, if Whitey had his way, heads would begin to roll. The portly psychologist had recovered somewhat from his cicada killer injection and was now madder than a wet hornet. He'd spent the last half hour counting the minutes until he could exact his revenge.

"Fifteen minutes and their time is up," he said to Ranger, who was perched in his pickup listening to the police scanner. He'd warned us that if he heard any chatter about Grayson or anything else suspicious, our gig would be up and our heads would come off.

Whitey paced around the hole intended as our grave, then circled back to us like a hungry buzzard. Earl and I were sitting about thirty feet away, propped back-to-back under the thin shade of a pine tree. Our hands were tied together with a tangled knot of nylon rope as big as a football.

"Fourteen minutes," Whitey said, flashing his hacksaw and licking his lips. As he wandered back toward Ranger's truck, I whispered to my cousin.

"I'm sorry about getting you into this."

"Mmm mmmy mmo," Earl answered, still muzzled with duct tape.

"Come on," Whitey whined to Ranger through the Ford's passenger window. "Lemme do one of 'em. You owe me that."

"Owe you?" Ranger said. "I don't owe you. Calm down." He glanced at his watch, then climbed out of the truck and walked over to us.

"You and your boyfriend are running out of time," he said.

I stuck my chin up proudly. "He'll be here."

"Nine minutes," Whitey announced with a gleam in his eye. "Just time enough for a pee break."

Ranger returned to the truck. Whitey sauntered off to a stand of scrub oaks.

"I knew he was your boyfriend," Earl said.

"You got the duct tape off!" I said.

"Yep. Don't let on, though. And don't you be sorry one bit. Chasin' monsters with you and Mr. G.'s been the best time a my life. You're also one bona fide prankster, Bobbie. Respect."

"You, too, Earl," I sniffed. "Respect right back at you."

"Five minutes," Whitey said, returning with a small tree branch. He leaned it against the pine tree and sawed it in half, just to torture us.

As he finished, he grinned at us like a maniac, then looked up at the road and hissed. "Damn!"

My heart leapt. Bessie was pulling slowly up the road into the clearing! Before he even brought it to a stop, Grayson leapt out of the passenger side and ran straight at us, two quart-sized bottles in his hands.

"Hold it right there!" Ranger said, pointing his Ruger at him.

Grayson stopped about fifteen feet shy of us.

"I did it!" he said breathlessly, as Rusty caught up with him. "See for yourself."

"Gimme those!" Ranger grabbed a bottle and opened it, then took a big sniff.

"This is shit," he said. "Get them to the pit."

"No!" Grayson said. "What you've got there is Pine-Solve-It's new crappy formula. I brought it along for comparison. The stuff I synthesized is in *this* bottle."

Grayson held out the second bottle. Ranger snatched it from his hand and took a whiff.

"Well I'll be damned," he said, taking a second sniff. "Smells just like Torreya pine. And strong, too." He shook his head, astounded. "You actually did it."

"Yes," Grayson said. "And there's plenty more where that came from. Now, just let them go, and the formula's yours."

"Not so fast," Ranger said. "Lemme see the formula."

"I brought half of it," Grayson said, pulling a slip of paper from his pocket. "The other half is hidden where you'll never find it. Let them go. You get half now, and when they're safely away, I'll lead you to the other half."

Ranger thought the offer over. "You're pretty clever after all. I respect that. But what's to keep these two from going straight to the authorities?"

"*I* am," Grayson said. "I'll be your hostage." Grayson turned to us. "Earl. Drex. I want you to swear to Ranger on my life that you won't contact any law enforcement of any kind about this."

I gasped. "But—"

"Do it," Grayson barked.

I crumpled. "I swear I won't."

"Me either," Earl said.

Ranger pursed his lips and nodded. "You see this, boys?" he said to Rusty and Whitey. "This is what real loyalty looks like." He turned to Grayson. "Okay. You got yourself a deal. Untie them."

"Aww, man!" Whitey groused. Suddenly his eyes lit up. He took a lunging step toward us, his hacksaw raised.

Ranger stepped into his path. "Not you."

"I was just gonna cut 'em free," Whitey said.

"Sure you were," Ranger said. "Rusty, you do the honors."

As the ropes fell away, Earl and I stood up and rubbed our wrists. But I felt no relief. Now it was Grayson who was being held against his will.

My heart sank.

"What should we do?" I asked Grayson as they held him at gunpoint.

"Go. Get out of here. And say nothing to anyone. That's the deal."

"But—"

Grayson shook his head. "It's done, Drex. Go on, now. Hopefully I'll see you again soon. If not, well, it's been a real honor."

Earl saluted. "It sure has, Mr. G."

Chapter Sixty-Two

R anger and his goons had all the weapons.

There was nothing Earl and I could do but wait. As we marched toward Earl's truck with our hands raised in the air, I knew that one false move could cause Rusty and Whitey to shoot us, saw us to bits, and bury us before we had a chance to blink.

"So now what?" Earl asked as he and I tromped along the edge of the mass cicada grave toward his waiting monster truck.

"Nothing," I said. "Just hold our breath and hope Grayson plays his cards right."

We climbed into Bessie and Rusty and Whitey backed off enough to let us pass.

"Here we go," Earl said, turning the ignition. The massive Hemi engine cut in, rattling the entire chassis.

Suddenly, the glovebox fell open at my knees, startling me half to death.

I gasped.

A piece of paper had been duct-taped to the inside of the glove compartment. As the door fell downward, the paper unfolded like an accordion, revealing a note.

I recognized Grayson's handwriting.

"What's going on, Bobbie?" Earl asked.

"Keep your eyes on the road and just keep backing out," I said as I read the note.

They won't shoot me.
Need to stall.

Take your time turning Bessie around, then initiate Operation Sexy Cicada.

Like a ventriloquist, I read the note aloud to Earl.

"Hot dog!" Earl hollered. "The man's got a plan!"

"Hush," I said. "Try to act normal."

"Okay. I'll try."

I stared at my cousin. "What the hell is Operation Sexy Cicada?"

"Crap!" Earl said. "How we gonna do that without Lamar?"

"How should I know? I don't even know what Operation Sexy Cicada is!"

Suddenly, a scraggly head popped up in the back window above the truck bed. A pair of beady eyes peered through the open, center pane.

"Lamar!" I whispered, opening the window. "What are you doing back there?"

"No time to explain," he said. "Earl, I'm ready when you are. Operation Sexy Cicada is a go." Then he disappeared under the blue tarp.

"What can I do?" I asked.

"Smile and wave," Earl said. "Smile and wave."

Then he shifted Bessie into first and hollered, "Let's roll!"

Chapter Sixty-Three

I thought Earl was going to punch the gas and send Bessie barreling over the field to rescue Grayson.

But I was wrong.

Instead, Earl took his sweet, country time completing an encore performance of the agonizingly slow, six-point turnaround he'd done at the ravine last night. Only this time, instead of a barren ravine, we were on a narrow dirt road with at least three maniacs pointing guns at us.

Earl played it up, grinding gears and grunting as the monster truck shifted and lurched. I tried to keep up appearances by smiling and waving at Whitey and Rusty. But the truth was, I was terrified that any second Ranger would change his mind and those two lunatics would start shooting.

"Hurry up, Earl!" I whined.

"Don't you fret," he said. "It's all part of the plan."

An eternity later, Earl finally had the truck turned around. The front end of Bessie now pointed away from the warehouse and Ranger's homicide squad. It was time for Earl to get us the H-E double toothpicks out of there.

But again, to my surprise he didn't gun the engine. Instead, he turned and whispered out the back window to Lamar. "You ready?"

"Yep," Lamar said.

"All righty then. Let her rip!"

Something moved under the blue tarp. Then a jolting buzz reverberated through the chassis of the monster truck. A generator had kicked on in the back of the bed!

Earl revved the massive engine to mask the sound. Then, keeping one foot on the brake, he slowly eased Bessie forward at the pace of a geriatric turtle.

"What's happening?" I asked.

"Operation Sexy Cicada," Earl said.

"I know that. But—"

Earl put a hand on my shoulder. "We got this, Cuz."

He turned and hollered out the back window. "Deploy the decoy!"

Lamar jumped to his feet and started popping bungee cords loose like a mad cotton picker. They flew up and away like broken slingshots.

Suddenly, the blue tarp fell away.

Something began to rise from the corner of the truck bed.

I turned around for a better look, but a sheath of light-pink plastic slapped against the window, obstructing my view. Painted on the plastic, a huge, googly eye stared back at me through the window.

What the?

Earl caught a glimpse of the plastic eye and hooted. "There she blows!"

The plastic squeaked against the truck. The pie-plate sized googly eye moved upward, revealing two odd, black circles.

"What is it?" I asked Earl as he slowly maneuvered the truck forward.

He opened his mouth to speak, but hit a giant pothole. The truck lurched down, then up like a bucking donkey. In the process, the plastic fell away from the window, revealing it was a pink balloon the size of a juvenile elephant!

The two black dots that had been trapped against the window jutted out from the flat surface forming a snout like the transformation from man to beast in a low-budget werewolf movie. Then the whole pink plastic figure jerked loose and floated upward like some deranged dirigible.

I craned my neck out the back window for a better view, and ended up with Lamar's scrawny butt in my face.

"Geez, Lamar!" I said.

He turned around. "What?"

"We ready for the tailgate?" Earl asked.

"I'm on it," Lamar said, crawling like a drunken sailor to the back end and releasing the latch on the tailgate. As it flew open, Lamar undid a final bungee cord, then grabbed hold of a piece of yellow nylon rope.

Attached to the other end of the rope floated a fully-inflated, six-foot-tall Piglet balloon.

I stared, mouth agape, as the secret to the pink duct tape was revealed. Earl had used it to fashion a bra and panties out of it for Winnie the Pooh's overgrown pink pig pal.

I shook my head in wonder and admiration. Grayson couldn't have asked for a better diversion. I couldn't keep my eyes off the thing.

Earl idled Bessie along at two miles an hour, allowing Miss Piglet to bobble along with her sexy self about five feet above the truck bed.

"Now what?" I asked.

"Miss Piglet goes for a stroll," Earl said.

"Yeah she does," Lamar said. He reached into the corner of the truck bed and grabbed hold of a small, radio-controlled dune buggy. He checked the knot on the yellow nylon line tied to its back bumper, then set the mini-car on the tailgate and fished a remote-control device out of his back pocket.

"What the?" I mumbled.

Lamar hit a button on the remote. The dune buggy leapt off the tailgate, dragging the yellow rope with it.

The dune buggy's fat tires hit the ground, kicking up orange dust. The rope went taught, and suddenly the little car was tugging the scantily clad Piglet float along behind it like the highlight of some post-apocalyptic Macy's Thanksgiving Day Parade.

"Here, piggy piggy!" Lamar called out, working the controls like a madman, his tongue lolling enthusiastically from one side of his mouth to the other.

I shook my head and turned to Earl. I had to know.

"Why Piglet?" I asked.

Earl shrugged. "It was the closest thing they had to a cicada at Party City."

"Of course," I said.

What could possibly top this?

As it turned out, I didn't have long to find out.

Chapter Sixty-Four

Earl inched Bessie further and further away from Ranger's private graveyard for pesky cicadas and humans—but he and his goons were still holding Grayson captive until he produced the other half of the formula to synthesized Pine-Solve-It. Or until they decided to do him in...

Suddenly, a loud bang sounded behind us. My heart leapt in my throat.

Grayson!

"They shot him!" I cried out.

"Naw," Earl said. "That's just the next part of Operation Sexy Cicada. Sounds like Lamar's commenced Phase Fancy Farts."

"Phase *what?*"

I stared out the back window. A stream of white gas was jetting from Piglet's rear end, propelling it forward like jet propulsion.

A moment later, Miss Piglet disappeared in the cloud of white fog emanating from its backside.

"This is crazy," I yelled. "How is this helping?" I unhooked my seatbelt. "I'm going back for Grayson!"

I reached for the passenger door handle.

"No, Bobbie!" Earl said, grabbing hold of the back of my shirt with a Hulk-sized hand. "Hold your horses. Give it a chance to work!"

I shook my head in dismay. "How could this possibly work?" I struggled to free myself from Earl's grip. A movement in the side mirror made me freeze—then melt.

Grayson!

His fedora-topped head appeared out of the white fog. Then his shoulders and knees. Grayson was running for all he was worth!

Before I could even utter his name, he was alongside Bessie. He snatched open the passenger door. I nearly toppled out on top of him.

"You escaped!" I yelled.

"That was the plan," he said, pushing me back into the truck. He scrambled in beside me and yelled, "Punch it, Earl," then slammed the door.

"Woohoo!" Earl hollered, and hit the gas.

"Argh!" a man's voice sounded behind us.

We heard a thump. The three of us glanced into each other's eyes. No words necessary.

Lamar had fallen out of the back of the truck.

"Crap!" Earl said, stomping the brakes.

"I'll get him," Grayson said.

"Hold on," Earl bellowed, reaching under his seat. "Better take this with you."

Grayson's eyebrow shot up. "A can of mace?"

Earl winced. "Better than nothin'."

Grayson shrugged. "True."

Suddenly, the truck lurched forward as if struck from behind. I turned to see Lamar scrambling up the truck bed toward us like a deranged crab-man.

"Get us out of here!" he shouted through the sliding window. "Now!"

Earl shifted into gear. The monster truck's front-end lurched upward like a tricked-out show truck.

"What in tarnation?" Earl muttered as the force sent the three of us flailing up and backward like crash-test dummies in an anti-gravity booth.

As we fell back into our seats, Lamar let out a blood-curdling scream. Bessie's rear shocks groaned and sunk down a foot as an incredible weight slammed onto her rear end. The whole truck listed to the back as if the rear tires had fallen into quicksand.

"Awe shit!" I squealed. "Another sinkhole!"

"No," Grayson said, staring at the side mirror. "Sinkholes don't have teeth."

My eyebrows met my hairline. "What!"

Earl and I both scrambled for a look out the sliding back window, causing our heads to knock together like a pair of coconuts.

What we saw left us wishing we were on a tropical island—or anywhere but there.

Chapter Sixty-Five

Incredibly, a huge, fanged beast had launched its massive body halfway into the truck bed, and was hoping to make a snack out of Lamar.

The wiry old man was hysterical, hanging onto the back window frame and kicking for dear life as the monster snapped its hideous, gaping maw at him like a land version of that horrible shark in *Jaws*.

"Earl, grab his left wrist. I'll get his right," Grayson yelled.

The men took hold of Lamar's arms while I pried his bony fingers loose from the death grip he had on the window frame.

"Clear!" I yelled as I pried Lamar's last pinky loose.

Earl and Grayson yanked the old man through the sliding back window of the cab, right onto my lap.

"What the hell is that thing?" I screeched, staring back at the ravenous monster.

Lamar panted. "Hit the gas! It's Hogzilla!"

Upon mention of its name, the massive, tan-colored boar roared like a lion, then gouged the air with its elephantine tusks.

I bopped Earl on the arm. "You heard the man. Get us the hell out of here!"

Dodging a tangled pile of elbows and knees, Earl shifted into first and gunned the engine. Bessie's back wheels spun in place, anchored down by a hog the size of a pregnant hippo. He let off the gas.

"We gotta get that hog off a us!" Earl said. "If I spin the tires any more, we'll be stuck in the clay till next Sunday."

"What can we do?" I yelled.

"Continue with Operation Sexy Cicada," Grayson said. He turned to Lamar. "You still have the remote?"

"I think so." Lamar patted himself down and found the remote lodged in his underpants. He pulled it out.

"Good," Grayson said. "How many farts has she got left?"

Lamar chewed his lip. "Two. Maybe three?"

Grayson nodded. "Okay. We're going to have to make each one count. Hand Drex the remote."

My nose crinkled. "Me? I don't know how to operate that thing!"

"It's easy," Lamar said, slapping the remote into my palm. "Just push the button marked F in brown."

"I only see one marked P."

Lamar took it and wiped away a brown smudge. The P became an F, and I became sick to my stomach.

"There you go," he said, pressing the remote back into my hand.

Suddenly, the truck jostled forward again.

Hogzilla had pushed its massive hulk further into the truck bed. I watched in horror as the creature's back hoof caught on the tailgate, then slipped off. If that foot found purchase, we were goners.

"Why in the world is that thing after us?" I asked.

"Thanks to Ranger's body farm, I think it's developed a taste for human flesh," Grayson said. "Earl, you keep a foot ready on the pedal. Drex, you release a fart every forty-five seconds."

"Why?"

"We need to keep the smoke screen viable. Right now, it's the only thing keeping Ranger and his goons at bay."

"Right," I said, and put a thumb on the F. I pressed down. I couldn't see Miss Piglet, but I noticed the fog behind us thickened. I pursed my lips and silently started counting to forty-five.

Grayson turned to Lamar. "I hate to tell you this, but you're going to have to go back out there, my man."

Lamar flinched. "What? Why *me*?"

"You're the only one who can fit through the sliding window."

"What about her?" Lamar asked, throwing me under the bus.

Grayson glanced at my hips. "Not a chance."

"Lord-a-mercy," Lamar said. "What do you want me to do?"

Grayson handed him the can of mace. "Spray Hogzilla in the face with this."

My nose crinkled at the mace. "What do you hope to do with that?"

"Make it angry," Grayson said.

I glanced back at the beast. "I think it already is."

Hogzilla lunged again, jerking the truck chassis forward. This time, its back leg caught on the tailgate. It heaved one side of its massive carcass into the truck bed.

"Oh, shit!" I yelled.

"Hurry!" Grayson said, shoving Lamar head-first out the window. "I've got your feet."

"Aw, crap," Lamar mumbled. But there was no escape. As Grayson shoved Lamar's head through the small window, his beard caught on the frame. Like a scene from a war-hero movie, the scrawny old man let out a rebel yell, ripped his beard free, twisted his torso until he faced the enemy, then shot a stream of mace straight into Hogzilla's horrible face.

Stunned, the massive boar stopped thrashing about for a moment. But then it came back to life with a vengeance. It let out a squeal that could curdle cheese grits in the pot, then stumbled backward and fell off the truck, taking Bessie's tailgate with it.

"Yahoo!" I yelled, watching the hog run off into the woods. Then I realized I could actually see the woods.

The white smoke from the decoy had faded. I'd forgotten to fart!

"Crap!" I yelled, and scrambled to hit the F button on the remote.

But it was too late.

Five yards behind the truck, Rusty and Ranger appeared, their guns drawn.

"Cut the engine or we start shooting," Ranger yelled.

"You heard him!" Rusty managed to say, right before Hogzilla rammed him clear across the road.

After flattening Rusty, the massive boar turned its sights on Ranger.

"What the—!" Ranger hollered. He got off one shot before the massive boar trampled him, then bolted off into the woods, its balls swinging like a pair of grapefruits dangling from a rearview mirror.

Chapter Sixty-Six

While Ranger and Rusty lay in trampled heaps on the ground, Earl and Grayson jumped out of Bessie and commandeered their guns. After yanking both battered men to their feet, Grayson held them at gunpoint while Lamar secured their wrists with pink duct tape.

"Let's load them up," Grayson said, marching the two men toward the back of the truck.

"Not so fast," a voice sounded from somewhere in the woods. I recognized it. It was crazy, hacksaw-happy Whitey.

Shit.

The pig-bellied, psycho-psychologist had found us. Now he was grinning and pointing a sawed-off shotgun right at Lamar.

"Looks like we got us a standoff," Whitey said.

"I don't think so," I muttered under my breath. Behind my back, I worked the joystick on the remote, shoving it into full throttle.

The toy dune buggy raced down the narrow lane and slammed into Whitey's ankle with enough force to make him holler. He glanced down at the culprit, then up again just in time to get a full body slam from a hot-to-trot Miss Piglet.

"Ung!" Whitey grunted, then hit the ground with a thud. As he fell, his shotgun flew up into the air. Lamar snatched it before it hit the dirt.

"Woohoo!" Earl hollered. "We done it! We got 'em all!"

Nearby, a loud, angry grunt negated that statement.

"Lookout!" I screeched. "Hogzilla's back!"

From the edge of the clearing, the massive boar chuffed and dug at the ground like a wounded bull in a crowded arena.

"Crap!" I yelled as it took a charging step toward us.

Then, suddenly, the hippo-sized boar stopped in its tracks and looked up—and licked its lips.

Floating above its head, her helium leaking badly, Miss Piglet was descending from the sky like an angel in a junkie's acid flashback.

Hogzilla let out an odd squeal, lunged for the balloon, and executed an enthusiastic rendition of the hokey-pokey with his new dance partner.

Poor Piglet never stood a chance.

Chapter Sixty-Seven

While Hogzilla had its way with the inflatable porcine love toy, we hustled the three bad guys—Randy, Whitey and Rusty—into Bessie's truck bed.

Grayson climbed in the back with them, keeping watch over the trio with Ranger's Rugar.

"What about Hogzilla?" I asked. "Don't you want to capture it or something?"

"No," Grayson said. "I had a porcine pal once. Randolph. He taught me that pigs are like people. They were born to be free."

"Huh?" I grunted.

"Long story," Grayson said. "Now, let's roll!" He slapped Bessie's side panel.

"Hurry up!" Earl yelled from the driver's seat.

Lamar and I jumped into the cab of the monster truck. "Let's go," Lamar said, "Before that horny hog comes after us next!"

Earl punched the gas pedal. Bessie lurched forward, struggling slowly up the side of the massive hole its huge tractor tires had dug into the clay.

"Hold your breath," Earl said as we reached the top, teetered on the edge, then began to slip back down into the crater. "Crap!"

Another loud bang sounded behind us. I looked out the back window, expecting to see more of Ranger's goons brandishing guns. Instead, a stream of white smoke filled the air like a low-lying cloud.

"There she goes," Lamar laughed, then elbowed me. "Which one of them burst first, you think?"

I grimaced. "Get us out of here, Earl!"

Earl gunned the Hemi engine, then stomped the gas pedal again. We churned our way out of the hole, then barreled half a mile down the narrow dirt road like a rogue bottle rocket.

"Woohoo!" Earl hollered as we rounded a curve leading to the main road. Then he suddenly slammed on the brakes.

"Whoa!" he yelled, as a grey sedan sped straight for us. A head-on collision was mere seconds away...

"Watch out!" I cried, and watched in slow motion as the sedan skittered sideways, then came to a screeching halt two feet in front of us.

"It's about damned time!" I heard Grayson yell from the back of the truck.

The driver's side window on the sedan rolled down. Officer Snyder stuck his head out and grinned.

"Better late than never," he said. "Besides, it looks to me like you didn't need my help after all."

Chapter Sixty-Eight

After backup units from the Sheriff's Department arrived, troopers hauled away Rusty, Whitey and Ranger while Officer Snyder took our statements.

By the time the paperwork was over and we were free to go, the sun was already setting over our campsite in Torreya State Park.

"There's something I've got to know," I said to Grayson, grabbing a slice of delivery pizza before Earl could eat it all. "That note you left us in Bessie's glove compartment. How did you know Ranger wouldn't shoot you?"

"He couldn't," Grayson said, reaching across the banquette for another slice. "Not if he wanted the secret formula, anyway. You see, I told him I'd committed the other half of the formula to memory." He tapped a spidery index finger to his temple. "The place I'd hidden it was inside my brain."

I shook my head. "Smooth move. But how in the world did you manage to synthesize the formula so quickly?"

Grayson smirked and grabbed the last slice of pizza, making Earl whimper. "Well, once Rusty and I got to the RV, I set up a mock chemistry lab on the banquette here. You know, TV stuff. A half dozen test tubes here, flasks boiling above Bunsen burners there. Real mad-scientist sort of things."

I laughed. "And you just happened to have all that stuff lying around. How surprising."

Grayson shrugged. "Like I said. Chemistry's a hobby of mine."

"Then what happened?" Earl asked, snatching my uneaten crust and shoving it into his maw.

Grayson smirked. "I gave Rusty a beer with a dose of my cicada stunner serum in it. It's basically 95% grain alcohol."

I shook my head. "So your plan all along was to capture this Cicada *Palaeontinidae* creature and then get it hammered on alcohol?"

Grayson shrugged. "I suppose that's one way to look at it. But I'll have you know the serum contains a few proprietary components, as well. At any rate, while Rusty was incapacitated, I called Officer Snyder and told him what was going on."

"He already knew," I said. "That's why you could tell us to swear we wouldn't."

Grayson's cheek dimpled. "Precisely."

"And he believed you?" Earl asked.

"Eventually. Surprisingly, it took less time to convince him than I expected."

I smirked. "But what about synthesizing the formula?"

Grayson grinned. "I didn't have to. I simply poured the contents of that old brown bottle of original Pine-Solve-It into the flask I set up at the end of my chemistry set."

I smiled. "Respect, Grayson. No wonder it fooled Ranger."

Grayson nodded. "Then I wrote the note for you two and put it in the glove box. By then, Rusty was coming around. I gave him the antidote to the serum—a cup of plain coffee. After Rusty sobered up, I pretended I'd synthesized the original formula. Then I wrote down a bunch of gibberish and claimed it was the secret formula."

"Rusty wasn't suspicious?"

Grayson shrugged. "A little bit. But I convinced him he'd only nodded off for a second or two. He was too groggy to argue. I told him if he'd really been out for any length of time, I surely would've taken the opportunity to escape, or turn the tables on him. He bought it."

"Okay," I said. "But you let him drive back in that half-addled state?"

"I didn't have a lot of choice," Grayson said. "Rusty was driving so slow I had to perk him up."

"How?" Earl asked.

"With adrenaline," Grayson said. "I got him angry. I tore the bogus formula in half and ate part of it."

"Geez!" I said. "What did he do then?"

"Went a little ballistic, just as I'd hoped," Grayson said. "But I convinced him I'd committed the formula to memory. And to keep him from getting in trouble with Ranger, I told Rusty I'd say I hid the other half of the note somewhere. That became my ticket to staying alive until Operation Sexy Cicada could kick in."

I shook my head. "So brilliant, yet so disturbing."

Earl beamed. "Puttin' panties on Miss Piglet was my idea!"

Grayson laughed. "And it worked like a charm. As they say, the more unexpected the event, the more effective the distraction. Ranger and his crew were stunned nearly into stupors. Before they could utter a word, I was able to skip out under the cover of Piglet's white fart cloud."

I shook my head.

Well, there's something you don't hear every day.

Chapter Sixty-Nine

I showered and slipped into bed beside Grayson. Earl had one last night to finish off what remained of my sofa-bed. From the squeaks and groans emanating from its springs, the poor thing was on its last legs.

"What a day," I said, then yawned and glanced at my phone. "Geez. It's almost midnight."

"Yes, it was an interesting day," Grayson said. "Even though Hogzilla doesn't count as a true cryptid."

"Why not?"

"It's merely an overgrown boar. A genetic anomaly, but not a genetic novelty."

"What's the difference?"

"Both recessive genes and environment can shape a one-off anomaly, while a true genetic *novelty* can be passed down to offspring and thus marking the start of a whole new breed," Grayson said.

"So you're saying Earl is an anomaly, but he's still part of the human race?"

Grayson didn't answer, but I saw his cheek dimple before he clicked off the light.

I fluffed my pillow and stared in the dim light at the mystery man beside me. Then I chose my words carefully and tiptoed as I broached a subject that had been plaguing my mind ever since Earl had snuck a peek in Grayson's cabinet of mystery concoctions.

"Grayson, you're a physicist, a cryptid chaser, and homeopathic physician. I had no idea you were a chemist, too."

"I'm not," he said, turning on his side to face me. "Chemistry is just a hobby."

I turned on my side to face him. "Right. But what's the allure?"

"Chemicals are much more powerful than most give them credit for. The right combinations can elicit infinite varieties of behaviors in test subjects."

My eyes widened.

Wait a minute. Is Grayson using chemicals to trick me?

"No," Grayson said. "I'm not using chemicals to trick you, Drex."

I gasped. "You can read my mind?"

Grayson laughed. "Sometimes."

Suddenly, the RV jostled.

Grayson bolted to sitting. "Did you feel that?"

"Feel what?" I asked.

"That bump."

The RV jiggled again. "Uh ... no. I didn't feel a thing."

Grayson leapt up out of bed. "Cicada *Palaeontinidae*! It's back!"

Aw, crap!

Grayson skirted around the bed toward the door.

"No!" I called after him, springing out of bed. "Don't go in there—"

But it was too late. I grimaced, then padded down the short hall. At the end of it Grayson stood staring, dumfounded, at the inexplicable spectacle before him.

The clock had just struck midnight, and Earl was standing in the middle of the sofa-bed doing jumping jacks like a grizzly bear in pajamas.

"Earl," Grayson said, taking a step toward him.

"Shh!" I whispered. "You'll wake him."

Grayson peered at my cousin in the dim light. "You're right. This is somnambular activity."

Earl flapped around a few more times, then laid back down as if nothing had happened.

Grayson shook his head. "Your cousin is nuttier than a fruit-cake."

"I know." I grinned. "But he's *our* fruitcake. Come on, let's don't wake him."

I took Grayson's hand and tugged him back toward the bedroom, a smirk nearly splitting my lips.

Screw chemicals.

Long live the power of hypnotic suggestion.

Chapter Seventy

"So there really *is* no secret formula," Officer Snyder said, sipping coffee at the picnic table outside our RV.

"No," Grayson said. "It was a ruse to buy time."

"And save our lives," I added.

Snyder smiled. "I guess that's more bad news for Gerold Bong, I'm afraid. Too bad. Couldn't have happened to a nicer guy."

"Did you check out Darryl's Dodge for Torreya tree tags?" Grayson asked.

Snyder nodded and put down his cup. "Yes. Found a couple stashed under the driver's seat. Looks like you were right about Dale and Darryl cutting down the Torreyas and putting the tags on other trees. One of our undercover officers found a tag hanging on a maple sapling. Those brothers weren't the brightest bulbs in the bunch."

"Undercover officers?" Grayson asked.

"Yes. We've had our suspicions for a couple of months."

"Did they ever find Darryl?" I asked.

"I suspect so," Snyder said. "At the moment, the crew excavating the cicada burial site have uncovered more bodies than heads. I suspect Darryl's will turn out to be one of them."

"What will happen to Ranger?" I asked.

Snyder smirked. "Well, he won't be running for mayor, that's for sure."

"He confessed?" I asked.

"Indirectly. His sister Pat wore a wire for us last night. Got pretty much all we need on tape."

I shook my head. "I thought they were close. Why would she turn on him?"

"It wasn't so much turning on him as doing her civic duty. Though she did admit she was angry. Ranger and Bong forced her to accept that godawful awning they put up on her restaurant. She knew the gesture was no gift, but an attempt to make her guilty by association. Well, let me tell you, Pat wasn't having any of it."

I smiled. "Good for her. Integrity is everything."

Grayson glanced at me, then looked away.

"And Whitey?" I asked.

Snyder chuckled. "Now *there's* an interesting fella. Come to find out the old kook's no psychologist. Just the opposite."

"What do you mean?" I asked.

"Whitey escaped from a mental health facility up near Chatta-hoochee a few months back."

I shook my head. "Why do I not find that hard to believe?"

"What about Rusty?" Grayson asked.

"He's deep in the poo, too," Snyder said. "We've got the goods on him as well, thanks to our undercover agent Carmella."

My head cocked sideways like a puppy's. "Carmella?"

Snyder grinned. "You probably know her best as Bonnie, or should I say Bondo?"

My jaw dropped. "You're kidding."

Snyder smiled. "Nope. She took a real liking to you, Miss Drex. Wanted to know if it'd be okay if she dropped by to say goodbye."

I laughed, thinking about the two of us sneaking out like SWAT agents to drink wine from a rusty deep-freezer. "Sure. I'd like that."

"Good. I'll buzz her. She's just up at the old Gregory Mansion, checking on the guard we've got watching over the last Torreya trees there."

"So, I guess that just leaves one more open question," I said.

Snyder's eyebrow flat-lined. "What's that?"

"Cicada *Palaeontinidae*," Grayson said.

I elbowed Grayson. "No. *Hogzilla*. What happened to that wild beast?"

"Oh." Snyder sat up and sighed. "Well, sad story, that. The trackers and hounds chased that hog for about five miles. It ended up at that junkyard compound of Rusty's. The men cornered it by a couple of camper vans soldered together. Hogzilla ran inside that thing, but its weight must've broken the last holds keeping that trailer home thingamajig anchored. It slid off its foundation with the hog inside it and tumbled down into the pit of that new sinkhole that opened up."

"That's too bad," I said.

"Indeed," Grayson said. "What a loss."

Snyder laughed. "You aren't kidding. I bet that hog was carrying a pure natural ton of bacon on its back."

Earl, who'd remained silent up to this time, let out a long, sad whistle. "You know that's right."

Snyder gave Earl a sideways glance. "That reminds me. That other lunatic, Roy Stubbs. From what we can piece together, he was working for Gerold Bong, tying up loose ends and loose tongues. We think it was most likely this Hogzilla creature Roy was running from when he dove into that pit toilet."

A car horn sounded. Snyder looked up toward the road. "Oh, there's Carmella now."

I turned to see a rusty, faded-tan Volkswagen Beetle pull up.

Carmella, aka Bondo, climbed out, patted her golden-brown, perfectly coiffed bun, and sauntered over to us.

"How we all doin'?" she asked, her Jersey accent blaring like a taxi horn.

"Fine," I said, grinning with admiration. "You know, you're great at your job. I had no idea you were working undercover."

She laughed, "Come on, girl! You think a hot bod like this is gonna settle for a scrawny bucket of country-fried freckles?"

I laughed. "Tell me. How did you hold it together when you woke up and saw Virgil's head lying next to you?"

"It wasn't easy. Especially since I wasn't actually drunk. I faked passing out."

I blanched. "Why?"

She rolled her eyes. "Ugh! I couldn't bear to look at that bug buffet another second. Compared to cicada cacciatore, Virgil's severed head looked like a Boston cream pie."

Grayson and Snyder laughed. I cocked my head.

"But I heard you say, 'Get away from me, pervert.'"

Bondo laughed. "Girlfriend, in Jersey, that's the same as saying 'How do you do.'"

Chapter Seventy-One

As I watched Snyder and Bondo drive away, a thought popped into my head that sent shivers down my spine.

The sinkhole at Rusty's.

Whatever I'd seen sinking into that pit—bubbling down into the water with the appliances and auto parts—*couldn't have been that rusted VW* because *Bondo was driving off in it!*

"Grayson!" I yelped.

"What?" he asked, concern in his green eyes. "Are you okay?"

I stared at him, wide-eyed. "I think you might've been right!"

Concern turned into a smirk. "Of course I was," he said. "But you're going to have to be more specific."

"About Cicada *Palaeontinidae*!" I yelled.

His green eyes flashed. "Go on."

"The other day, at Rusty's place. I ... I thought I saw Rusty's VW at the bottom of that sinkhole."

"So?"

"It couldn't have been because Bondo just drove off in it!"

Grayson turned and stared down the road, trying to catch a glimpse of the RV.

"What if what I *actually* saw was the back of Cicada *Palaeontinidae*?"

"Intriguing," Grayson said, turning back to face me. "But even if you're right, the creature's gone now. Buried deep in that sinkhole."

I nodded. "Perhaps. But there may have been more than one creature."

Grayson's eyebrow hooked skyward. "What makes you say that?"

"If you recall, more heads were found after the sinkhole opened up at Rusty's."

"Correct. So?"

"In nature, isn't it usually a mated *female* who bites the male's head off?"

Grayson's cheek dimpled. "I plead the fifth on that one."

"I'm serious!" I growled.

"Hey Mr. G!" Earl called out, waving the fishing rod in his right hand. His left hand was weighted down by a giant tackle box. "You ready to go fishin'?"

"You know, I think I'll skip it," Grayson said, locking eyes with me. "I've still got a few things to sort out before we take off tomorrow."

"I have to go with him," I said. "I promised Earl a fishing trip to Ocheesee Landing. It's now or never."

"You sure you don't want to go Mr. G.?" Earl called out. "You don't know what you're missing!"

"Come on. Let's get a move on," Lamar said, loading a cooler into the back of Bessie. "It's already after ten in the morning. Time's a wastin'!"

AFTER GETTING MORE mosquito bites than fish nibbles, I was glad to leave Ocheesee Landing behind. And, after sitting sandwiched between Earl and Lamar in a boat for four hours, I was looking forward to a conversation that didn't include the words stumpknockers, vittles, or corn squeezin's.

On the ride back to Torreya State Park, we made a quick detour to Walmart to return the unused half a case of new-formula Pine-Solve-It. I seized the opportunity to pick up some necessary traveling provisions—a family-size bag of Cheetos for Grayson, and a box of Tootsie Pops for me.

As we headed back to Earl's monster truck with our Walmart loot, I spied a twenty-dollar bill on the ground.

"Hey, today's my lucky day!" I said, sticking the money in my jeans pocket.

"Now, now, Miss Drex," Lamar scolded, eyeing me with a furrowed brow. He glanced down at the found money. "What would Jesus do?"

I nodded. "You're right, Lamar."

Then I marched right back into Walmart and turned that twenty dollar bill into wine.

IT WAS LATE AFTERNOON when we got back to the campsite. As the guys emptied the fishing gear, I headed for the RV to wash up.

Grayson opened the door as I approached. "It's about time," he said. "I was getting worried."

"My fault," Earl called out. "We got into a mess a stumpknockers and I didn't want to go home. Got me a whole cooler full of 'em on ice. Gonna make for some great vittles!"

I smirked. "I didn't catch a thing. But the fish started biting fast and furious for those two, especially after Earl snagged that head."

Grayson's eyebrows rose an inch. "A *human* head?"

"Yes." I winked. "But this time, it turned out to be part of a mannequin."

Grayson sighed. "Good."

He turned to step back into the RV. I followed him inside.

"Hey, Grayson. You wouldn't happen to know anything about that line of military vehicles that blew past us on our way here, would you?"

"Perhaps," he said, rinsing a glass in the sink.

"So? What's going on?"

He shrugged. "Let's just say I think the fine people of Bristol might be getting a new fishing hole soon."

My nose crinkled. "What do you mean?"

He turned to face me. "You remember my FBI contact, Chief Warren Engles?"

I made a sour face. "Other than you telling me that information about him was on a 'need to know basis,' *no*."

"Sit down," he said, motioning to the banquette. "Maybe it's time you knew a little more."

"Like what?" I asked, scooting into the booth across from him.

"I relayed the facts about your observation of a possible giant cicada trapped in the sinkhole at Rusty's place."

"And?"

"Chief Engles heads a special division that takes care of things like this."

"*Special division?*" I gasped. "Takes *care* of things? *What* things?"

Grayson cocked his head and shrugged. "That's on—"

"I got it," I said. "A freaking need to know basis."

Chapter Seventy-Two

Grayson and I waved goodbye to Earl and his cooler full of stumpknockers, then turned to walk back to the RV.

"I think it's time," Grayson said.

I stiffened. "Time?"

"Yes, Drex. Now that the dust has settled, I think it's time we did that long overdue EEG."

"Aw, geez, Grayson," I said, climbing the steps into the RV. "I just washed my hair!"

"Then I think you'll be pleased. I sent away for a newly developed testing device. It measures alpha waves using pulmonary pulse probes as opposed to galvanic skin response."

I scowled. "First off, what the heck does that mean?" I tore open the box of Tootsie Pops and grabbed a chocolate one. "And secondly, what's it got to do with the fact that I just washed my hair?"

"This new technique doesn't require electrodes be pasted to your scalp," Grayson explained. "It employs a finger-pulse accumulator instead."

"Oh." I stuffed the Tootsie Pop in my mouth and shifted the sucker to my left cheek. "Well, that's cool."

"Have a seat at the banquette. I'll show you."

"Fine."

As I slid into the booth, Grayson wheeled out his old EEG monitor. Wired to it was a new device—a white contraption about the size and shape of half a honeydew melon.

Like something from a sci-fi movie, the top, rounded side of the device had a molded silver inset in the shape of a hand. At the ends of the fingers and the base of the palm protruded oval, button-like things roughly the dimensions of the vitamin capsules I took every morning.

"Place your right hand on the device," Grayson said, setting it on the table.

He walked behind me and turned on the EEG machine. As it hummed to life, I slipped my hand into the silver mold. It fit like the bottom half of a glove.

Grayson hovered over me and fastened the device's red, Velcro strap across the back of my hand, securing it in place.

"Try not to move your fingers," he said as he placed his laptop on the table in front of me.

He clicked a button and the familiar, blue-and-yellow smiley face popped up on the screen. I knew it was the initial calm before the storm of horrific images to come. Their purpose was to frighten me and engage my innate fight-or-flight mechanisms.

By now, I knew my part in the process well. I was to use the experience to practice overriding my fears. As I'd come to learn, this was no theoretical exercise. It was basic job training. Working for Grayson, not freaking out in the face of bizarre phenomena was a skill I truly needed to master.

"Ready?" Grayson asked.

I took a deep, calming breath. "Yes."

Suddenly, the side door popped open. Earl stuck his head in. "What y'all doing?"

I glanced over at my cousin.

Every hair on my body pricked to attention.

"Aarggh!" I shouted, as rapid-fire pulses, like a tiny, electric Uzi, shot through my hand and up my arm.

"Ow!" I yelled, and flailed my strapped-in hand, trying to free it from the device. But the dang thing hung on like a hungry snapping turtle.

Suddenly, the electric pulses stopped.

As the ringing in my ears subsided, I heard an ape-like howling.

I glanced over at Grayson. He was bent over the EEG machine, convulsing with laughter.

Earl's staccato, woodpecker laugh echoed through the main cabin like a lunatic's mating call. I shot my cousin a glare that could melt ice inside a double-hulled igloo.

"What the hell's going on here?" I yelled, yanking the device off my hand.

"We got you good, that's what!" Earl said. He pulled a small box from behind his back.

My molars nearly cracked.

It was the carton for a kid's lie-detector toy.

My eyes followed the wire Grayson had told me he'd attached to the EEG machine. He'd lied.

The device wasn't hooked to the EEG machine. It was hooked to the same damned 9-Volt battery I'd blown Earl's Pop-Tarts with.

I shook my head.

I'd been double-teamed.

"Respect," I said. "Now Earl, get the hell out of here!"

Chapter Seventy-Three

After the numbness faded from my fingertips and my homicidal urges abated to a more civilized level, I decided to join Grayson at the banquette for a case wrap-up.

"If you ask me, we're witnessing the end of one legend, and perhaps the birth of another," Grayson said as I scooted into the booth opposite him.

I took a swig of holy wine. "What do you mean?"

Grayson shrugged. "When one belief dies, it makes room for another."

I let out a little laugh. "That's how we evolve, I guess."

"Or *de*volve."

I winced. "That's a discouraging thought."

Grayson studied me with his mesmerizing green eyes. "How are you feeling?"

I shrugged and held up my glass of wine. "Actually, pretty good, thanks to this new miracle juice I got at Walmart."

"No headache or pain?"

"Nope."

"Good." Grayson's eyes locked on mine like twin laser beams. "Is there anything *else* you want to share with me?"

Emboldened by booze, I decided to make a confession. "Yeah. I tried to get inside your cabinet."

Grayson's eyebrow angled up like Spock's. "*Tried?*"

I winced. "Okay. I *did*. But I have to say, for being head of security, you sure put a flimsy lock on the door."

Grayson frowned. "It was a test, Drex."

"To see if I could pick the lock? Any kid with a—"

"No," he said, cutting me off. "The lock on the cabinet wasn't a test of *security*, Drex. It was a test of *integrity*. I told you it was off limits, and that should've been enough to keep you out."

I winced again. "I'm a curious person," I backpedaled. "And I wanted..." I stopped and shook my head. "No. I *needed* to know about something you have inside there."

Grayson's shoulders straightened. "What?"

I looked down at the table. "Your ... uh ... nubbin."

"My *nubbin*?" Grayson said, nearly choking. "So *that's* what all this sneakiness has been about."

I glanced up at him, eyes wide. "You *knew* we'd been in your cabinet?"

"I knew *someone* had. Wait. We?"

I cringed, but held my ground. "Yes. Earl broke into the cabinet first. He told me you kept your scorpion tail thing in there ... in a jar labeled 'Nubbin.'"

Grayson stared at me. "Geez, Drex. Do you really think I'm the kind of person who would keep an extraneous body part in a jar?"

"Absolutely."

Grayson's cheek dimpled. "Fine. Why don't we go have a look?"

My gut flopped. "Uh ... okay."

I swallowed hard and trailed behind Grayson as he walked over to the locked cabinet in the hallway. He produced a key, undid the small padlock, and pulled the handle. To my surprise, the door didn't squeak when he opened it.

"So, which jar is it that's supposed to hold my nubbin?" he asked.

I grimaced. "You *know* which one. It's all the way in the back. The tall jar marked Nubbin?"

"This one?" Grayson asked, pointing to the jar in question.

"Yes."

He lifted the jar and held it up to the light for my examination.

Inside, floating in amber fluid, bobbed a withered-looking, dark object roughly the size of a kosher dill pickle. It was bulbous on one end. The other end was tapered, with spikey protrusions on either side, similar to an anchor.

The hair on my arms prickled. "How the hell do you explain *that*?"

Grayson turned the jar around until the label faced me.

Hello! *My Name Is:*
Nubian Fertility Talisman

"I DON'T KNOW," GRAYSON said, letting out a sigh. "I bought it on a whim."

"What?" I gasped. "Why?"

He shrugged. "I thought it might come in handy in case I ever wanted to produce offspring with a barren Nubian."

My lower jaw hung open, refusing to close.

"Satisfied?" he asked.

I nodded, mouth still agape.

Grayson put the jar back inside the cabinet, closed the door, then held the tiny padlock between pinched fingers. "I guess there's no point in using *this* anymore."

"I ... I'm sorry," I muttered, lowering my gaze. "I have no integrity."

Grayson smiled. "Actually, you have more than most, Drex. And I can understand your motivation."

I gulped. "You can?"

"Yes. You were concerned I was harboring some deep, dark secret that would jeopardize your chance to complete your private investigator internship with me."

Not even close.

"You got me," I said, my gut flopping with an odd mixture of relief and hope.

I still didn't know what the hell was going on with his nubbin thing. But Grayson's explanation *did* solve one mystery for me. At some point in his life, he'd actually thought about having sex with someone.

I smiled up at him weakly. "Sorry I broke into your cabinet. We all have our issues. I guess mine is trust."

Grayson's cheek dimpled. "You think?"

I smiled sheepishly. "Hey, nobody's perfect."

"True. But don't forget, Drex. It was curiosity that killed the cat."

Grayson tossed the padlock into a drawer, then turned and smiled mischievously at me. "But on the other hand, a cat has nine lives. It might as well use them in interesting ways."

I TURNED ONTO MY SIDE in the sofa-bed, hoping to avoid the spring that was jabbing my kidney like a dull knife.

In less than a week, my giant bear of a cousin had turned the thin mattress into a literal minefield of things that went poke in the night.

I glanced up at the clock. It was a minute before midnight. I grinned and envisioned Earl doing zombie jumping jacks in his own bed. I laughed to myself.

I don't care what Lamar says. Revenge really is sweet.

In six or so short hours, Grayson would rise, fully rested and up and at 'em, ready to set off on some new hair-brained adventure.

At least I know now that he isn't part scorpion.

The thought made me giggle, causing another busted spring to jab into my ribcage.

"Ugh!" I groaned, and turned onto my back, only to be jabbed yet again—this time where the sun don't shine.

"Oh, forget it!" I groaned, and climbed out of the ruined sofa-bed.

I tiptoed down the short hallway. Grayson's bedroom door was ajar. I pushed it open a bit further and blinked into the pitch-black space.

Suddenly, like a prowling cat caught in a flashlight, two glowing green eyes blinked on in the darkness.

My breath caught in my throat.

That crack Grayson made about the curious cat. Could it be that he's part—

"What's up, Drex?" Grayson's voice sounded from the darkness.

"Uh ... nothing. Sorry I disturbed you. It's just that Earl ... well, he did a number on my bed."

"Number one or number two?"

"What?" I asked, then burst out laughing. "A sense of humor. Wow, Grayson, I didn't think you had it in you."

"Really?" he said. "Not even after our prank?"

"A prank is something entirely different."

"If you say so."

I chewed my lip. "Grayson, do you think there's more of them out there?"

"More what?"

I strained to see him in the dim light. "Cicada *Palaeontinidae*."

"Doubtful. I have a feeling they were the last of their kind. One lone male and female, looking for love in all the wrong places."

I sighed. "That's kind of sad, really."

"Like so many tragic tales of love, the thing that attracts us is also what kills us in the end."

Grayson a romantic? I didn't see that coming.

I swallowed hard. "What are you saying, Grayson?"

He blinked his green eyes. "That Pine-Solve-It is both attractive and lethal to cicadas."

My gut flopped. "Oh."

"What did you *think* I meant?"

I groaned. "Nothing."

I turned to go, but something compelled me to turn back around. "Grayson?"

"Hmm?"

"My bed's shot. Would it be okay if I—"

"Of course. Climb on in."

Ready for More *Freaky Florida Investigations?*
Find out where Bobbie and Grayson go from here. Check in book 6, Scatman Dues!
HTTPS://WWW.AMAZON.com/dp/B08MD7PRYX

*I hope you enjoyed **Weevil Spirits**. If you did, it would be freaking fantastic if you would post a review on Amazon, Goodreads and/or BookBub. You'll be helping me keep the series going! Thanks in advance for being so awesome!*

https://www.amazon.com/dp/B08BZT95TW#customerReviews

Get a Free Story!

DON'T MISS ANOTHER sneak preview, sale, or new release of *Freaky Florida Investigations!* Sign up for my newsletter for insider tips. I'll send you a free copy of the Welcome to Florida, Now Go Home *as a* welcome gift!

https://dl.bookfunnel.com/ikfes8er75

For more laughs and discussions with fellow fans, follow me on Facebook, Amazon and BookBub:

Facebook:

https://www.facebook.com/valandpalspage/

Amazon:

https://www.amazon.com/-/e/B06XKJ3YD8

BookBub:

https://www.bookbub.com/search/authors?search=margaret%20lashley

Thank you! Now, please enjoy the following excerpt from: Scatman Dues, Freaky Florida Investigations Book 6!

Scatman Dues Excerpt

P rologue

I'm Bobbie Drex, and I have a confession to make.

Becoming a private investigator wasn't exactly a profession I chose. At least, not *intentionally*—and certainly not while in complete control of my faculties.

If you want to know the truth, I'd been knee-deep in a vodka bottle when I'd ordered an online P.I. training course from a cheesy, late-night infomercial. I'd been even more out of my mind the next morning, when I'd sobered up and discovered the credit-card charges were non-refundable.

Fueled by frustration, stubbornness, and an inability to throw away hard-earned cash, I'd gone ahead and completed the course. I'd figured what the hell—it might've come in handy for my glamorous job as a part-time mall cop.

As it turned out, I never got the chance to find out.

A few days later, a ricochet bullet popped me in the forehead, putting an end to my glorious security-patrol gig. I'd returned home from the hospital with my head shaved, my health insurance cancelled, and my family's auto repair business in the crapper.

Awesome.

The only bright spot had been finding my training course certificate in the mailbox. But after reading the fine print, that bright spot had turned as dark and unwelcome as a suspicious mole.

I'd discovered that, in and of itself, my new "Private Investigator Intern Certificate" was barely worth the paper it was printed on. In order to become a full-fledged Florida private eye, I'd also have to complete *two years* of on-the-job training with a licensed investigator.

(Insert expletive of your choice here.)

Anyway, I was wadding up the stupid certificate and hurling it into the bin when something *even more* aggravating happened.

An oddball named Nick Grayson showed up at my door.

The mysterious, green-eyed stranger sported a vintage fedora and a shiny private-eye badge—and he was on the hunt for two things.

One was repairs to his ratty old RV. The other was ... uh ... *Mothman.*

And he'd wanted my help with both.

At the time, I couldn't tell if Grayson was a gift from the Universe or another sick joke at my expense. But back then, my life was so deep in the dumpster I'd decided to take him up on his offer.

I'd joined his weird crusade tracking down cryptids for cash.

As Grayson's P.I. intern, I've spent the past seven months roaming the dirty backwaters of the Sunshine State in a rundown Winnebago—with a guy whose own human pedigree was as sketchy as the creatures we investigate.

If all that weren't bad enough, we operate our research deep within the stomping grounds of Florida Man—where it's doubly hard to tell a monster from a maniac.

Sometimes, it's darn-near *impossible.*

They say hindsight is 2020. Well, let me tell you. That infamous year's got *nothing* on the unbelievable crap that's gone down since I climbed aboard Grayson's magical mystery motorhome.

Little did I realize, I hadn't seen anything yet ...

Chapter One

I cracked open a sleepy eye and groaned. It was official. I was the only grown-ass woman in the entire universe who was "sleeping" with her boss—*literally*.

As in, "snoring-in-your-face, no-sexy-time" *literally*.

Worse yet, I couldn't decide if that was a good thing or a bad thing.

Ever since my big lug of a cousin came and wrecked the sofa-bed I usually slept on, I'd been forced to share a queen-sized bed with my irritatingly handsome boss and partner, Nick Grayson.

My cousin Earl had headed back to Point Paradise a week ago, leaving me with a murdered mattress and a busting headache. While the headache came and went, the ruined mattress persisted. So did Grayson's fixation on using *me* to fine-tune his wacked-out brain-wave contraption.

According to my mad-scientist partner, Grayson's modified EEG machine was supposed to measure my brain's alpha-wave activity in response to threatening stimuli. What that meant for *me* was regular sessions of having my skull plastered to the contraption via electrodes, then being blasted with images designed to scare the living crap out of me.

Through sheer willpower and deep-breathing techniques, I was supposed to override my instinctual flight-or-flight responses and remain calm in the face of fear. The higher my alpha waves remained, the better I was doing.

Good times...

Besides learning how to not freak out in the face of carnivorous cryptids and cantankerous crazies, Grayson was also instructing me on ways to escape unforeseen attacks by vile, blood-sucking creatures.

Not that I needed the practice.

After swimming in the deep end of Florida's dating pool for the past two decades, I'd joined his team fully equipped with my own armor-plated life raft and an arsenal of moves that could blow an entire army of despicable, handsy parasites clean out of the water.

Not that Grayson *himself* had tried to put the moves on me, mind you.

While there existed an undeniable chemistry between us, we had yet to perfect the formula.

Who am I kidding? Maybe there isn't one.

During the two weeks we'd become unintentional bedmates, the closest thing to a romantic gesture I'd witnessed from Grayson was when he'd gone and cleaned the toilet without me asking.

As a bona fide Earth woman, that action *alone* had been enough to make me question whether Grayson was a real human male, or some kind of evolved mutant clone.

Not that I didn't already have enough suspicions about the guy. Given Grayson's strange diet, odd way of speaking, and secondary bellybutton, I had some pretty serious doubts about his family tree. Was the weirdo a mere mortal? Or was he some lost, alien life form trying desperately to phone home?

An ET from Venus sporting a Freddie Mercury moustache...

Not exactly a combination to send a girl over the moon. Still, part of me was dying to find out the truth. The other part of me was worried about dying *if* I found out.

Talk about your cosmic quandaries... Ugh!

I ROLLED OUT OF BED and padded barefoot to the main cabin of the old Winnebago we traveled in. As usual, my bedmate and boss was wide awake—annoyingly alert and fully dressed in his neat, never-changing uniform of black T-shirt, black jeans, and black boots.

Perched in his favorite spot at the small banquette across from the kitchen, Grayson was working away at the only thing more annoying than his apparent prime directive of lifelong celibacy—

That stupid EEG brainwave machine.

"Ah. You're awake," Grayson said, never looking up from his precious contraption. He fiddled with a few knobs, making the needles on the monitors jerk around like a Richter scale in an apocalypse.

"You noticed," I grunted.

"You're just in time."

A frown pinched the corners of my mouth. I scrounged in the kitchen cupboard for a clean coffee cup. "Just in time *for what*?"

"To test my theory."

I shot Grayson some caffeine-deprived side-eye and poured myself a cup from the pot on the stove.

"Theory?" I asked, then took a sip.

"Yes."

Grayson looked up from fiddling with the EEG machine. "You've been displaying unusually high alpha waves on the last few tests. I'm trying to determine if this means my program is indeed desensitizing you to strange phenomena, or if the test itself is influencing the results."

I groaned. "Grayson, if you don't let me drink this coffee in peace, *I'll* be determining the results of *your lifespan*."

Grayson's eyebrow formed a Spock-like triangle. "Duly noted."

I ripped open a package of Pop-Tarts and slammed them into the toaster. As I waited for them to heat up into warm, life-saving rectangles of blueberry-flavored salvation, my curiosity got the better of me. "What did you mean when you said the EEG test *itself* could be influencing my results?"

Grayson's mesmerizing green eyes locked on mine. "Non-objective anticipatory response, of course."

I stifled another groan. I should've been used to this by now. "More human-oriented data required, robot man."

Grayson studied me for a moment, then winced slightly as I took a savage bite of Pop-Tart.

"I merely meant that your *anticipation* of viewing shocking images on the test program could be subconsciously tempering your response," he said. "Your expectations could be putting you into a sort of 'prepared state,' thus influencing your reactions to the images themselves."

I sucked blueberry goo from my front teeth. "It's seven a.m., for crying out loud. Could you dial down the science talk one more notch?"

Grayson chewed his lip. "How's this? You know what's coming, so you mentally brace for it."

"Ah," I said, and flopped down across from him at the banquette. "Forewarned is forearmed."

"Exactly." Grayson's cheek dimpled. It was the only tell he was smiling, as his lips were perpetually obscured by his bushy moustache. "This 'mental preparation' could be skewing your alpha-wave results to a falsely high level."

"Or, it could mean I'm finally getting the hang of dealing with otherworldly creeps."

"Hmm." Grayson rubbed his chin. "I suppose that's *one* of the other possibilities."

"*One*?" I set my coffee cup down and noticed the edge of a manila folder tucked under his laptop. The label sticking out read, *Experiment #5.*

I frowned. "What other possibilities *are* there?"

Grayson shrugged. "Quite a few, actually. Elevated alpha waves could be symptomatic of the vestigial twin lodged in the center of your brain."

"How so?"

"The mass could be exerting pressure on your pineal gland, inducing an unwarranted state of bliss."

"Bliss?" An image flashed in my mind from a week ago, when I was yanking legs off grubs for a bug barbeque. I let out a jaded laugh. "Well, it sure isn't from this job."

Grayson shook his head. "No. The bliss I'm talking about would be totally unassociated with your current reality."

I smirked. "It'd *have* to be."

I jabbed a finger at the folder peeking out from beneath his laptop. "What's experiment number five?"

Grayson covered the label with his hand, then studied me for a moment. "That's on a need-to-know basis, Drex."

Frustration shot an arrow at my temple. "Come on, Grayson! I thought we were supposed to *trust* each other."

Grayson cocked his head and raised an eyebrow at me. "Is that why you broke into my locked cabinet last week?"

I winced. "I already apologized for that. Besides, Earl did it first."

Grayson eyed me coolly. "If Earl jumped off a bridge—"

"Fine!" I blurted. "You win. I shouldn't have done it. Sorry."

"Apology accepted."

I glanced down at the mysterious folder and chewed my bottom lip. I couldn't stand not knowing. "Aw, come on, Grayson. Just give me a hint, okay?"

Grayson sighed. "Very well."

I smiled and took a victory sip of coffee.

Grayson cleared his throat. "It involves *hot bodies*."

Coffee spurted from my mouth like a busted lawn sprinkler. "*Porn?*" I hacked, wiping my chin.

Grayson studied me clinically, then put a spidery hand on my forehead. "Drex, are you experiencing a headache?"

I blanched and yanked his hand away. "No. Why?"

Grayson stared at me oddly. A thought stabbed my brain making my ears grow hot.

"Grayson, is this your attempt at *foreplay*?"

Grayson's handsome head tilted slightly to the left. "*Four* play? Impossible, Drex. We're not equipped for that."

My eyebrows met. "What? Why not?"

"Because there are only *two* of us."

Either Grayson stole a joke book from a ten year old, or he was using an outdated guide to intergalactic dating. As I ground my teeth to powder contemplating whether he was human or not, there was only one thing I knew about him for certain.

The guy sure knew how to pull my chain.

Check Out What Bobbie and Grayson are Up to Next!
Order Scatman Dues now!
https://www.amazon.com/dp/B08MD7PRYX

More Freaky Florida Mysteries

by Margaret Lashley
Moth Busters
Dr. Prepper
Oral Robbers
Ape Shift
Weevil Spirits
Scatman Dues
Smoked Mullet
Half Crocked
More to Come???

*"The things a girl's gotta do to get a lousy
P.I. license. Geez!"*

Bobbie Drex

About the Author

Why do I love underdogs? Well, it takes one to know one. Like the main characters in my novels, I haven't lead a life of wealth or luxury. In fact, as it stands now, I'm set to inherit a half-eaten jar of Cheez Whiz...if my siblings don't beat me to it.

During my illustrious career, I've been a roller-skating waitress, an actuarial assistant, an advertising copywriter, a real estate agent, a house flipper, an organic farmer, and a traveling vagabond/truth seeker. But no matter where I've gone or what I've done, I've always felt like a weirdo.

I've learned a heck of a lot in my life. But getting to know myself has been my greatest journey. Today, I know I'm smart. I'm direct. I'm jaded. I'm hopeful. I'm funny. I'm fierce. I'm a pushover. And I have a laugh that lures strangers over, wanting to join in the fun.

In other words, I'm a jumble of opposing talents and flaws and emotions. And it's all good.

I enjoy underdogs because we've got spunk. And hope. And secrets that drive us to be different from the rest.

So dare to be different. It's the only way to be!

Happy reading!

Made in United States
Orlando, FL
24 May 2025